HAPPINESS OF FISH

To Robert
wishing you
some.

Best wishes

Fred Armstrong

HAPPINESS OF FISH

A NOVEL

FRED ARMSTRONG

JESPERSON PUBLISHING

JESPERSON PUBLISHING
100 Water Street
P. O. Box 2188
St. John's, NL
A1C 6E6
www.jespersonpublishing.nf.net

Library and Archives Canada Cataloguing in Publication

Armstrong, Fred, 1947–
    Happiness of fish / Fred Armstrong.
ISBN 978-1-894377-25-6
I. Title.
PS8601.R584H36 2007   C813'.6   C2007-904808-0

We acknowledge the financial support of The
Canada Council for the Arts for our publishing
activities.

We acknowledge the support of the Department of Tourism, Culture
and Recreation for our publishing activities.

Printed in Canada

To Elizabeth.

"I wish you'd write a
book," she said.

Acknowledgements

I should like to thank the Writers' Alliance of Newfoundland and Labrador for its support of this book through its mentorship program. As that mentor, Ed Kavanagh deserves my heartiest thanks for his critical eye and helpful suggestions as he hacked his way through early drafts in the winter of 2005. Finally, thanks go to my editor at Jesperson, Annamarie Beckel, for what still seems a surreally gentle final treatment of the manuscript and its author.

A gentle snow is starting to bury the orange extension cord that leads to Gerry Adamson. The cord begins at a plug on a post in a boatyard by a quiet, black little river that swallows the snowflakes before the sea swallows it. The river is starting to freeze along the banks.

The cord runs past a dark, boarded-up clubhouse, around and under cradled boats, their summer personalities mummified in plastic tarpaulins, netting and old tires on ropes. Back by the dark spruce trees at the corner of the yard, the cord comes to a boat that has had its tarp cocoon partially peeled back. A ladder is tied to the rail and a snow shovel stands in the corner of the cockpit. Like scat or new-dug earth around a burrow, they proclaim that this boat is inhabited.

The cord leaves the snow and snakes upward and onto the boat. Secured to a cleat with a bit of line, it dives through a tape-muffled notch in a hatch. Inside, it is joined by three other cords. One leads to a small ceramic heater that looks like a hot radio. Another powers a small table lamp. The third, with an adaptor, is hooked to a laptop computer on the tiny galley table. Sitting on his sleeping bag with a cup of sweet tea beside him, Gerry Adamson pokes the keys.

The boat's cabin is small and Gerry can reach out and touch most of what he thinks he needs just now. The kettle on the galley alcohol stove is close enough beside him that he's aware of its heat. His bed is one of the cabin seats. He has piled one gym bag of clothes and another of papers and small red and black notebooks in the V-berth. A shit, a shower or a telephone call is an outing, an excursion down the ladder, through the wintry yard and into the silent clubhouse with the ghostly notices of last summer's barbecues gibbeted on the bulletin board.

Gerry shuffles through the notebooks or scrolls through the electronic guts of the laptop. He wonders and tries to write down how, in the last year or so, he's managed to get his world this small.

one

NOVEMBER 2003

T he woman on the telephone is on the cusp, somewhere between a nanny-ish desire for precision and ethnic cleansing. "You're not from here, are you?"

"No. Not originally," Gerry admits, wondering how far he should go with this. After all, this is somebody trying to jump the queue on an open-line show by calling an office number. He doesn't actually have to produce his papers or pedigree. Just put her through to bother the technician and have her say about offshore oil revenues or Churchill power. "But I've been here for thirty years or so."

"I knew it. You're not a Newfoundlander," the woman says fiercely.

"Would you like me to put you through to the studio?" Gerry asks, deciding that it's better to roll over and play dead.

"Do you think they fly the Canadian flag in the Quebec House of Assembly?" she demands. "Where are you from anyway? Where do you belong to?"

"Sort of all over the place," Gerry says, rustling papers to make a distraction and going for busy-jovial. "I've got another call coming in now. I'll put you right through."

Gerry pushes a couple of buttons on the phone and hopes he's inadvertently (or not) cut the old hag off.

Old hag, except she's probably younger than he is. You can't count on crotchety people to be older than you are when you're pushing sixty and have still managed to avoid getting a grown-up job. Once upon a time he could have been confident that she was a cardigan-draped pillar of the altar guild, a million years older than he was. Now he's not so sure, and besides, her question rankles. Where is he from?

When Gerry was a child, he liked books with maps of where the characters lived. *Winnie the Pooh* and *House at Pooh Corner* had maps on the inside of the covers. They showed the topography of the Hundred Acre Wood and Eeyore's Gloomy Place. The North Pole, as discovered by Pooh, was helpfully indicated.

Wind in the Willows was the same, with the river snaking past Toad Hall and Rat's and Mole's houses and the Wildwood and the town in the background. Pan's Island split the river in that circumspect way maps have of not giving away the sacredness of what they show.

Gerry mentally designs the map for the inside of his personal book covers. There is the town wrapped around the harbour behind the palisade of Signal Hill and Gibbet Hill. The south-side is the other doorpost of the secret seaward entrance. A couple of times Gerry has approached the city from the sea, and he is always surprised at how secret it is, the narrow entrance opening only as you bring the range lights on the wharf and the church-toothed hillside into line. Inside the harbour, hanging like laundry from the washing lines of the map contours, are the places Gerry mostly lives.

In the pigeon canyon of Water Street are two coffee shops. On good days they are the drawing pins that anchor his mornings to his world. On bad ones, they're the nails, crucifying him on the street for premeditated idleness. One coffee shop is comfortably unkempt and all its employees seem to do something else as well. They disappear from time to time to be in bands or to have photographic exhibitions or to read their poetry in bars.

Gerry calls the other The Coffee Shop of the Debutantes From Outer Space. It has enormous, slightly mouldy looking, velveteen armchairs that are hugely comfortable. The girls who work in it are improbably beautiful. They seem to speak Earthling as a second language. However, the space debs sell you your second, and all further cups of coffee, at half price. The first coffee shop offers no half-price arrangement, although from time to time a coffee becomes entirely free. The system is entirely random. The chairs are also hard. Gerry suspects it may be some kind of levy on those who want their caffeine in a bohemian milieu.

Up the hill from the coffee shops is the radio station where Gerry is fairly frequently employed. It is a large grey building that sticks up out of the jumble of clapboard row houses like the stone you would choose to hop to in crossing a brook. It looks broad enough to land on safely. Many times through the years, Gerry has hopped back onto it, but, as is the problem with comfortable stepping stones, he finds it difficult to hop to something else. He sometimes feels he has been standing paralyzed in midstream for years. Only the rush of the current around him gives his life any sense of movement at all.

In other wrinkles and folds of the rocky town are the other places Gerry lives. There is his house in what was suburbia forty years ago. It's on a street of forty-year-old trees. Thirty years ago a younger Gerry Adamson lived in the downtown and walked through his future neighbourhood, scorning it on his way to work.

"Little houses made of ticky tacky…" He would hum the old Malvina Reynolds' song. "All made of ticky tacky and they all look just the same."

In those days the trees hadn't been planted long. It still amazes Gerry, if he takes a walk on a wet fall night, how grown-in and leaf-tunnelled the neighbourhood has become.

Over a brook, in one case, and some low hills in another, are two shopping malls where Gerry has been known to dither, hide, scribble in endless morning notebooks, or shop for presents and peace offerings. Many of his presents are peace offerings.

Beyond the malls the spruce and bog make forays into the strip malls and the subdivisions. Tim Hortons coffee shops dot the scrubland, guard towers on the frontier of Suburbia. In summer Gerry sometimes ventures farther. He leaves the sea of the harbour mouth behind to discover the other sea of The Bay, behind the town and 'round the corner. It's a smaller-yet-bigger world, like the world's best imaginable electric train set with miniature harbours interspersed with adventures of sensible scale.

Beyond that lie the places that can only be flown to: Upalong, Away, and The Old Country. Gerry comes from Upalong. He has visited Away and The Old Country, but the jury is still out on where he belongs.

In a dim late-fall afternoon, when the open-line show has been herded off the air, Gerry sits in the coffee shop of the space debs. He's got the cryptic crossword from *The National Post* and a little black and red Chinese notebook. He buys the notebooks from a bookstore that also sells pewter wizards and dragons, Tarot cards and tin toys from Taiwan, knock-offs of toys Gerry had fifty years ago. He keeps a sporadic sort of journal in the Chinese notebooks and stows them in bookshelves and desk drawers against the time he needs them to help write the novel he says he's going to write.

"Alchemist is an anagram for St. Michael," Gerry informs the space deb in low-rise pants who's clearing tables. He moves his crossword to let her get on with it. Her skin has an unnatural bright-bronze look, like statuary in an MGM '50s bible epic.

"Have you been south?" Gerry asks. Asking about holidays is about the limit of any intimacy that has established itself between him and the polished alien waitresses. He thinks *between* and not among because he suspects they have one shared intelligence. What planets consenting adults vacation on is their own business. However, holidays are something the waitresses are programmed to discuss if they're in a forthcoming mood.

"No, I was in a bodybuilding contest on the weekend," she says and strikes a flexed pose. Between the bottom of her short shirt and the top of her low pants, the bit of her stomach that shows becomes a narrow, vertical rectangle like the box an expensive bottle of liquor comes in. Its sharp edges are softened by being lightly upholstered in microscopic peach fuzz and artificially bronze goose flesh.

"How did that go?"

"I got third. A whole bunch of us got third. It was the first contest they'd had. I think they want a lot of us to keep working out."

"Will you?"

"No. I don't know. Maybe…but hey, I mean, like I got a third, you know."

Gerry thinks he knows all about coming third.

The coffee shop is decorated in elaborate garlands of evergreen and those new space lights of such an intense blue that they seem to radiate dark. It is supposed to be almost Christmas and has been, it seems, for months.

Gerry puts the crossword aside and scribbles in his notebook: *Whatever happened to November as a month?* He also jots down a note that St. Michael is an anagram for alchemist. The space waitress may not be around to remind him if he ever needs to know.

Gerry arrived in St. John's in November 1972 and he doesn't remember it feeling like Christmas then. Late one Sunday night, he and his ex, Patricia, rode into town at opposite ends of a CN bus. They weren't married yet. They had left Ottawa hand-in-hand. After four days on buses, broken by a rough night on the ferry, they had found separate seats where they could stretch out more.

"Don't touch me. I think I've got bugs," Patricia announced tightly, after a taxi took them from the train station bus stop to a hotel they thought they could afford. She spent a long time in the shower.

He had paid for the room in advance while she was in the lobby washroom. It cost sixteen dollars. They were supposed to be on a strict budget.

"How much was the room?" Patricia asked as they went upstairs. It was close to midnight and they'd been off the boat since early morning, but she still had a seasick pallor. She looked like she needed to lie down.

"Ten bucks," Gerry said. It was the first time he had lied to her.

The first but not the last, he thinks now.

When they felt better and started to explore the town, Gerry remembers it as being like the Novembers from early childhood, a separate, pre-Christmas winter season of its own. It was a gentler, English picture book winter, made of first snowmen and last robins, with inglenooks and cherry-bright fires in elaborate hearths. December was more intense because November was separate.

Gerry thinks the orphanage raffle was the first sign of approaching Christmas back then. He looks out into Water Street and remembers the kids with handbells clanging away for the Mount Cashel draw. They stood in front of a shop with a floor full of ticket stubs and slush and cigarette butts. The air was full of smoke and the bells and the endless whir of the big, numbered wheel.

"Win a turkey, mister," had a Dickens ring to it. "A turkey bigger than me."

The bells don't ring now and Mount Cashel is a subdivision and Gerry covered the abuse hearings and a couple of the trials a dozen or more years ago.

There was always a lot of Dickens that he hated, Gerry thinks, but he sort of misses the handbells.

two

DECEMBER 2003

I f tonight is any indication, it will be a green Christmas. There is a hard, slanting rain driving against the house, rattling the vinyl siding that Gerry still thinks of as new, although it's been on the house for about five years now. The siding has a louder, tinnier rattle than the old cedar it replaced. Gerry had fought with Vivian to keep the cedar.

"I painted it," he said.

"It's falling apart," said Vivian. "Everybody's got vinyl now. You don't have to look after it all the time."

He still expects the vinyl to come off on wet windy nights like this.

The vinyl wars are behind them tonight. Gerry and Vivian are pottering in their kitchen. She is re-hanging a Christmas garland that has come partially unstuck over the kitchen door. Gerry is washing their few supper dishes. They've had a run of Christmas parties to go to and have been pigging out. Tonight they've been fighting a rearguard action, eating soup and a salad. They've been toying with the idea of a movie.

"It's a rotten night out there," Vivian says, tottering on a kitchen chair in her stocking feet. The joints in her toes whiten under nylon as they flex to maintain her balance on the chair. Life is unconscious acrobatics. "Do you really want to see a movie? We could stay in. I'm up to my arse with Christmas stuff and I've got a lot of paperwork to sort out." Vivian sells real estate. She climbs off her chair and they move around each other, straightening the kitchen. Vivian is workout trim and still in black slacks and a good sweater. Her hairdresser has given her short hair a red streak. Gerry is taller, bulkier, bearded and dressed in old cords and a sweater. She moves around him like an escort around a battleship in the kitchen. The rain rattles the siding again.

"I'm happy this Christmas," Vivian announces. She climbs down off her chair, crosses the kitchen and leans into him. "Are you happy?"

This is the sort of question that can explode. Gerry approaches it cautiously. He knows he's supposed to be happy.

"After all, I live in a vinyl house that I don't have to paint."

Gerry sometimes thinks Vivian sees happiness the same way she sees cleanliness and takes it far too seriously. She pulls spot checks. If there is a suspicion that the standard is slipping, the housecleaning can be worse than a bit of squalor. Confessing to the most trivial angst can land you in a fit of emotional attic cleaning.

"Be happy, damn you!"

"Pretty content, I guess," Gerry says. "Not actively suicidal over the outdoor lights or anything."

Christmas traditions are another minefield. He knows he should shut up now, but the notion of not belonging anywhere has sneaked into the kitchen like a guilty wet dog. He can't stop himself adding, "I feel a bit itchy sometimes. You know, fidgety."

"Not about us?" Vivian's touchy sea-urchin spines stir in the sluggish post-supper current of the kitchen.

"No. God no!" Gerry says, then adds, "I'm going back at the book, I think."

He has surprised himself. Through nearly twenty years with Vivian he's threatened to write a novel. He has filled filing cabinets with notes and scribbles and the dead Chinese notebook journals. He's made starts that disappear like rivers in a desert after fifty pages, but it's been months since he sat down to write anything long.

"I'm a radio writer," he jokes when pressed. "I get to three pages and expect somebody to give me money."

Two tatty folders of typescript that once claimed to be finished products lurk in the bottom of a filing cabinet in the basement. Gerry's ex, Patricia, had found them in the bottom of a trunk and sent them back. He wondered at the time what her motive was: prosecution exhibits to justify her going perhaps. Judged by length, they could charitably be called novellas. They were written back in Gerry's drinking days when he thought every word was god-given. There are polite but firm rejection slips tucked into them too. Thanks, but no thanks. They made better recitations at the ends of house parties.

"Anyway," Gerry says, "I'm thinking about getting at it again, trying to make sense of it all, and sort of trying to explain how I got here."

"I'd love it if you'd do that," Vivian says, putting the soup pot away under the counter. "But I don't want to push you though. I think you're afraid of failure sometimes."

"I am not," Gerry retorts, making a flurry with the dishcloth. "I revel in it. I have failed consistently and creatively for thirty years now. Anybody who hasn't failed has never tried to do anything hard."

"You haven't failed," says Vivian. Her office wall has a poster of a cat struggling to cling to a rope with "Hang in there, baby!" on it. "I mean, you're always working. You haven't failed."

"Or tried," mutters Gerry.

Some years ago, when Gerry thought the bottom was falling out of the freelance radio journalism market, he went out and rented himself an office to become a man of letters. He imagined Virginia Woolf and Alice Munro turning cheerleader cartwheels as he took the little room on the back of a strip mall. He furnished it with two Wal-Mart filing cabinets with a door blank across them for a desk. He took in a brand new swivel chair, a coffee maker and his computer. His office window looked out on a dumpster, a rear parking lot and a cemetery over a fence. The rent was satisfyingly low and idiosyncratic, seventy-three dollars a month. Vivian had gone to see the office the first spring he rented it. He was proud of its starkness, like the orderly room of a puritan battalion in a front-line attic in some urban guerrilla war. The computer had a tool-like, weapon-like practicality. It was like a lathe, drill press or machine gun under the pale fluorescent light of the little room. He felt he should be able to take it apart and put it together blinfolded. In the office, he hoped to make tangible, workman-like words out of his drifting life. It was a place for invention, stripped to its industrial guts, with a cheque-cashing service and a mini-mart next door.

Unfortunately Gerry always preferred gathering the oddments of raw material to sitting down and putting them together.

"Why do you pay rent on that darn room?" Vivian asked after a year or two. She had a point. Gerry hadn't been near the place in a couple of months. Its equipment and purpose made it too accusatory a place to get away from home in. It was easier to sit in the coffee shops with a notebook, or just drive around.

"It's not costing you anything, is it?" he demanded. "You haven't been asked to contribute to the rent. Besides it's a tax write-off."

The book and the office failed to thrive. After several years more, the office was abandoned. The filing cabinets, the door blank and the computer got moved to Gerry and Vivian's basement. So did the malaise they produced in Gerry. A laundry basket on top of a file cabinet could scare him back upstairs in an instant.

"It's too nice a day to lurk in the basement. Let's go for a walk," he'd say. He found a walk in the park or through the nighttime neighbour-hood took his mind off the accusing scraps of paper and stale notebooks. Vivian found it was just as well to go with him for the walks. He was less irritable around the house.

She took over the door-blank worktable to sew new living room drapes.

"How the hell am I supposed to write with all that crap there?" he demanded, waving at her table and lapful of pale heavy cloth. "What the hell's wrong with the drapes we've got?"

"They don't match the room, you poor fool," Vivian shot back. "They haven't matched the room since we painted and it needs doing again. I hate that goddamn room."

"A zoo," he yelled. "I live in a fucking designer zoo."

"Oh, go on with you, boy," Vivian said. "By the time you get around to doing anything, I'll be out of here. I'll take the damn drapes and go on with them if you need to write something."

The "new" drapes are three years old now.

People who don't go to church often, go at Christmas. Gerry doesn't go to Alcoholics Anonymous often anymore, but on an evening in mid-December he finds himself driving through the dark streets to a '60s-modern church not too far from home. He feels he needs a booster shot against the Christmas spirit. The parking lot is too full to be all AA people, and when he goes in, he can hear the organ from the sanctuary and the coughing that suggests a full house. He goes to the church library for his meeting.

There are AA meetings and AA meetings. Gerry has been to some that have the smell of puke, piss and desperation still strong in the room. Then again, once in Ottawa he went to one so calm and existential it was rather other-worldly.

"Hi, my name is Gerry and if I exist and alcoholism exists, I'm an alcoholic," he described it to Vivian later.

The people Gerry listened to at that meeting, and talked to over gritty carrot cake and coffee afterwards, seemed to imply that they'd only become drunks to further the cause of addictions research.

This meeting isn't like that. It's got a good mix of people, long-timers and newcomers. Gerry sees people he used to carouse with when George Street was just starting to be a bar ghetto and before that, when the neighbourhoods of town seemed to be a network of booze capillaries and alcohol nodes he could navigate like a sodden corpuscle. There's some grey long hair at tonight's session and some fashionable clothes and the talk is generally pretty bright.

There's only one first-timer, a scared-looking woman accompanied by a pretty woman with white hair parted in the middle, but a surprisingly young face that looks like it came off a '60s album cover, peering over a dulcimer perhaps. Gerry remembers her when she hung around the bar where a lot of reporters and actors hung out in the '70s. He sort of remembers that she tried to cut her wrists with a broken bottle in the toilet one night, He looks at her wrists but she has long sleeves and bracelets.

The chair asks the newcomer if she wants to speak. She's got a narrow face collapsing into the black holes of her eyes and she's twisting Kleenex and paper napkins into tight, white worms.

"My name is Lori—"

"Hi Lori," the room booms for her.

Hi Doctor Nick, thinks Gerry, who watches *The Simpsons* before the news comes on at suppertime.

"I just want to…I don't know, just feel better, I guess."

"You're in the right place, Lori," the chair tells her. "Just sit back and listen."

And hope you recognize somebody, Gerry thinks. He remembers coming to a first meeting fifteen years ago and being surprised at the number of people he thought were dead who were there, apparently alive and well and sober. He'd lost track of them when they disappeared from the pieces of the bar scene he inhabited. Any program that could raise the dead had something going for it.

The chair knows his crowd and turns the evening into a sort of greatest hits night for Lori's benefit. He's a square-set man with a grey ponytail. Gerry remembers that he's some kind of geologist and used to play rugby. He remembers singing hymns and rugby songs with him at a keg party somewhere a million years ago.

A few people looked askance at Gerry tonight because he didn't identify himself as a newcomer. That's how seldom he goes to meetings anymore. There are people at this meeting who consider themselves regulars and have never seen him before. The chair must remember their singing together though, because he remembers Gerry's name and calls on him.

"Hi, my name is Gerry and I'm an alcoholic and I'm glad to be here tonight." Gerry's not a hundred percent sure he is glad to be here but, what the hell? Something brought him. He could have stayed home or gone shopping or whatever. Besides, he used to be glad, unbelievably, unbelievingly glad when a week of doing the impossible and not taking a drink stretched into three months and he got a copper medallion like a licence tag for a big dog. He lost the medallion somewhere, but the months have turned slowly into years.

He decides it's important that Lori should be glad to be here, so he talks indirectly to her.

"The first time I came in here I'd walked around town all day to keep moving so I wouldn't have a drink. I couldn't make up my mind if I wanted to admit I was a drunk or go to the Waterford Hospital and say I was crazy. I decided to be a drunk because I was afraid that if I got in the Waterford, they'd never let me out or they'd zap my memory. I write and I figured I needed my memory. Once I came in here, I sort of knew I'd made the right decision. It gets easier."

Gerry sits down.

"Good words there," the chair intones.

Gerry sits back and wonders who he is trying to convince by mentioning that he writes. He does his journalistic writing of course, but he suspects he could do that zapped or lobotomized or whatever. He doesn't do anything very challenging.

The meeting flows on around him and he looks at the room. This library has bemused him before. It's richly lined with books from religious publishing houses. Gerry has sometimes wandered around looking at titles before meetings, or afterwards, during the coffee and cookies. They range from studies of the obscure miracles of obscure saints to '50s *Readers Digest*-style things like *Switchblade and the Cross* and Doctor Tom Dooley's medical missions in Indo-China. There are how-to books on daily devotion and "issues" books like *God and Globalization*. As far as Gerry has been able to discover through casual browsing, Saint Rose of Viterbo and Saint Beatrice da Silva have Thomas Merton heavily outnumbered and there's no sampling of other philosophies.

He remembers going to parent-teacher night, back when there was still denominational education and Tanya, Vivian's youngest daughter, was in school. For reasons that made sense to Vivian when she took the kids and got out of her first marriage, Tanya was in the Catholic system. At one session, her homeroom teacher enthused about the new religious education text that had come out that year. In the meet-and-greet afterwards, Gerry had suggested the book didn't give much space to anything but the home team.

"Couldn't it be taught like herpetology?" Gerry asked the teacher, a youngish version of Dr. Bunsen Honeydew on *The Muppets*, round and bland and up-to-date.

"How's that, Mr. Adamson?"

Gerry could see him riffling through a mental card file of "ologies," trying to place herpetology.

"Snakes, right?" He looked at Gerry hopefully, expecting a joke perhaps.

"I mean," Gerry said, "that it's a grand thing to know all about snakes and have a serious enthusiasm for snakes, but the goal isn't necessarily to graduate snakes at the end of the course."

The faux Honeydew said that was an interesting point and went on to talk to somebody else.

Gerry has a friend, Philip, who hangs out in the coffee shops and is a sceptic who wants a funeral. He says most religions demand that he take on faith the existence of a giant pink rabbit. Empirical evidence of the big pink bunny strikes him as being in short supply, so he's moved away from organized religion. Still, he says, there's no reason that a sceptic shouldn't have some inspiring words read over him. On and off, he is cherry-picking his way through the ancients, east and west. He's gathering snippets of text that he says should do for a humanist send-off. However, he feels classic Buddhism is bleak, and Taoism and Zen are a bit slap-dash and happy-go-lucky.

"Lackadaisical even," he says, looking at the Chinese notebook like Gerry's, where he writes down his snippets. Gerry told him the shop to buy them at.

Gerry also has a story about "lackadaisical." At his work, he tells Philip, they have to transcribe the clips of people speaking that they put in radio pieces. Some reporter, who went to school after spelling stopped being a subject and apparently didn't read a lot, transcribed "lackadaisical attitude" as "lack of daisy-go attitude."

"That's what I suffer from," Gerry told Philip. "A lack of daisy-go attitude. I can't remember the last time I had even a touch of daisy-go attitude."

Philip continues to gather final-sounding aphorisms. At the moment though, his hypothetical funeral features a lot of Marcus Aurelius and Confucius.

Sitting in the church library listening to people stay sober through Christmas, Gerry feels that Philip's pink rabbit is over-represented on the bookshelves. There should be more Marcus and Confucius and a section on what to do when your daisy-go goes.

When the meeting breaks up and Gerry goes outside, it has started to snow. He brushes off his grubby little SUV and drives home through big snowflakes like flower petals, daisy petals maybe, daisy petals going.

On a Saturday when Vivian has gone Christmas shopping, Gerry goes to the basement, passing under the plywood duck-shape he cut out and stuck over the stairs as the international symbol for "duck." He roots in his cabinets and desk drawers for the scribblers, notebooks stamped with glass and cup rings like old passports. He makes piles of paper, sorting by period, mood, or degree of physical damage, reconstructing how he got here.

Call this the CFA pile, Gerry muses as he unearths a nineteenth-century looking duplicate notebook that he'd found in his mother's house on a visit a couple of years before. It's the kind with one-sided carbon pages that automatically left a copy of what was written. In it he'd printed a bunch of poems by hand. Today it seems impossible that there was a time when he didn't type, when ballpoint and carbon seemed the best way to leave smudges of a human-shaped animal on the cave wall.

Gerry pours a coffee and looks at his come-from-away self before he knew he was a CFA. His 1960s and early '70s lurk between the blue marble-pattern covers.

> *Cupid is a fascist*
> *With shiny black jackboots*
> *Smeared with small pieces*
> *Of hearts he's machine-gunned;*
> *A thousand valentines*
> *Flap wildly in his camp,*
> *Battle flags abounding.*

"Christ, this kid!" Gerry says softly to himself. The oil furnace cuts in with a breathy, but probably sympathetic sigh. He wonders if he goes upstairs and finds the Leonard Cohen anthology Vivian gave him a few anniversaries back, will he be able to track what he was reading when he wrote some of this. Then again, maybe it wasn't that profound.

> *I was walking my serpent in the garden*
> *And I let him off the leash*
> *To frolic among the flowers and lovers,*
> *When up came a silver-wingèd cop*
> *Who said all serpents must,*

Must be kept on the leash, not
Let frolic et cetera et cetera;
So I sadly took my serpent and went home
To eat apples in my room.

"Record jackets," Gerry says aloud, "I must have been reading frigging record jackets."

In another pile of paper, Gerry finds himself in St. John's for the first time. At some point over the years he has transcribed some of the stuff he wrote when he and Patricia, his first wife, lived in the east-end.

Why is the night?
Because of the dog, child,
Obscene fat doggy,
Soul beneath his waggle:
He licks the sun
From the pavement
Like ice cream;
Dirty, mouldy dog,
Like a hairy Dutch cheese,
Dreams all gurgly
And burps another morning;
Nice fat doggy.

Gerry had written that the first autumn he and Patricia had come to St. John's. It occurs to him that you no longer see the packs of almost mythologically ugly crackies that used to drift up and down the hilly streets in the older parts of town. Dogs are tied on now and belong to recognizable breeds and, for all Gerry knows, health clubs and spas and new-age churches. Their owners walk them with pockets full of shopping bags to pick up the dog shit. Gerry sometimes argues that picking up dog shit is making humanity stupider. A basic lesson in watching where you're going has been removed. Shuffle along any old way. Never mind the dog poop. There's no need to be watchful or learn the steps in the dance of life.

"Don't be silly," Vivian tells him. "It's not sanitary."

At any rate, the weird dog creatures are no longer around, but they were when he and Patricia were setting up housekeeping in 1972 or so. Maybe they huddled together for safety from the mythological crackies. They'd only just learned the word and could conjure with it. Maybe when the crackie packs disappeared they had no further need of each other and fell apart.

The house is ghostly quiet and Gerry goes upstairs to make a cup of tea. He feels like a museum visitor, sidling past the baroque splendours of Vivian's Christmas decorations. The few cars that pass in the street make soft noises like rotten old flags tearing. He makes the tea in the pot rather than in the cup and takes it back to the basement with him. Somewhere over the years he had come by a mini electric pad, a tiny hot plate for keeping a mug warm. He plugs it in, balances the teapot on it and returns to thirty years ago. Pawing through the snippets and false starts in his middle-class basement, he compares then and now.

It seems to Gerry that he and Vivian dress quite a lot alike now. They both wear khaki pants in summer and blazers when they dress up. They buy sweaters and suburban sweatshirts at Work Warehouse. He and Patricia may have shopped in the same stores but their look was different.

Patricia wore a lot of Danskin leotard tops and he remembers a short suede skirt. They'd joke and call it a wide belt. On other days she went to the opposite extreme and wore a maxi-length jumper that he called her one-legged overalls. In the winter she piled an antique raccoon coat over it all.

Gerry wore high-top work boots and cords under old tweed or leather sports jackets or the sailorish, vinyl-shouldered donkey jacket he'd bought in the UK after university. He bought a salt-and-pepper cap and wore it. They had a gypsy air as they walked to and from the bus stops of the east-end. Gerry has an old picture of them in an album Pat sent back when everybody had divorced and remarried and settled into amiability. In the picture they look as though they might be about to break into some sort of street performance at any moment.

All we needed was a tambourine and a dancing bear.

Gerry is being good today. He actually turns on the computer and transcribes bits of stuff and looks at old scenes he's written. Often he doesn't get that far and curls up with a book on the couch.

"I don't know what you do all day, "Vivian will say. "I wish I had time to just sit and read."

"If you don't read, you can't write," Gerry retorts, but with his fingers slightly crossed. You do have to stop reading at some point to start writing. As it is, he works enough odd hours and relief shifts in radio to find excuses for not doing much personal writing. That, and the fact he usually has supper on the table when Vivian gets home, save him from being accused of being lazy, a major sin in Vivian's world.

"People like you enjoy painting stones white in the army," Gerry says, only half-teasing.

"So what?" says Vivian. In fact there is a ring of small white-painted beach rocks around a tree in their backyard.

Gerry has tried to trick or coerce himself into putting something substantial down on paper, to jump-start his creativity. Some time ago he joined a writing workshop, although he doubted that it would do anything about the real problem of sitting down long enough to put the bits together.

At first the workshop felt slightly odd, with a home-and-school-meeting flavour to the cups of coffee and the homemade muffins, notebooks and journals. Then it became the first day at the nude beach. People tended to look over each other's shoulders, obliquely at the walls, or at the pattern in the carpet and wonder if everyone else was doing the same. Then came the old dressing room cliché, the sideways comparative glances. People began to learn either to pay polite attention to each other's naughty bits or to forget about them entirely.

As the writing sessions went on, Gerry watched his group-mates.

There was the woman who always arrived at the last minute dressed in running gear. Her name was Pamela and she had a slightly explosive look. Gerry would wonder if she was going to read or break dishes or burst into tears. She had a full knuckle of wedding and engagement rings, but talked about having been dropped off by her boyfriend. She seemed to be doing the workshop either as therapy or as a form of martial arts training in preparation for some great retributive war.

"My ex would kill me if he knew I was going to write a book," she said. Then she asked, "You can't get sued if you change the names, right?"

Pamela seemed to be deputizing the group to be on guard for prowling former husbands or their spies. She wrote and read angrily and fast in the first person. She didn't seem to understand any discussion of synthesis in fiction and made no bones about being her own protagonist, in fact, her own heroine.

Walking home on nice nights, or driving on miserable ones, Gerry would wonder if he was his own hero in his writing. Mostly he felt he was only the stage things were acted out on. He felt littered by bits and pieces of other people, like the traffic jam of corpses at the end of *Hamlet*.

As an assignment Gerry tried to write about himself and Patricia in their early days. He called them George and Paula.

"Hey hey, Paula," he hummed as he wrote.

Fragment: Streets

It seems to him that they spent a lot of time on the streets then. He supposes it was a function of not having a car. They walked a lot for cheap recreation and for the buses they needed to take them to their jobs and sometimes to the mall. The mall was still new then. When people heard you'd just arrived in town, they'd ask if you had been to the mall yet.

George and Paula were new to St. John's and childishly delighted with what they found in its streets. They'd compare notes on the mute shoeshine boy who gargled a greeting at them as they walked to the bus stop or to the narrow liquor store opposite the war memorial for a bottle of cheap wine. The shoeshine boy had a gaudy painted box to rest your foot on. It was decorated with hand-painted American flags and Union Jacks, harking back to the war days when the shoeshine boy had started in his trade and had really been a boy and not a gnarled little man with a lot of grey showing under his cap. The shoeshine box also had religious medals tacked onto it.

"They say he doesn't really give a very good shoeshine," George reported to Paula. "He'll polish your socks if you're not careful."

George got a job with a newspaper that let him hang out in bars a lot and get the lowdown on the street characters. Paula was working in a boutique. She didn't want to teach just yet and get into that whole middle-class thing. The boutique was called The Vales of Har. In the basement they had a second-hand bookstore called The Books of Thel. They got a fair number of customers who didn't get the Blake references and were looking for science fiction. They got enough that they finally had to stock some.

Often, as George walked Paula to work, they'd meet the two little musical winos who used to dance the length of Duckworth Street. They were jockey-sized men who wore old suit jackets over layers of shirts. In cold weather they pulled the lapels shut across their chests with one hand. One played the harmonica, not-too-badly. The other did a shuffling step-dance to the music. They never stayed in one place but shuffled along like some archaic sky-driven street-cleaning device. At times the wind seemed to propel them around the corners.

In the evenings, George and Paula built a papier maché wino. They made a frame of chicken wire that George bought at Neyle-Soper Hardware, crimping it together with pliers. Then they made flour and water paste and slathered strips of newspaper over it in layers. It dried poorly in the apartment and grew some spots of mould. They thought that was great.

"Wino-rot, far out!"

"Intimations of mortality built right in…"

They dressed their wino in the same sort of thrift-store clothes they bought for themselves, including a salt-and-pepper cap like George's. They darkened the eye sockets and sketched features with magic marker, but in the end they decided against painting their creation. His complexion was a fog of smudged print and dried mould. They stabilized the surface with artist's spray shellac. The wino had a small loop of wire protruding above his collar at the back that let him be hung bashfully in a corner. A cigarette butt, smoked to a filter stub, was glued to his lips.

When they didn't have a major project like the wino to work on and neither had to work in the evening, they'd sit in their crow's nest top-floor apartment that creaked like a ship when the wind funnelled through the narrow harbour entrance and swept up the street. Paula painted watercolours at the kitchen table. She painted pitcher plants and bunches of dogberries and sold them on consignment at The Vales of Har. They actually sold quite well. Paula painted in a mock-Victorian, ladylike, tidy style that middle-class housewives, slumming at The Vales, thought pretty.

George read or settled at his Woolco Smith Corona portable at a shaky worktable in the corner of their living room. His two-finger typing made the table wobble as he wrote. They had a cork bulletin board on one living room wall, an organic collage of whatever they were doing. When George finished a poem he'd pin it to the board for contemplation next to the doodles and *evil little caricatures that Paula did. She drew the ladies in fur coats who bought Mexican and Indian jewellery for the nights they were being Bohemian or who played art patron by acquiring her watercolours.*

"Don't you have one with more green, dear?" she'd mimic. "I'm doing the kitchen avocado."

They also clipped George's stories out of the newspapers and put them on the wall. They still weren't used to seeing him validated in print. It seemed incredibly grown-up to have words you'd written available on doorsteps and under newsboys' arms every morning.

"Why should we care about these people making a chicken-wire wino?" asked Leona, the woman who ran the writing workshop. She had written a novel about the Labrador coast.

Because we did, Gerry thought. Because we thought the world was new and wonderful, warts and all. We wanted to build wart monuments.

He was tempted to add that no polar bears ate their children and, in fact, they didn't have children. He said something else though, something a bit disloyal to his Paula/Patricia and George/Gerry.

"It's setting a scene," he said. "It's showing how naïve they are."

He reflected that it wasn't the first time he'd betrayed Patricia, or himself. We were together then. We still came home.

"I had two kids just starting school then," Vivian said, when he tried to tell her about how the group is going and how his Paula and George were received.

Another member of the writing group was a short, boiled-looking man who used to be a purser on a coastal boat until booze got the better of him. His name was Nish and Gerry had met him before at AA meetings. Nish wanted to write about some of the funny things he'd heard or seen on the boats. He wrote larger-than-life snappy endings that sometimes got away from him. One night he read a story that Gerry remembered having heard somewhere else from some of his coastal boat acquaintances.

"The mate was a hard-spoken man, common as pig shit," Nish read. "And when the owner's wife and family were coming aboard, the captain told him to watch his language. He told him to refer to the toilet as 'the facilities' and ask if the ladies would like to wash their hands."

Nish gripped the school notebook he wrote in, readying himself for the climax of the story.

"The mate was nice as pie as they all came aboard," he said, seeming to swell with anticipation. "Then he says, 'Ladies, the facilities is right this way, and if you wants to wash your hands, you can piss in this bucket here.'"

One wet night, Gerry gave Nish a ride home. He was living in a bed-sitter in Rabbittown.

"The wife and me split up," he told Gerry. "I'm going to write a book and show her I can do something."

Gerry wondered if that was what he was trying to do himself, but he kept going to the workshop. It had an optimism he liked. One night a woman announced she had just sold a radio commentary. Her name was Jan and she normally did something clerical in a theatre company.

"It's a program for people who've never been on the radio before," she said. "It's great. You just write it and read it and they give you money, it's neat."

Gerry had heard of the program. He wondered if she'd sell another piece or learn to lurch from one short radio gig to the next the way he did. Then he realized he was a hooker listening to a bride. Jan didn't care. She had done something and got it out there in front of an audience. She was immortal. Gerry envied her the feeling. The millions of words he had spilled onto newsprint or into microphones over the years didn't delight him much. He wanted that first-time feeling compacted into an artefact. He wanted to jump out of the aimless archaeological dig of his life and wave it and yell, "Eureka."

On another drizzly morning Gerry sits in the more austere and bohemian of his two coffee shops and lets the random thoughts come.

How many of us are writing in here today? he writes. *At least three: the blonde girl in the T-shirt at the window, the guy with the chef's clogs and the laptop at the back table, and me.*

Gerry's little notebook fills pleasantly fast. There's something to be said for writing tiny thoughts on little pages in a small book. It seems to bridge a stylistic gap, poetry ripening into prose, he hopes.

The pages look pleasantly cluttered and busy, like bird tracks in snow under a bush that still has a few berries in early winter. He wonders how you translate bird tracks into characters.

"A circle is defined by its tangents," Gerry says half aloud as he writes it. He wonders what a circle being defined by its tangents would look like modelled on a computer screen.

It starts as just the line circle, the circumference. Tangents dart out of nowhere at the edges of the screen and glance off it, spermatozoa with bad aim bouncing off an impermeable round egg in some existential sex-education class. As many points as exist in the circumference, there will be tangents to touch them. The space around the blank circle becomes a weave of crosshatched tangents getting infinitely darker and denser. In time there is only the blank circle on a black field.

How about the inside of the circle? What happens there? What's going on with all the chords and secants?

What the hell is a secant? Gerry asks himself. He sort of thinks he knows, but he'll have to check in the frayed high-school geometry book he lugged back from his mother's house in case it might help him learn navigation. He tries to relate what goes on inside and outside the circle. Imagine chords drawn in between all the points the tangents touch, then all the equal angles subtended by the chords. The inside of the circle blooms in a million equiangular petals, layer upon layer. It seems to Gerry that more is happening inside than outside the imaginary circle.

Geometry as a first cause, he writes. *What do the math people say about that? What about inherent darkening of enclosed circles, insides innately more mysterious than outsides?*

The coffee grinder roars beside him and there's a fine dark smell of coffee.

Dark sucks when surrounded by a circle, he writes, but can't resist adding, *There's a fine piece of obscure wankery.*

three

DECEMBER 2003

Gerry and Vivian are waiting at the airport for two-thirds of her kids
to come home. By some miracle of on-line booking, Tanya, the
youngest, and Duane, the eldest, and his family are both arriving
on the same plane from Toronto. Tanya is coming in from Alberta, and
Duane and his family can get to Newfoundland from where they live,
near Ottawa, quicker by flying to Toronto and meeting her there.
They're all travelling on one of the one or two-syllable airlines that seem
to pop up like mushrooms on the arrival screens these days, Zip or Zap
or Bingo. It amazes Gerry that, if he shops around, he can get to places
on the mainland as cheaply, or even more cheaply, than he could
thirty years ago. In some cases he thinks he's even flying on the same
planes. Bingo, or whatever line it was he last used to get to Ottawa,
flew the old familiar Boeing 737's like the ones Eastern Provincial flew
in the old days. They had tall, pretty young flight attendants who sang
summer-camp-style songs to their passengers. Unlike thirty years
ago, though, they charged for everything. Cheezies cost a dollar.
Dubious-looking sandwiches cost five bucks or more. Gerry wondered
if they had antique value. Maybe they had been discovered, stashed in

the old planes. Bottled water had to be paid for and people did. Gerry remembers free double Scotches and being blissfully buzzed by Halifax.

Gerry and Vivian wait by the arrival gate. She's craning and stretching in her leather coat to look for Duane and Gretchen and their kids, Joshua and Natalie. Gerry looks at her beside him, hair short and recently gone redder, big hoop earrings and a good scarf tied around the strap of her bag. The snow is still holding off and she's wearing low, black walking shoes, jeans and a sweater.

"We look good for breathless grandparents," he says. He's being conciliatory. They'd argued over when to leave for the airport. They often argue about when to leave for things. Gerry likes to go early and hang out. Vivian favours a last-minute dash. When they go somewhere together, they both manage to feel rushed and pressured.

"There they are," Vivian says, neutrally. A truce has been arrived at. "Wave. You're taller. They'll see you."

Gerry waves and watches the family come down the steps.

Vivian had Duane when she was eighteen, so now he doesn't look all that much younger than the reception committee. He's a short, square man, with his mother's snub nose. After Vivian's divorce from his father and before Gerry came along, Duane had fixed things around the house and kept his mother's beat-up car running. She'd been clerking in a store then, studying for her real estate licence, and money had been tight. Duane put himself through technical school by joining the militia, where he worked on radios with the communications squadron. Early on, Gerry always thought of him as "Master Corporal Duane," the rank he achieved before he landed a job in Kanata, just outside of Ottawa, and moved out. That was shortly after Gerry and Vivian got married. He laughed in a guarded way at Gerry's stories about his unsuccessful year in the navy. He laughed in the right places, but seemed wary of the fact that Gerry had been an officer and that he had failed some courses and emerged again as a civilian. Duane hadn't the luxury of trying things on. That said, he didn't socialize with his militia buddies and dropped out entirely when the job in Kanata came along. Gerry grew up in Ottawa and gave Duane some names of people to look up. Duane called on Gerry's elderly mother a couple of times, but other than that, did little to get in touch with anybody Gerry knew. Instead he got in touch with Jesus.

Gerry doesn't remember Ottawa as a born-again kind of town but he supposes it's changed. He knows, for example, that a building which won a Massey Medal for Architecture when it was a brand-new Chinese restaurant in the '60s is a "community temple" now. He saw its scruffy hand-painted sign when he went to Ottawa to visit his mother in her retirement home. He supposes that it's probably no stranger for it to be a church than it was for a Chinese restaurant to go out and hire an architect and win a design medal back when he was in high school. He knows it won the award because he and his buddies, Doc and Mort, were hanging out in the art gallery on the night of the presentations. They were dressed up in sports jackets and skinny ties, trying to look older and cool and not spend any money. They tagged along behind a crowd of people in evening clothes to get free sandwiches and coffee and look at photos of the winning buildings. It occurs to Gerry that Ottawa was a very small town when he lived there. People would put on evening clothes for coffee and sandwiches.

At any rate, Duane started going to church and met Gretchen and got married. Gretchen sounds German but isn't. She comes from Trail, B.C., and her parents just liked the sound of the name. She always strikes Gerry as a bit like Duane in drag, not fat but slightly thickened, with thick, shoulder-length hair. She makes her own clothes and wears a lot of denim. Tonight she's wearing winter boots with thick light-coloured sponge soles. They have a '70s, bargain-basement look to them. Gerry suspects Duane and Gretchen don't waste much money on shoe leather. She and Duane and the kids don't actually live in Kanata. They've bought a place somewhere in the country beyond Richmond, and Duane commutes. They have a horse and are thinking about getting some sheep. Gretchen looks after the horse and a big vegetable garden.

The kids are quiet and big-eyed, half hiding behind their parents. Gerry wonders what they've overheard about Vivian and him. Are they the grandparents from hell?

Joshua is ten, delicate featured. Natalie is eight and carved more like her parents, round cheeks, a Cabbage-Patch-Kids look to her. Vivian wades in with hugs. Gerry grins but hangs back a little.

"How are you doing, guys?" he asks.

He wishes he could do an *Exorcist* head rotation for them and then wink to show that demonic possession isn't really so bad. He shakes hands with Duane and kisses Gretchen on the cheek. She smells of oatmeal and airplane. Gerry wonders if economy airlines can possibly serve porridge, or did she bring her own?

Tanya is making her way down the stairs now. She is the child Gerry had the most to do with. Duane and Melanie, her older sister, moved out fairly early on in his and Vivian's life together. Tanya, now twenty-five, was only eight or so when Gerry appeared on the scene.

"You raised her," Vivian will say. Gerry wonders how true that is, but she arguably is raised. A couple of years ago she went to work in a hotel in Banff. Later she stayed for a while with Vivian's sister in Calgary and got interested in a wildlife technology course that was being offered there. She took it and now she's back in Banff counting elk. When she calls or e-mails she says how much better she likes it than the business courses she started at the university at home.

"Hey kid," Gerry gives her a hug. Tanya's lean and blonde. She has become the type of woman Gerry associates with patting a whippet, fine bones just under the surface. She's wearing a Michelin Man down ski-jacket and jeans and her old air cadet boots. She'd e-mailed to have the boots found and shipped out.

In case I decide to have a formal wedding, she wrote, followed by: *Joke, ha ha!*

She hardly feels there when Gerry hugs her in her marshmallow coat.

"Still wrestling elk there, Hulk?"

"Oh yeah. Bears too, except they're all asleep now."

Gerry tries to picture Tanya doing anything with a bear and gives up. When they lived in a townhouse in an outlying suburb he used to have to walk in front of her to the bus stop on windy snowy days. He broke trail in the snow and cut the wind that held her back in the long pink parka Vivian had bought her that year.

Gerry had been puzzled about being a late-blooming surrogate parent to Tanya. He never knew how much he was supposed to give or expect. Before her teens they had mostly been pals, co-conspirators. He had told her to call him Gerry, reasoning that she already had a father, whether or not he was still around. He sometimes wonders now if he should have left well-enough alone and let her decide what she wanted to call him.

How he and Tanya got along was often an irritant between him and Vivian. He tried to be what he hoped was reasonable, supportive, civil. Vivian was louder, more bloody-minded. She acknowledged no need to be consistent.

"Go! Get! Get upstairs before I smack you!" Vivian could shout. She also invoked unspecified threats. "You're in trouble now, maid! Just you wait!"

Gerry felt he couldn't threaten because he didn't know what he could realistically carry out. He was pretty sure smacking other people's kids wasn't an option.

"You leave all the discipline up to me," Vivian would complain. "Support me a little, can't you?"

However, she'd threaten dire punishments when Gerry got home if he wasn't there when things went wrong.

"You blow me up into some kind of monster," he complained. Then Tanya and a friend got picked up for stealing lipsticks at K-Mart and Vivian thought he over-reacted.

"There's nothing worse than a sneak," he'd grated. "It's not like you needed the stuff. You've got pocket money, you could have bought it. One of these days you're going to be living with other people at university or somewhere. Are you going to steal from them?"

Tanya said nothing. She just looked down, hot and red. She wasn't much of an arguer-back, not with Gerry anyway.

"Kids steal," Vivian had said, shoes off, relaxing with a beer in front of the late news after the cops had left and Tanya had been sent to bed. "She's just acting out."

Gerry wondered if he was just a property-worshipping, middle-class wimp. Was his homily on sneaks hypocrisy and a wimpy cop-out? Maybe he should have congratulated Tanya on taking on the system, becoming a lip-gloss commando, a make-up martyr.

Gerry supposes the ripples of the incident are still expanding off into outer space somewhere, gone to reverberate in some elk pasture in Alberta. He thinks of the times he's been startled when he opens his mouth only to hear a ventriloquist's rendition of his genuine, born-in-

1898, Victorian father. Maybe some wayward elk or back-sliding bear is in for the lecture of its life when Tanya starts channelling him from some buried memory.

Gerry takes charge at the baggage carousels, positioning people where they can spot their bags easily and give warning so the rest of the tribe can snatch them from the circling current of Samsonite, duffel bags and Canadian Tire tool boxes with locks and rope and duct tape. It's a small family myth that Gerry is a practical traveller, familiar with airports and all their mysteries. They load a cart and head out past the triage of cab companies and rent-a-car reps sorting the incoming passengers.

Outside the pinball-machine brightness of the terminal, it's gone drizzly. The tall lights in the parking lot are haloed in drifting sodium-yellow haze. Duane and Gerry pack suitcases into the boot of Gerry's mud-and-salt-stained Honda wagon and crowd five into the back seat, kids on laps.

"It's only a minute to home."

"Can you breathe back there?"

"Yeah, we're fine, we're good…"

The third of Vivian's kids is waiting for them at home. Melanie is the middle child. She lives across town with her husband Darren, who isn't with her tonight. He runs Darren's Donair and Pizza and he's working. Gerry privately calls him "My Other Brother Darren," a reference to Brother Darrel on the *Bob Newhart* TV show.

Melanie has brought her daughter Diana with her tonight. Diana's eight and has been told she can stay up to greet her cousins. She's dozed off on Vivian's basement couch in front of the cartoon channel and Melanie has made corned beef, tuna, and peanut butter sandwiches and put on a pot of coffee.

Melanie is a slim, tallish woman with a bit of last year's purple-red to her hair. She moved out, not long after Duane, and spent half a dozen years waiting tables and partying. In the course of the partying she met Darren, who was in the process of setting up Darren's D&P, as the family called it. Vivian contended that Melanie married Darren because he was such a hapless goof, a stray.

"He's just like Jack," Vivian would complain.

Jack was her ex, who had gone bust running a gas bar in Grand Falls and taken it out on her and the kids until she loaded them on the bus and came to town. Darren is often in debt, behind on his payroll or broke because he likes to play the video gambling machines.

"The government doesn't need to worry about him being behind in his sales tax," Vivian pronounces on Darren from time to time. "They're getting it back triple in those damn machines."

"You've got to pay your stupidity tax," Gerry says.

"You should talk to him," Vivian says. "He'd listen to you."

"What makes you think that?" Gerry says. "The man's thirty-five years old. He's a grown-up, supposedly. How much advice did you take from your mother when you were thirty-five, or eighteen, for that matter?"

"Melanie should pack up Diana and move out," Vivian will say, shifting to her other tack in the ongoing Darren debate.

Darren, for his part, rails against the government.

"They shouldn't have those old machines," he complains. "They ought to be illegal."

Mostly Melanie appears to let it all roll off her. She spends as much time as she can with Diana, ignores Darren when he's morose, and sweeps around in a patter of sneakers. To Gerry, Melanie sometimes seems to be playing in some internal madcap '50s comedy like *I Love Lucy*. She's unnaturally bright and breezy and does the smallest things with Diana with a decisive toss of her head. Melanie has an expressive head. She nods when making points and shakes when saying something isn't so or didn't happen. The toss is a physical exclamation point.

"Right…" Melanie will announce, shaking her autumn-dyed hair aside. "We are going to the store for ice cream!"

Gerry sometimes wonders if all the head movements aren't an effort to look over her shoulder at what might be gaining.

When they arrive home, Melanie has turned the outside Christmas lights on. Gerry doesn't care for Christmas lights but Vivian says it's not Christmas without them. A couple of Christmases, the light debate has ended in tears and slammed doors. He got them up early this year, un-asked, as part of his personal campaign to make Christmas as painless as possible with everybody home. The eaves drip electric icicles and a big lit wreath makes a ring of fairy lights.

"A dartboard to throw reindeer at," Gerry said when he put it up.

The tree is lit-up in the living room. Vivian had it up by the fifteenth of the month.

"It's the best tree we've had yet," she says.

"Every tree is the best we've had yet," Gerry jokes. "It's inevitable, fore-ordained, an endless succession of trees that become perfect the minute we get them in the door." He knows he sounds shallowly avuncular when he talks like this. He finds the jovial-old-cynic role distasteful, but he can't think of another one.

Duane and Gretchen's kids are tired and grumpy from the flight and Diana is out-of-it from being awakened to see them. They all tend to hang on their mothers and whine in vague, distant voices while the grown-ups sit at the kitchen table.

Duane asks a blessing on the sandwiches, "...for this food, thank you, Lord Jesus. Amen."

Vivian looks mildly perplexed. She was an Anglican as a kid, a low-enough Anglican that sandwiches didn't rate a grace. She's pretty much a nothing now.

Gerry has been eating officially unhallowed sandwiches for years and feels that being hungry is grace enough. If he was being all Taoist and Lao Tzu-ish about it, he'd say that eating and being eaten are as much a part of "The Way" as the automatic perfection of Christmas trees. Gretchen, however, seems relieved that the snack is divinely sanctioned.

"No promiscuous, unsanctified sannies for our Gretch," Gerry says to Vivian at the sink.

Gretchen avoids the ham sandwiches. "I'm on the Scripture Diet," she says.

Gerry can't remember tuna or peanut butter in the bible but apparently they pass muster for Gretchen.

Everyone is hungrier or less hungry than they thought they'd be, so the sandwiches and a plate of Christmas cake work out approximately right and get eaten up. The kids are put to bed and the grown-ups sort out bags and rooms and couches and follow them.

Outside, the drizzle slides diagonally through the naked tree branches and rings the street lights. Along the street the Christmas lights throw out the cheesy welcome of long-ago summer hot dog stands and disco lighting. About two in the morning, when Gerry gets up to go to the toilet, the house is silent and the occasional sound of tires from the parkway at the end of the street is like a distant whir of grouse wings far away in a leafless forest. You're not quite sure you heard them.

A little bit of family goes a long way with Gerry. By the next afternoon he's hiding in the basement, pretending to have to write. Vivian sniffs, but he smoothes things over by cooking a big, late breakfast and fussing over them as they plan to go to the mall and go visiting. Gerry hints at writing that must be done and presents that have to be wrapped. He's practically dancing from foot to foot by the time he gets them all out the door. He isn't totally lying. There's always something he ought to be writing.

Sitting at his computer with a cup of coffee, Gerry thinks that he's always found excuses to put distance between himself and the people close to him. Trying to write something was often the excuse. Today he's holed up in the cellar. Thirty years ago he'd hang out in bars and collect what he hoped were legends. He'd tell them to Patricia. He wonders now just when she got bored with dressed-up bar gossip and when she stopped caring how long he spent away gathering it. Still, he had to play the literary druid and go off to the word-woods by himself to gather the herbs for the potions, even if he only grabbed a few weeds and took a nap under a tree.

Gerry has been working on a piece about his early legend gathering for his writing group. He dusts off his characters, George and Paula, and wanders in thirty-year-old east-end fog.

Fragment: Bars

In those days, George remembers, St John's still had neighbourhood bars; in fact, their apartment was on top of one, a third-floor aerie reached by an anonymous door from the hall next to the pool table.

The bar was the sort where middle-aged locals dropped in for a drink at noon hour or a couple of beers after supper. George hung out there in the daytime if he was working nights. He and Paula would drop down in the *evenings sometimes, or they just bought a couple of beers and took them upstairs with them. It meant paying bar prices for beer you could buy at the beer store a block away for half the price, but there was something about having a bar and bartender in your basement.*

Frankie, the bartender, opened every day at ten-thirty in the morning and shut at midnight. He and his wife Veronica were the whole operation, except for Veronica's ancient Uncle Tommy who swept and mopped up. He'd be given a beer when he was finished and then Veronica would drive him home to his boarding house somewhere in Rabbittown. She'd leave Frankie in charge until two o'clock. Then she'd take over until five when he returned. From five until closing, Frankie would be behind the bar, with Veronica coming back later in the evening if things got busy.

Frankie was a townie, but with Syrian immigrant parents, a round little man like a comic grand vizier or court astrologer in some Hope and Crosby road-to-the-harem movie. He'd have looked at home in a fez. The younger neighbourhood layabouts, who thought fifty-five cents was too much for a beer, said Frankie was a Jew, but in fact, "Frankie" was short for Francis Xavier, and he was a pillar of the Basilica and a Knight of Columbus. Frankie gloried in a dinner jacket, cocked hat, cape and sword on high occasions.

His older customers liked Frankie and disapproved of the neighbourhood youngsters taking liberties, but they couldn't resist pulling his leg about being tight with a dollar either.

"The Assyrian came down like a wolf on the billfold...," said the barbered insurance agent. He'd been praised for his recitations as a boy and he still sang John MacCormack Irish songs in the bar rather than make calls in the afternoon.

Others told the story of Frankie and Nicky Dolan. Nicholas Dolan lived across the street from Frankie's bar. He was a thin, vague man with what he believed to be the Irish manners of another age.

"You don't say," he'd encourage the person he was talking to, leaning back expectantly and peering through the smoke of a carefully cared for briar pipe. "Did you ever hear the like?"

He became vaguer and more polite as the evenings wore on and he sipped India beer until he disappeared into a sort of warm black hole of civility and floated back across the road to his numerous family and grim-looking wife.

One day, so the story went, Frankie was driving up Military Road when he spied Nick Dolan and pulled over. He bought big black American cars he could barely see over the dashboards of, and he was proud of the way he kept them.

"Can I give you a run, Mr. Dolan?" Frankie asked.

"That would be very kind of you, Francis, very kind indeed," Nicky said. "I'm just going up the Basilica, you know."

Frankie would finish the story himself. "And that's just where I took him, dropped him right off at the door. Then the old shagger goes in and takes the pledge and stops coming in for a beer or a swally. If I'd have known, he could have walked, the old bugger. Very kind of you, Francis, me arse!"

Since Paula and George had arrived in town they had been trying out the local beers and picking their favourites. In Ontario, when they were first going out, she had drunk Fifty and he had drunk Red Cap. He still occasionally sang the Red Cap hymn from the commercials that had been on TV when he was in university.

Cans or draft or bottles,

It's our favourite brew.

We drink Carling Red Cap.

We are drinkers true…

Now they were trying to make up their minds over India and Dominion.

The writing group gave Gerry an easy ride on that chapter. They like local colour and nostalgia.

Vivian read the piece after he brought it home.

"They liked it," she said. "You must be happy."

Gerry was actually sadder for writing the piece. What's stayed with him from his and Pat's first year is pub stories. He knows there were cozy nests of sleeping bags and her old fur coat because they had no blankets at first. Now, he can remember walks to bus stops under giant snowflakes. Still, what stuck were the pub stories.

When did she stop coming with me to gather them?

Sitting in his basement now, Gerry finds time running together. He remembers the cartoons that advertised Dominion which Patricia favoured. He seems to remember that they featured the Duke and Duchess of Duckworth and the forger who painted the frescoes in Government House while he served his time. He thinks there may have been Johnnie Burke and Father Duffy and his holy well. However, he can't remember if the cartoons ran when they first got to St. John's or later on.

"India, India, India Beer, India that's the brew," Gerry hums. "India Beer's the best there is and it's all because of you!"

A few days later, Gerry is hiding out in a coffee shop again. It's early afternoon. He worked an early morning shift and he's in no great rush to go home. A police car pulls up outside. It's the silly/cute little Pacer the Constabulary use for community relations, a little 1930s-looking car that always makes Gerry feel it escaped from *Who Framed Roger Rabbit*. Two cops, a man and a woman in the utilitarian new black battledress uniform, feed the parking meter and head off down the street.

Gerry remembers cops from thirty years ago, when he was cutting his teeth as a court reporter.

The Newfoundland Constabulary weren't "Royal" yet when he came to town, but their black delivery-van paddy wagons had a big crown flanked with an ER on the side. You're not supposed to call paddy wagons "paddy wagons" now, Gerry reflects. You're probably supposed to call them Celtic conveyances or something, but they were paddy wagons then. The back of the wagon was separated from the seats by a nautical-looking barricade of painted grey boards with a bright orange life-saving ring buoy hung on it. Two little foot plates were welded at the back of the van and a set of handles onto the roof so that two officers could ride outside like footmen on a coach or the Keystone Kops, waiting to be hurled off on a sharp turn. When the shifts changed, Gerry would watch the paddy wagons roll sedately and grandly up the hill to Fort Townsend, the cop shop, with a couple of constables standing on the foot plates.

For police grandeur, though, you couldn't beat Inspector Jimmy Hayes coming down the hill. Gerry isn't sure now if he remembers him, or imagines the sheer glorious anachronism of him on a sunny morning. He wore the belted tunic the Constabulary inherited from the

Irish Constabulary, with black buttons with silver highlights and a short cape swinging. Square on his head was a cap that was a hymn of braid and polish and, in his gloved hand, an ebony and silver swagger stick. His boots were a heel-tap oratorio of black.

At the opposite end of the police fashion spectrum was Inspector Alphonsus Collins who shared the police prosecuting duties with Hayes. When Gerry started covering magistrates' court in the 1970s, the police still did most of the prosecuting.

If Jimmy Hayes came down the hill like an Orange Lodge triumph, Gerry had no idea how Phonse Collins got to work at the court house. He suspected he slept in the walled-off prosecutors' cubicle at the side of the court room. He looked like a giant toad swelling out of the blue-black uniform with the military, outside patch pockets. Leaning back in a swivel chair, looking at the world over the mound of his gut, he patted cigarette ash into his tunic, and Gerry, although he's rationally convinced it didn't happen, could swear he remembers Collins using the dangling tunic pockets as an ashtray, even popping glowing butts into them as the magistrate emerged from the panelled door behind the bench.

At Frankie's bar, Gerry got lessons in Constabulary ancient history from a marinated giant of a former cop. Lately he writes about him as "Patrick Driscoll." According to legend at Frankie's bar, Driscoll got into an epic punch-up with Phonse Collins when they were new constables in the late '30s. Collins had got the worst of it. He'd landed in hospital and complained, so Driscoll had left the force. He'd gone to sea for a bit, joined the heavy artillery during the war, and afterwards become a traveller for one of the old Water Street business houses until he retired.

Gerry heard his favourite cop story from Pat Driscoll as they drank Beck's beer in Frankie's bar. He has tried to sketch the scene for his writing group.

Fragment: Cops

"We were picked for big, not smart, you see," Driscoll said. He was big and dark and beetle-browed and always wore a suit and tie and a good dark overcoat in winter. "There was this big young fellow and he found a dead horse on Waldegrave Street. He couldn't spell Waldegrave in his notebook so he carried the horse 'round the corner onto George Street."

The bar at Frankie's would kindle into cop and court stories.

"There was this old fella, see, who used to get himself thrown in the pen every fall to get through the winter…" The audience pours its beer from the small bottles into the short tooth-glass tumblers that Frankie uses for both beer and drinks. "…Anyway, he chucked a rock through a store window down on Water Street and then he got worried that might not be enough to get him put away for the whole winter."

In the diagonal afternoon sun of Frankie's, the dust motes and smoke danced in anticipation of how the story would come out.

"I knows what comes next. I knows what comes next!"

"Anyway, the police bring the rock into court as Crown exhibit 'A' and the old fella pleads not guilty and challenges their evidence. He says he may have thrown a rock but he didn't throw that rock."

The storyteller became both magistrate and accused, his voice dividing into an imperial boom for one and a corner-boy crackie yap for the other.

"How big was your rock, man? Was it as big as my fist?"

"Bigger than that, Your Honour."

"Bigger than my two fists?"

"Bigger than that, Your Honour."

"As big as my head?"

"About as big as that, Your Honour, but not quite so thick."

"Guilty! You are sentenced to six months in His Majesty's Penitentiary! Next case!"

Somebody else has a story about a street character: Tommy Toe.

"There was buddy used to hang around with Tommy, see, and they were up in court for something and the judge asked Tommy where he lived, and he told him, 'no fixed address.' Then the judge asks buddy where he lived."

The bar would hang on the imagined question. Lips wet themselves with beer.

"I lives right alongside of Tommy."

The answer completed the lunch hour liturgy and the drinkers would drain glasses and straggle down the hill back to work.

Gerry thinks of Patrick Driscoll during this year's Christmas shopping. He has to go to a warehouse outlet in the industrial park out by the overpass to look for some kind of range hood that Vivian thinks they need. She said it could be their present to themselves. Gerry thinks half a range hood is a crummy present, but more and more often now, they find each other hard to buy gifts for.

Back when the railway track still ran through the scrubby spruce, Driscoll had a cabin there and a mistress who was not much older than Gerry was back then. Mistresses were officially a rarity in the working-class east-end. If they existed at all, they were more likely called "the lady friend" or "the girlfriend," but Gerry always thought of Driscoll's lover as a mistress. She and Driscoll had that kind of old-fashioned tang to them. Gerry remembers going to Driscoll's cabin to meet her. He has added the scene to the on-going remembrances of George and Paula.

Fragment: Mistress at the Overpass

Driscoll drove them to the cabin in a large black car that moved like a battleship through lesser traffic. After dropping Mrs. Driscoll off at her bowling league, they made their stately way across town, out of the narrow street canyons of the east and out to the Breughel-landscape scrub around the overpass. There, they drove down snowy ruts among the rabbit tracks and rail sidings.

The mistress, whose name was Yvonne, arrived in her own small car. She was the widow of a man who had died in a hunting accident. She said she could never understand why he hunted because he didn't like moose meat very much although she did. Anyway, his buddy killed him, shooting blind, somewhere down around the Horse Chops.

The three of them drank Scotch through a late winter afternoon. Around Driscoll, Yvonne had the air of a guide at some historic monument. They had a full set of weights and a weight-lifting bench in the cabin. Driscoll lifted weights to keep fit and Yvonne had taken it up. They both took vitamin B from a huge plastic jar.

"Good for the liver," Driscoll told George. "You can drink what you like if you eat right and take those."

It was fully dark when George finally excused himself and left them *alone. He had to give a cab very elaborate instructions for finding him in the overpass wilderness. Twice, corrections had to be telephoned to the taxi company and relayed by radio to the cab which had gone up the wrong dead-end lane.*

Driving across the overpass, Gerry looks down and scans what's left of the woods by the old railway right-of-way, trying to find a sign of the cabin or even the track that led to it.

He remembers that Patricia disapproved of the visit when he told her about it.

"The man's married for God's sake! Think of his wife!" She stopped short of saying something to Mrs. Driscoll. That would be too much tampering in Gerry's supposed literary laboratory, a spoiling of his experiment. However, afterwards, she seemed to examine Gerry for symptoms of having affairs. Perhaps it was contagious. He realizes now that she was right. In a few years they both caught it, but he just caught affair sniffles from time to time. She got a terminal case and married somebody else. At the time, though, he just made a mental note that if adultery upset her, best not to tell her.

Words to live by, he thinks.

There's no sign of Driscoll's cabin now, or at least Gerry can't find it. Neither can he get the range hood, or at least not by Christmas. The people at the warehouse know the one he means but it's out of stock and they're not even sure it's made anymore. They say the people at the main store should have been able to tell him that.

A few years ago, Gerry read in the paper that his Patrick Driscoll had died. He hadn't seen him in twenty-five years or more but he went to the funeral home. It was a soft spring night, one of the first warm ones of the year, and Gerry went up in the gathering dusk. He wore a blazer and a button-down shirt and tie with khakis and boat shoes. Once upon a time it would have been called irreverent but no one seems to change to go to funeral homes anymore.

Gerry's "Yvonne" was the widow. The original wife had died years ago and she and Driscoll married. The children seemed to have accepted her, although some of them were her age. They stood around her protectively. Gerry knew some of the kids from the first marriage.

There was one daughter who acts, and another, Siobhan, who took up public relations for some government department years ago. When he met her, Gerry had never seen "Siobhan" written as a name before and referred to her privately as Shaboom. Once he told her that at some office party and she thought it was cute. Now she greeted Gerry at the door. He introduced himself but found he didn't need to.

"You're still on the radio?"

"Until a grown-up job comes along, I guess. I'm still trying to decide what I want to be when I grow up."

"Who says you have to grow up?" she asked. "He never did. Not so you'd notice anyhow."

She inclined her head to the long casket where the slightly yellow face reposed, propped up a bit in the satin ruffles. Except that his eyes were closed, Driscoll looked like he was trying to see the TV without too much effort while lying on the couch. Gerry looked at the yellow face and wondered if the vitamin B kept working. In his head floated a line from his drinking days: I know my liver redeemeth.

Siobhan told him she was living in Toronto now, working at a public relations firm. She had to be close to sixty but she looked fit and tanned. Her fingernails were painted a smooth cocoa brown.

Gerry had to be introduced to Yvonne.

"We met at Pat's cabin," he told her when Siobhan took him over. They could have been sisters, one of whom had had a harder life. Yvonne seemed to have blended into the role of an old man's wife.

"Oh my, the cabin..." she said. "That's been torn down for years."

It wasn't a very sad wake. Driscoll was old and had been sick the last few years. Gerry was re-introduced to the other kids, all of them his age at least. There were two sons with Florida golfers' tans. They seemed somehow impressed that Gerry could have drunk with their father and still be alive to tell the tale.

"Here's a man who used to go down to Frankie's place with Dad."

"I remember him boasting about you the year you won some big golf tournament, a junior club championship?"

"God! That must have been what, '73, '74?"

Later, Gerry drove home with the window down for the first time that year. You could tell it was really spring. The dotted lines and arrows on the streets bloomed bright white in the headlights, repainted and vivid after fading to nothing in the winter's salt. Visibility of street markings is becoming what Gerry has now learned to call "an issue" with him. On wet nights in late winter and early spring, he sometimes wonders what lane he's driving in. Recalling the brightness of the lines that night, Gerry reflects that now they're starting to fade again under this year's December salt.

"Tempus certainly does fugit," he says aloud.

four

DECEMBER 2003

G erry is in the mall for his final rush of Christmas shopping. He
has a strategy for mall-stalking in the last days before Christmas;
catch it while it's still asleep. He gets up in darkness and drives
through the quiet streets where there are only a few luminously striped
joggers. The ones he sees are the skinny Spandex variety with the bright
glowing V's that seem to point to the middle of their backsides. Is it
supposed to focus attention on the fitness of the bum or give you a
central aiming point? Gerry is an inconsistent jogger at best, and, when
he does jog, he wears a pair of ancient Zellers sweatpants and an old
sweatshirt. The black long-underwear look of this morning's joggers isn't
for him. If you're going out in tights you have to hark back to the
Tudors, he thinks, although even they needed a sort of post-feudal
ferocity to carry it off. Essex or Drake or some of Lady Jane Grey's tribe
could get away with it because they'd thunder into your courtyard and
impale you on your own maypole over a slow fire. At the other end of
the scale, Malvolio and Osric come down to us as fashion fools.

"A hit, a very palpable hit," Gerry mutters, mowing down joggers in
his imagination.

The parking lot is almost empty when Gerry pulls in. With no cars, you can appreciate its bald topography, actually rolling over a low rise in the middle so it sheds rain. The ploughs and salt crews have been out and you can see the painted stalls on bare pavement, although the hills all around are ghostly with light new snow on the trees. Gerry parks carefully between the painted lines in the centre of the empty lot. He points the front of the Honda out into the hypothetical traffic lane for a quick getaway in case the shoppers turn nasty.

"S-A-S parking," Gerry says to himself. Years ago he bought the Special Air Service survival book and learned to avoid snakes like tai pans and bushmasters if they ever slithered into Newfoundland. He read up on how to boil the goldfish and drink the water as you tried to outlive the neighbours after nuclear Armageddon. So far the need hasn't arisen. However, he parks, nose-out, for a quick getaway.

In the mall, he finds one coffee shop open earlier than the others. He carries a foam cup with him to the barber shop that is part of this morning's plan. The barber opens at seven. A haircut and the morning papers will occupy him until Wal-Mart opens in an hour or so.

The barbershop is a transplant from downtown and is old-fashioned in a modern sort of way. According to framed clippings on the walls, when it started up in the '50s it was ultra-modern. It had low, swivel easy chairs instead of high barber chairs. It gave the short back and sides haircuts, the Sal Mineo comb-backs and crews and brush cuts that still grace framed photos on the walls. Some of the photos are advertising shots, showing what you can do with Wildroot Cream Oil or Brylcream. Others are sports teams, hockey and softball mostly, wearing narrow-lapel jackets and skinny ties with big clips that go past the width of the tie. Team members sport the haircuts in the pictures.

When Gerry first came to town he wouldn't have gone to this barbershop. They were slow to get the hang of long hair. Besides, they were busy watching their sports teams grow up and move to the suburbs. By the time the long-haired had taken over the downtown sometime in the '80s, the barber shop moved to the mall.

Gerry fancies he can recognize some of the ancient sports teams in the chairs in the barbershop yet. There are retired faces under haircuts that are renewed weekly, although they don't need it. Gerry himself gets monthly haircuts. He started coming here in the '90s, well after he'd begun keeping his hair shortish and after there had been a sort of convergence of styles. The barbershop has given long cuts for years now. Some disco-flavoured pictures of mullets and shags have even joined the ducktails and buzz-cuts on the wall. They all look about equally antiquated now.

Gerry gets his Christmas trim with the minimum of fuss. The conversation is morning, Christmas and minimal.

"Have you got your shopping done?"

"Just about, I should have it clewed up today."

"You got your boat up for the winter, I guess?"

Gerry is not a sports follower so talking about his sailboat is his occasional key to some sorts of small talk. "Oh yes, got it up in October, Thanksgiving weekend."

"The snow's holding off a bit."

"Just enough for a white Christmas would be okay with me."

One day in this barbershop, Gerry had a long chat with a man who was waiting for hospital results. He didn't seem to expect them to be good.

"I've only just got enough hair again to need cutting," he complained. "Now I'm going to have to start chemo again."

The man was about ten years older than Gerry, thin and golf-club smart-casual. As he was leaving, he introduced himself. Gerry recognized the name. Twenty-odd years ago when he and Pat were falling apart he had spent some time with the man's ex-wife. The man had left her for somebody younger at work. She'd complain about her stretch marks as they smoked cigarettes in bed after making love. Gerry would trace them with a dismissive finger, or kiss them. He felt plagiarized when the movie *Shirley Valentine* came out and made a thing out of stretch-mark kissing. Sometimes he would lie with his head cushioned on her small belly while she would lay elaborate curses on her ex: biblical plagues and disasters. Sitting in the mall barbershop, it appeared to Gerry that the statute of limitations for those curses hadn't yet run out.

"Chemo's the shits."

Today the barber vacuums his collar and holds the mirror up behind his head.

"Okay for another couple of weeks."

"Yup, I ought to be safe from the dogcatcher for a little longer."

Gerry pays and leaves a five instead of his usual three-dollar tip for a fifteen-dollar haircut.

"Merry Christmas if I don't see you before the day."

"Yes, you have a Merry Christmas now too."

Conscious of his glowing, new-shaved neck and a few hair-ends in his collar, Gerry sets about his shopping. Last night he asked Vivian to reconfirm sizes for him. It's the sort of attention to detail that pleases her and can expiate other failings. He thinks he has the liturgy down pat. Vivian is medium. Melanie is smallish medium and Tanya is smallish small. Gretchen is large medium or smallish large. Duane is large and Darren is medium. Vivian offered to size the kids too, but Gerry has a personal rule against clothes for Christmas for little kids. Because Vivian has already shopped for all the grandkids once, he can relax in the knowledge he's doing extras.

For Joshua he finds a little radio-controlled car. It's not much bigger than the Matchbox toys he played with in the '50s. It sits on a little battery pack to charge itself and costs less than forty dollars. Radio-controlled stuff has got a lot cheaper. Gerry anticipates getting to play with the car himself when the kids are in bed. He buys a big economy-size box of spare double-A batteries.

AA batteries from Grampa in AA.

Natalie and Diana both get do-it-yourself jewellery kits. They're cheaper than the car but Vivian had told him she had only got Joshua a sweater so he could go a bit wild on boy-toys to even things out.

Despite the warnings from the police about stowing stuff in your car, Gerry shuttles bags out to his Honda and conceals them under seats and under the roll-out cover for the boot.

Trotting back inside, he hits Eddie Bauer and buys sweaters for the girls and shirts for Duane and Darren. That exhausts his mall shopping. When the Christmas range-hood project fell through, Vivian said she could use new winter boots and he'll have to go downtown to get what she has said she wants. He takes himself to a Second Cup for an espresso and a chocolate croissant to celebrate his efficiency.

With only the expensive trendy stores left, the downtown at Christmas seems unnaturally quiet to Gerry these days. In late afternoon he watches the streets clear. Vivian has taken the kids to the mall and they plan to stay and have supper and go to a movie. Gerry is back in the old street canyon of thirty years ago, watching the traffic thin out.

He remembers early Christmases, when he and Patricia finished up their shopping on foot, zigzagging between Duckworth and Water Streets. They'd bought each other's big presents at a war-surplus store in the east-end. He got her a submariner's roll-neck jersey and a gas-mask pack for a purse. She bought him a long-skirted trench coat with bottomless pockets and a 1950 date tag sewed into it.

For their families on the mainland, they bought presents at her store, The Vales of Har, and at places that sold homemade trigger mitts and itchy toques and little souvenir killicks made out of twigs and beach pebbles. Some of this stuff drifts around Gerry and Vivian's house now. It came home to roost when he cleared out his mother's house and she went into an old-age home.

"You gave us that," she'd say. "I won't have room for it. Take it home with you."

Accordingly, the stuff that was supposed to evoke Newfoundland as exotic in Ontario drifted home to occupy odd corners of bookshelves or spare-room dressers, a sort of underlining of some mythical subtext of the everyday.

Gerry gets Vivian's Christmas boots in a store that was once a restaurant. They went there to eat when they were dating in the '80s. It still has some of the '80s brass and glass, but now it frames expensive shoes. The light is still restaurant dim. The leathers look roasted, glazed and edible.

"What would you recommend as a good, middle-of-the-road wine to go with those?" Gerry asks the clerk, looking around at the brick and stained glass as he puts the boots on his bank card.

"A nice Cabernet Sauvignon," the clerk says without missing a beat. This is an upscale store.

Gerry meets his friend Philip in the street as he heads back to the wagon with the boots. Philip has just got off the bus, heading home from a shift at the call centre where he works. He's wearing enormous troll-foot snow boots with felt liners spilling over the tops and a big shapeless parka. He's carrying a plastic shopping bag full of books, probably the homework for the humanist funeral or whatever else he's into at the moment. Philip reads heavy and smart. Gerry finds it's good exercise to even try to keep up, but it can get pricey. He paid better than full price for an out-of-print copy of Julian Jaynes's *Origin of Consciousness in the Breakdown of the Bicameral Mind*. He needed to get up to speed on the voices of gods as auditory hallucinations.

"Can you join us for Christmas dinner?" Gerry asks. "I need someone to help keep the family at bay. Otherwise we'll be playing Born-again Barbie versus the Whore of Babylon on Game Boy all afternoon. I'll get you home at a civilized hour, I've got to drop down to the office and see if there's anything that needs doing. I'm on early mornings on Boxing Day."

"I'm sure your family isn't that bad," Philip says. "Dinner sounds very nice."

Philip lives in a top-floor bed-sit in an old house downtown. He's been a regular at Christmas dinner with Gerry and Vivian for a couple of years. He's another come-from-away, although at a less-assimilated stage than Gerry. He's been around for five years and still gets more delighted and angrier with the place than Gerry does. He says he can't afford to live in St. John's. He originally came to be a hermit in an outport and not live in town at all. That never happened, so for months he's been mailing books home to his family in Toronto and saying that someday he'll follow them. Gerry points out that it would be cheaper to send a part load with a moving company, but there is something about the scale of making up the weekly book packages that suits Philip, tucking his literary soul into boxes and shipping it out a piece at a time. Unfortunately he keeps buying books, so the process has stretched out, even when he tries to short-circuit it and gives books away. Gerry's bookshelves have had several windfalls from Philip's proposed move.

Philip's job at the call centre is to field complaints for an American phone company. He talks to people in California about their internet service. He says the call centre is like a spaceship.

"The mother ship is in stationary orbit right over you," he tells Gerry over coffee as afternoon turns into early solstice-time night. "I can see your computer and it isn't fucking-well plugged in."

"Where are you?" people on the phone ask Philip. Gerry kids him that new-age women in California want to party with an alien.

"We're only allowed to say Canada," Philip tells him. "Explaining where Newfoundland is would take too long."

Gerry can identify with the Californians a bit. He once listened to one end of a surreal cell-phone conversation in a sailboat, motoring in circles in Conception Bay. A friend of his was trying to get a fancy wind-direction indicator calibrated. They followed the instructions that came with the thing. They motored into the wind for a bit and then went around in circles but the instrument didn't want to lock in. The service call centre appeared to be in Singapore. Gerry's friend said the guy on the other end didn't seem to realize he was talking to a boat at sea. He just ran down a checklist of questions.

"He probably had another couple there, in case my coffee maker or my vibrator didn't work," Gerry's friend remarked. "He only knows what he's servicing by model number."

The day had been brilliant with a crinkled tinsel sea throwing diamonds in the air and a warm breeze blowing off the land and up the legs of Gerry's baggy shorts as they did their circle dance in the bay. A couple of minke whales came by to watch them go round and round in the summer sun.

Gerry thinks about the whales and the summer sun after he says goodnight to Philip and drives home though the winter dark, punctuated with the neon Morse of the Christmas lights.

Christmas Day is grey and mild with hardly any snow down. Gerry and Vivian had invoked their "Gran's House" rules so that the kids stayed up late and opened whatever present they wanted just after midnight. It keeps them in bed longer on Christmas morning while Gerry and Vivian get up early, put on a pot of coffee and stuff the turkey.

The turkey is big, but flawed. It had been selected, frozen-solid, out of a bin at the Dominion store. Now, it turns out to be a utility model, missing a drumstick although the thigh is still there.

"A children's Christmas classic is born," Gerry says. "Stumpy the Christmas Utility Turkey, hopping along on his little crutch."

"You're evil. You know that?" Viv says.

"God bless us every one!" Gerry says, hopping. "Then he settles down in the roaster and closes his eyes in blissful surrender. O Death, where is thy sting, or Gravy, thy victory?"

"Go on with you."

The kids wake up for their second round of Christmas and everybody unwraps and nods and thanks. Melanie, Darren and Diana turn up from their house and the living room disappears in a welter of paper.

Gerry gets his sock, deodorant and aftershave supply topped up. It's a standing joke that, although he doesn't shave, he gets aftershave every year. As well, he gets a couple of shirts and a sweater from Viv. There are also a couple of books. Darren gives him a Tom Clancy thriller and Duane and Gretchen give him *The Purpose Driven Life*. They've given him a number of Christian books over the years. He's never quite had the nerve to counter with a copy of the *Tao Te Ching*.

When the gifts are dealt with, Duane and Gretchen and their kids take Vivian's car and head off to church.

Darren goes to sleep on the basement couch because he worked late on Christmas Eve. Melanie, Tanya and Vivian take second coffees into the living room and watch Diana try stuff on and play with her presents.

Gerry, meanwhile, finds that the salt meat has been overlooked in the Christmas shopping. It gives him a chance to sneak away for a bit. He hops in the car and heads out on a whirlwind tour of twenty-four-hour service stations, looking for a bucket of riblets.

The city is enclosed behind its curtains this morning, wrapped up in its families and presents. The streets aren't busy except around the churches. Gerry tries a couple of Irving stations for his riblets.

"We forgot the salt meat. Everything's on hold, veggies, pease puddin', the works," he tells the girls at the cash.

At the first service station he draws a blank, but at the second, the clerk gets into the spirit of the emergency. She has long black hair and has gold bars diagonally through the rims of her ears. They remind Gerry of the skewers that used to transfix pickled pork-hock bar snacks.

"Can't have that," she says, when he explains his problem. "We haven't got any, but I'll call Water Street West."

She dials the phone, yells a Merry Christmas down it and asks about the riblet supply.

"They've got one bucket," she says. "Will I ask them to hold onto it for you?"

"Yes, please," Gerry says. "Thank you and Merry Christmas." He drives across town, picks up the riblets in their little plastic bucket and heads home to pop them in the pot.

Around noon, Gerry is out and about again. He drives down to Duckworth Street to collect Philip. Philip comes with a large net bag of walnuts and a book each for Gerry and Vivian. For Gerry he has *Mistress Masham's Repose*, a kid's book Gerry read as a child and has been hunting for since somebody pinched his copy at a party he and Patricia threw. He has told Philip of this hunt several times.

"I hope you didn't already find it," Philip says. "I'm sorry the cover's a little water-stained. It's the only one they had at the second-hand store."

Philip's gift to Vivian is also from the second-hand bookstore. It's a coffee table book of Gothic carved angels in cathedrals. Philip is never quite sure just what Vivian is into. He accepts a large glass of wine and sits on a stool in the kitchen while Gerry cuts up apples and celery and mixes them with raisins for Waldorf salad. This is his CFA contribution to the family Christmas tradition.

"I wish I could cook," Philip remarks. "There's something about home-cooking."

"Like you're required to maintain a home to do it," Gerry says. "You could have this tribe move into your bed-sit for a month and you'd start to cook just for the excuse to have a large sharp knife in your hand."

About two in the afternoon they sit at the dining table with the kitchen table pushed against one end for the kids.

"That's the biggest turkey I think we've ever had," Vivian says.

"It's the perfect Christmas trees that attract them," Gerry says. "The biggest turkeys always roost in those magic best-we-ever-had trees. Poor old Stumpy here just couldn't resist."

Vivian roots in the cabinet drawer for her camera and dinner passes in a series of snapshots.

Gerry proposes a toast to them all in cranberry juice and soda water.

Duane gets to ask another blessing.

Darren pours himself a shot of single-malt Scotch that Gerry bought for his more discriminating guests.

"That's the real good stuff," Darren says and then mixes it with ginger ale. Gerry doesn't say anything because it's Christmas.

"I don't want the salad. There's black things in it," Natalie says of the Waldorf.

"You don't have to eat it, dear," Vivian says.

The plates of food have a mediaeval look with their heaps of boiled root vegetables and chunks of Stumpy, the primordial utility turkey. Gerry reserves the pope's nose and the gizzard as his special share for cooking and carving. He wonders how the politically correct handle the pope's nose/parson's nose debate. It's probably clergy person's nose if you're being picky. He remembers an aunt of his who was a giblet fan when the family had turkey when he was a child. His other aunts, her older sisters, would recall her saying she wanted "the lizard and the gizzard and the heart."

"To the lizard and gizzard and the heart," says Gerry, raising a glass of cranberry and soda.

After dinner the kids produce a board game, The Game of Life. It's like monopoly with career choices thrown in. Gretchen and Vivian do the dishes and Darren returns to the couch. Gerry has spirited the single-malt out of sight and left a bottle of Grouse out. Everybody else, singly and in syndicates, plays the game in that haphazard, only-read-the-rules-when-you-have-to way that new board games are always played. Philip rapidly becomes a Game of Life shark. He becomes a brain surgeon, grabs the biggest mansion with a collection of art and retires to a private island in luxury while some players are still struggling with loans to pay for their education. He smiles and sips the good single-malt as his board game successes pile up.

"I don't believe your son-in-law knows what he's missing," Philip says.

"I'm glad someone appreciates it," Gerry says. "You're sure you wouldn't like Pepsi or whipped cream or a handful of Gummi Bears in that?"

In late afternoon Gerry drives the eminent retired brain surgeon back to his bed-sitter and drops by the radio station to make sure he has some updated news for Boxing Day. On desks in the office there are catering trays with sandwich crusts and wrinkly grapes and limp broccoli around empty dip dishes. There's the heel of a two-litre bottle of red wine on a filing cabinet. Gerry makes himself a coffee in his heat-saving thermal aluminium cup and gets on the phone.

There's a little secret society of people working on Christmas. Gerry's only a sort of honorary member because he has just dropped in for an hour or two. Still, the people on the other ends of the phone don't know that. He wishes Merry Christmas to the Constabulary and the Coast Guard search-and-rescue duty people and to the woman on the RCMP switchboard for the province. She's a familiar voice.

"Merry Christmas. Is that Stacey?"

"Yes it is. Merry Christmas to you too."

Gerry checks to make sure that he's not missing any of the faxed news releases that have come in. It appears that he hasn't, so he thanks Stacey and settles down at the computer to write the terse little stories that will fit tomorrow's short holiday newscasts.

A forty-three-year-old man from Berry Cove is dead as the result of a single-car accident on Christmas Eve... Gerry taps the final little formulae of distant despair onto the screen. *Police believe alcohol was a factor,* he types. Carve that on his monument or mine.

He's been doing this for thirty years. It comes easily and it's almost relaxing. He writes the stories of the untended chip pan that burnt down the house and the robbers who stole the Christmas presents in a laconic, almost comforting way. It's the journalistic equivalent of the pilot's voice: "Good morning, folks. This is the captain speaking. We're experiencing a little wing-falling-off difficulty here, but nothing to be alarmed about."

It will make people at an early breakfast tomorrow quietly glad that these tragic clichés didn't happen to them. Perhaps they'll even feel a little proud that, through superior care or foresight, they've avoided being the protagonists in one of Gerry's trite little two-finger-typed summations.

It's a mild night, with patches of starry sky showing, when Gerry leaves to go home. A few taxis prowl the streets now, and cars, moving slowly, wear invisible banners that proclaim they are on official family visit business.

He goes to bed early because he has to be up early in the morning. Melanie, Darren and Diana have gone home. Tanya, Duane and Gretchen are watching *Miracle on 34th Street* on TV. Vivian is sitting at the desk in the kitchen with a glass of white wine. She's talking to her brothers and sisters around the province and the country. He kisses her on the top of the head as he heads off to bed. Sometime late that night he feels her settle beside him with a tired little grunt. He leans back against her and sleeps.

On a cold, bright Saturday morning, Gerry is up and doing odd jobs. The project for this morning is taking the Christmas tree to the pile in the park where the city mulches them. Vivian took the tree down the day after Old Christmas, but then it snowed and now Gerry has to pull the snow-clotted tree out of its drift by the front walk. This isn't a bad thing. He's dressed for the cold, and the snow that falls on him as he heaves the tree onto the roof rack of the Honda is a diamond shower. There's something vaguely satisfying about the boatswain work of throwing ratchet tie-downs over the tree and cinching it down tight to the roof. Gerry believes the ratchet tie-down is right up there with the opposable thumb in humankind's ascent from the swamp.

The world seems a comfortably loose fit to Gerry this morning. The kids have gone home, leaving Vivian and him alone. This morning he walked from the bedroom to the bathroom naked, something he couldn't do for the two weeks of Christmas. One morning, Gretchen had found him in the kitchen in his underwear, making coffee. He's used to being the earliest riser and had thought everybody was still asleep. She gave a startled herbivore squeak and ducked back down the hall in her long housecoat and red-top grey work socks. Through the rest of the day she avoided meeting his eyes. Gerry had no idea grey Stanfield Y-fronts were so sinfully disturbing, but, out of respect for her sensibilities, he wore old sweatpants and a T-shirt to make the coffee for the rest of the holidays.

In any event, Gretchen and Duane and the kids have been herded onto one plane, and a couple of days later Tanya left on another. When she went she took a down-filled peaked cap with knitted earflaps that had somehow followed Gerry since he had worked in Labrador.

"You never wear it," she said.

"Who would?" Gerry asked. The hat had been a joke, presented to him at a Christmas party where everyone exchanged gifts under ten dollars. There was a knitted "willy warmer" with it. He'd modelled that for Patricia. They were in one of their patches of getting along at the time. It was a lot too big.

"It's nice to know you didn't have a personal fitting," she said as they climbed into bed. "Maybe you'll grow into it."

"I believe I am right now," Gerry said. "See what you think."

"Hmmm…"

However, later on, she vetoed the hat.

"It lowers your IQ by thirty points," she said when he proposed to wear it to go snowmobiling. "You look like the Mackenzie Brothers, *Great White North*."

Gerry drives the Christmas tree to the park and tosses it on the pile. It lands with a dead rustle. Around the main pile of trees, some people have dumped theirs at a distance. He wonders if they feel they're unworthy of the main heap, or if they're shy. Some of the set-apart trees are wrapped in those giant, plastic tree condoms that are supposed to contain the shed needles. Maybe their fastidious owners expect special treatment for their trees, designer chipping.

Gerry gets back in the Honda and heads for the mall.

A little later that morning, Gerry sits in the mall food court, drinking Tim Hortons coffee and eating an apple fritter. The sugar sticks to his fingers like candy leper scales. The too-hot paper cup melts it into a thin suburban varnish, a tacky morning shine he's not displeased with.

The tall, accordion-stalked cherry picker that the mall staff uses to reach the ceiling putters around. It purrs electrically through the pinball-machine décor of the food court. The maintenance people are taking down the last of the big hanging Christmas decorations. The mall is getting busier. Eventually the machine whirrs off to hide, kneeling in an alcove, a depressed, agoraphobic, electric giraffe.

Gerry eats his fritter and looks around at people packing away the doughnuts and oily wafers of hash browns. They treat their arteries to three-egg breakfasts. In a morning mall you can pretend to be grown-up enough to eat anything with impunity.

In the food court, Gerry writes in his Chinese notebook, *the pleasures are all guilty.*

Gerry is drowning some guilt of his own in apple fritter sweetness. Walking to the food court through the mall, he has dodged an old drinking buddy. He spotted the man, and the woman who looks after him, and angled behind a pillar, keeping a mall-width between them. The man's name is Paul. He wears pastel, elastic-waisted jogging suits and sneakers with Velcro fasteners because other people dress him now. There is an egg-sized dent, edged with shiny white scar, in the side of his head. It shows through the prison haircut that Paul has grown back since they whipped him into hospital to make the dent and scar, to remove the tumour and pull down the shades in his eyes.

The woman with Paul is his daughter. Her name is March, and Gerry supposes she must be in her late forties now. She leads Paul around the mall with a competent hand on his elbow. Gerry recalls that March is a potter. She has practical hands. On this sunny Saturday, under the skylights, she moulds their slow way around the mall out of plastic air.

Gerry hopes today's cowardice is temporary. On other days he has stopped where March sits Paul on the wide ceramic edge of a flowerbox while she fetches them cups of tea. She blows on his, making sure it's cool enough, like a drink for a small child. On other days they have spoken, although it is the same conversation each time.

"It's Gerry," March says, nodding at him, willing him into existence for her father. "Gerry Adamson."

"Gerry?" It is always a question.

"Yes, Gerry," Gerry says helpfully, joining in to see if force of numbers can help win the argument behind the furrowed brow.

"Oh yes, Gerry…That's right."

Paul is always pleasantly surprised, even relieved. He always says that it's right, as if to convince himself that he's solved the puzzle. Still, he seems a bit shy, a bit embarrassed about how long he's had to let Gerry's name wander in his mental pitted no-man's land before it could be recognized as a friend.

The mall has been redecorated now, but some years ago it was hung with huge banners of puffins. Gerry used to jot down notes about them. They struck him as immensely remote, ethereal and smug, looking down on the mall with their heraldic silken eyes with the accent *çirconflex* marks over them. Quizzical, avian Groucho Marx stares followed Gerry as he waltzed a sense of his own mortality around the mall.

In another bright January some years ago, Gerry got confirmation that he was not going to die right away. He had suspected as much, but the fact that there was doubt had created what he still thinks of as "The Longest Fall." It's a bit of a silly play on words really, fall the season and falling, vertigo dream-falling where you watch the world rush up, at, and past you. He pictured falling where you waited an agonizingly long time for it to end with a thump, a splat, some cartoon noise or sudden black silence.

"The Longest Fall" actually began in late July in a fit of conceited altruism that Gerry now thinks of as tempting fate. The blood donation centre called to remind him he hadn't given blood in more than a year. It was the summer holiday season. Wouldn't he please drop by?

Gerry was babysitting early morning newscasts that summer while someone was away on vacation. He went to work early and had the summer afternoons off. He would shiver in shorts at four-thirty in the morning and emerge into a noon like a warm shower. Warmth and steady work made Gerry feel benevolent in a summertime-smug sort of way, full of life, sneakily inclined to flaunt it. It was good to be finished work for the day and the only one in shorts and boat shoes among the people in ties giving blood on their lunch hours.

He filled in the new, longer questionnaire at the clinic. He was vaguely smug that none of the dangerous behaviours of the past decade seemed to apply to him.

Certainly not the last decade.

Gerry gave his pint quickly, chatting with a man from the offshore business in the next armchair. Gerry had interviewed the man a couple of times, but on this day they talked about boats. The little agitator machines rocked the blood bags beside the chairs as they chatted. Afterwards he ate a couple of doughnuts and drank a cup of sweet tea. Then he drove to the sailing club and spent the afternoon fitting a new oil lamp in the cabin of his elderly sailboat.

The letter arrived about three weeks later among a handful of bills and fliers. It was bravely bureaucratic. *Anomalous result in test for humano-T-cell leukemic virus*, it read. The writer told Gerry he shouldn't worry. He should contact his family doctor for another blood test. If that came back the same, a DNA test should be arranged. The writer jumped to a wrong conclusion about what might be worrying Gerry just then. *We regret we are no longer able to accept donations of your blood.*

Gerry was sitting in the kitchen, waiting for the kettle to boil when Vivian came home. He was sitting still with difficulty. He wanted to fuss or move, if not actually run. Vivian had been showing a house. She looked reassuringly businesslike in her khaki slacks, blazer and short, easy-care hair.

"What's the matter with you?" she asked, although he hadn't said anything.

"Intimations of mortality," he said, trying to joke. "Look at this."

He passed her the letter. He wondered if he had this thing. Had he given it to her too? They'd been married for ten years, the second time around for both. Now he wondered wildly about the drunken inter-regnum, "my midlife crisis," as he called it. Had he done something murderously stupid? How latent was latent?

Vivian read the letter while he poured tea for them.

"There's nothing wrong with you," she said. "I'd know. I'd know or I'd have it too and I just got my insurance medical and there's nothing wrong with me. So did you. There's nothing wrong with you."

"I guess I'm not that worried," Gerry said, hoping for a virtue he wasn't sure he had a claim on. "For once in my life, I've got a clean conscience. I haven't sowed any wild oats for a while."

Clichés like "wild oats" seemed to be what were called for. He meant fucking around. He had done his share when he was married to Patricia, but this time it was true, he had nothing to confess.

But what about before? a sly, legalistic mental voice demanded nastily. Do you have a conscience or a calendar?

Gerry wriggled mentally, skewered on internal gallows humour.

"It's going to be a nasty shock to the insurance people if they let a terminal case of Dutch elm disease slip by them," he said. "This could cost them big bucks."

"There's nothing wrong with you," Vivian repeated, a blunt, affirmative mantra.

There'd better not be, Gerry thought, or I've given it to you. How can I be sure I haven't killed us both?

The need to prove themselves right or wrong made them touch, then hug in the kitchen as the afternoon sun made diagonals through the Venetian blinds over the sink. Vivian always said she wasn't a fan of passion in daylight, but now they were tugging at each other's clothes. They did a conjoined, clumsy bear-waltz down the hall to their bed and almost frightened themselves with their fierceness. They were amazed at how much they wanted each other, at how they shouted when they came. They yelled like swimmers jumping into the ice-coldness of their mortality, daring the letter to be everything it threatened.

Afterwards, they lay and listened to the sibilant whisper of the neighbour's lawn sprinkler. In the early evening they felt the sweat and tears dry on them in the breeze from the open window.

"There's nothing wrong with you," Vivian said again with her face against his neck.

It took all autumn to prove Vivian right. Their family doctor did another blood test for Gerry and got another anomalous result. Gerry asked him what it was he might be getting.

"There's the good kind we just treat as ordinary leukemia," the doctor said. "The other kind paralyzes you."

Leukemia good, paralysis bad, Gerry thought in a Homer Simpson voice. The doctor went on to tell him that people who have had unprotected sex in Japan are the most likely candidates.

"But you do have gout," he said, studying Gerry's records.

Gerry gathered that something about protein levels, or maybe the gout medication, caused funny test results. He hoped he'd been diagnosed with a case of excess gravy or lobster. The doctor seemed a bit disappointed, scientifically speaking, that Gerry hadn't been fooling around in Japan. However, he sent him off to the hospital for a DNA test.

Gerry turned up at the hospital lab on a Monday morning and ran into half the people he knew. There seemed to be any number of greying boomers in to be jabbed or scoped or X-rayed.

"Just in for a little blood work," Gerry said for the fifth or sixth time.

"Me too. My damn cholesterol is through the roof."

Somebody else complained about the smell of bacon and eggs leaking from the hospital cafeteria into the lab waiting area.

"I've been fasting since suppertime."

Gerry reflected on what constitutes a fast. He'd only had a cup of black coffee since yesterday's supper.

Eventually he was shown into a little stall and gave a piece of paper to a harried-looking, plump woman in a lab coat and rubber gloves. Did they wear rubber gloves all the time now, or was it just for people suspected of picking up Japanese cell rot in the fleshpots of Tokyo? Gerry felt toxic.

The woman wore a chunky crucifix pendant.

It's a judgement on you, you pervert! he imagined her thinking. Her eyes and lips seemed tight as she whipped a rubber tube around his bicep. Still, she filled a vial of blood with mosquito painlessness and her rubber touch on his wrist was human and comforting.

In the end he had to go back three weeks later and give another sample. It seemed that the wrong sort of container had been used to send his blood away to a lab in Ottawa and they needed a fresh specimen. On another Monday, a cheerful girl with a stud in her nose and a green streak in her hair smiled at him warmly, took another vial and the waiting started again.

While he waited out the tests through the fall, Gerry thought about being nine years old and realizing he was going to die. He'd been home from school, sick, and watching old tear-jerker movies on TV while he lay under a blanket on the couch. He can't remember the name of the movie now, but someone was being brave about dying. It didn't fizz on Gerry at the time, but late that night he awoke, sweating, terrified and terribly aware that he was going to die. It was not the first he had heard of death. His father's mother had died when he was four.

"Your nana's gone to heaven," his father had told him early one morning. "She just went to sleep."

He had accepted that, but never related it to himself. Now the full realization struck.

"It's a bad dream," his mother said when she heard him crying and came in.

"Nothing to be afraid of," his tobacco-scented father said and sat on the side of the bed with him, waiting for him to go back to sleep.

Gerry couldn't say what frightened him. He couldn't bring himself to tell anyone. Maybe he was the only one in the world who had realized the awful truth or maybe his parents knew and had been keeping it from him. He couldn't decide which scenario was worse. Eventually the terror tired him enough to sleep.

Like gradually fading echoes, the terror returned at longer and longer intervals through a year or two. Gerry listened to Sunday school portrayals of heaven. Their eternal family reunion had some attraction, but late at night he tried to imagine just not being.

In his "Long Fall," Gerry woke late at night again. Sweating and scared, he waited to put a face or name on fate. He knew he was afraid of pain. If death was going to hurt, he was afraid of it. He felt guilty too. He was terrified that he'd shared his mystery plague with Vivian. He worked as much as he could, threw himself into putting the boat away for the winter, and watched himself for symptoms, physical or spiritual. He watched himself for a tendency to bargain: Can anybody reasonably say more than 'This is what I want to happen, but if something else happens, I hope I'm unconscious'?

On weekend mornings, Gerry wandered the fundamentalist fringes of TV, trying to keep himself appalled into disbelief. Duane and Gretchen had just joined a new congregation back then. When Duane called home, he was hot to trot about someone called Pastor Bob Herder.

"He's from home," Duane told them. "And there's always something going on at his services. There's music and it's all sort of simple and clear. You're with The Lord or you're not. Pastor Bob spells it all out."

Vivian and Gerry hadn't told the kids that Gerry was waiting out a test for possible biblical plagues. He wished someone would spell it all out for *him*. Whoever was going to do it, it wasn't going to be Pastor Bob. One day, Gerry found him in a non-prime afternoon spot on the religion channel. He was a bossy-looking, puffy man in a suit, yelling about Jesus. A soft-cover bible splayed out of one hand like a doomed sandwich. Gerry thought he looked like a clothing clerk complaining about a spoiled hamburger. Bookmarks dangled like derelict lettuce. Pastor Bob's auctioneer yelping was muted by the clicker in Gerry's hand, but visually he seemed to pulse towards the screen. He'd radiate little auras of sweat in bursts at the camera. Then he'd recoil behind his pulpit to appreciate the importance of what he'd said.

Gerry watched the congregation with their hands held aloft like roller-coaster riders showing off. To improve the reception, like moving the rabbit ears on an old TV? he wondered. To show you're open to catch the ball? He listened to the commercial-paced pulse of the music. He hated it, but it wasn't just churches like this one, what his parents would have called holy rollers. He found he was getting less and less tolerant of churches, period.

When he was drinking, Gerry had found himself capable of sliding towards a belief in some hypercritical Presbyterian deity with a grudge, particularly towards him. He pictured a giant Ian Paisley on methamphetamines.

Sober, Gerry had found the human edges of his gods blurred and faded. He worried about anthropomorphizing gods. The more he looked at religion, the more he thought of Mickey Mouse and a real mouse. Why was a three-fingered, glove-wearing mouse who behaved like a human the archetype? Mickey was only remarkable as a literary figure, aping people. A real mouse that could pass like vapour through a wall crack or found a dynasty in a nest of rags was surely a truer god.

Without drawing any very definite conclusions, Gerry began to contemplate the infinite and came up with a sort of Mobius strip of reasoning. There might be one god, and everything, real and imagined, was part of it. On the other hand, every thing, real and imagined, might be a god in and of itself. The gods would be like bacteria, omnipresent, simultaneously infinitely weak and strong, a benign presence in your gut or an epidemic wiping you out.

Gerry slid through the last months of "The Longest Fall" in a growing fatalism. In January, after the lab got their containers right, the DNA testers told him there was nothing wrong with him. He started a new year with a mental Wile E. Coyote *whew* of relief. The falling boulder had missed him. The brakes had grabbed at the edge of the cliff. Still, the fatalism stayed in what he hoped was a kind of positive way. It made Gerry leery of anybody who traded on the fear of death or offered help in transcending it.

"Shouldn't religions just say we're all going to die? We're in good company so get over it." Gerry and Vivian were talking over coffee one night. "Isn't dying a miracle too?"

"I'm not going to worry about it," Vivian said. "When you go, you go." She went to the cupboard and took down a package of Oreo cookies and put them on the table between them. "I knew there was nothing wrong with you," she repeated her mantra. "I would have known."

"I didn't know," Gerry said. "Everything felt sort of unreal for a long time there, like this thing was the reality and everything else was just illusion."

Time makes you cocky. Sitting in the mall *now*, Gerry recants a bit on what he said *then*. The mortality of then seems less real or maybe mortality is getting less real generally. Maybe the line is blurring. Gerry thinks of the sweaty preacher, shouting in his geometrically pressed suit, verbally trying to re-draw, indelibly, Gerry's line.

Gerry doesn't deal with the line, or Oreo cookies or long falls the next time he writes something for his group, but he does have a go at bringing his George into the more recent past.

Fragment: Mortality at the Mall

There was a piece of the AIDS quilt on display at the mall, under the floating banners of the optimistic puffins. The puffins looked bullet-proof, smug that they don't get AIDS. They just get their heads stuck in the plastic rings off six-packs and strangle or get oiled and freeze. Those are the occupational hazards of the heroic life of a small bird in a big ocean.

George looked at the quilt, which was made up of squares dedicated to the dead. He found he knew two of the squares, both mourned by families who had embroidered clouds and mushrooms and a smiling pink *and orange cat. Brothers and sisters and a mother did those squares for two men who were a poet and a teacher, respectively. The loves of their lives don't seem to be mentioned, unless they're squares themselves, names that George doesn't recognize.*

A pretty, youngish woman was passing out literature at a folding table. She worked at something or other at the university and George had known her for several years. Still, he did not know what her relationship to the quilt and the people on it might be.

"It's so sad," she said. "There are so many."

Undeniably there was a quilt-full there on display. George thought he recalled having heard that the national quilt was football-field size. He had a First World War vision of emerald soccer pitches full of Flanders Field crosses. Still, he felt vaguely that the dozen or so friends or acquaintances of his who had died, or were dying, of AIDS, didn't nearly match the numbers he'd lost to other life-style martyrdoms, heart attack, gunshots, pills or crossing the street three-parts pissed.

With a twinge, George realized that, flying in the face of reason, fewer people he knew were dying anymore. There was a time in the early '80s when he seemed to go to a wake every week. He had been drinking then and he hung out with older men with stories to tell. He brought his wife Paula along for them to be courtly to. They told their stories and he sponged them up with the beer, although sometimes the sagas were cut off in mid-cycle. Paula, whose father died when she was fifteen, wept at a number of funerals for men who would have been about his age.

Somewhere along the line, though, all the older men had gone.

"You're like the medicine man of a lost tribe," she told George as he kept scouring empty tables for myths in the beer puddles. Eventually he was starting to act out the sagas himself. At thirty-five or six George was acting very middle-aged. He drank too much too often and steadily in-between.

"You're the scribe for a civilization that only has a past," she said, variations on a theme. By that time, she may have been quoting the man she eventually left him for.

In the Saturday mall, the pretty girl from the university handed out her literature and mourned or quasi-mourned on the shopping centre frontier of mortality. George wondered if, perhaps, she was going through her wake-a-week period now, as his had slowed. He wondered if that was reason to rejoice. If you hang out with people who do not die, does immortality threaten? George remembered the silly twist of logic they had played with in high school when they talked about deductive reasoning. If you haven't died on any day so far, on the basis of the statistical data, it should be less likely you're ever going to.

George sat at a Tim Hortons table and prepared a list for the next Saturday supper stir-fry in a potentially eternal series: shrimp, snow peas, broccoli...

six

JANUARY 2004

S itting in the Honda on the bald hill over the sea, Gerry feels the buffet of the wind outside the closed windows. He listens to the wind bang at the wire garbage container in a wooden crib that keeps it from flying off this hilltop to Ireland. It's like a boxer warming up on the heavy bag, tentative shots at first, placing the target in space and muscle memory. Then it settles down to a piston-regular hammering.

Gerry has the radio tuned to CBC FM and has his notebook open. Vivian would say he is wasting time. Patricia would have too. If the two of them ever decide to get together and hold a seminar on Gerry, his tendency to go off and do nothing by himself for hours could provide the keynote address.

"Where have you been?" Vivian asks. "How can you just drive around all day?"

"Where did you get to?" Patricia would ask. She'd ask after late nights at the legislative press gallery, or election road trips, or when she came back from visits to her family in Toronto or the summer courses she did: painting for the handicapped, French immersion in Quebec. Eventually, though, she stopped worrying about the answer. She joined an amateur drama group. They were doing Bolt's, *Man for All Seasons*. She designed the sets and costumes and played a servant. When the play went out of town to the provincial drama festival, she went to bed with the man playing Richard Rich.

Where did you get to? Gerry thinks now.

Whatever the women he has married think, Gerry would deny doing nothing. Today, for example, he's chronicling the toughness of the garbage container in the wind. He's keeping an eye on the sea to make sure it's still there. He comes from a family that took a proprietary view of the universe. It's not that they felt they owned it. The arrangement was more of a long-established stewardship. It strikes Gerry that they should have had esoteric job descriptions like the titles in some Confucian bureaucracy. They should have been "The Comptroller of Fog" or "The Warden of the Sunrise." He takes a childhood fragment to the writing group.

Fragment: Ancestral Voices

In spring, in the city in Ontario where he grew up, George's family joined the flow towards the river. They joined the clumps of twos and threes and the giggling, officious tribes that went to watch the swollen river. They went to see the ice break up. They went for the annual morality play of the river flooding the house-of-cards shacks where people had camped on the edge of the wartime boom and stayed.

In the prissy '50s, the shack dwellers seemed shabby, tattered and hung-over for whole seasons. However, in the summer when the ice was gone, they jumped triumphantly off bridges and ramshackle docks. They yelled defiance, with green Liberty torches of foam-trailing beer bottles in their hands. Their summer-night ferocity made their spring inundations seem a small price to pay.

In the spring melt, the shabby-heroic cabins occupied a perilous no-man's land between the gnashing ice teeth of the river and the road where the water lapped complacently, halfway across one lane. Here and there, front and back doors were left wide open to let the water flow through.

A five-year-old George walked in incongruous new galoshes beside his father, sidewalk superintendents of the flood. Years later he wonders why galoshes should have been new in the spring. He decides it was because they were on sale at winter's end.

In summer, George and his family roamed the woods and dusty back lanes where the grass grew between the ruts. They commented on the wildflowers, the dust, and the frog chorus backstage in the marshes. They timed the long electric-razor swan song of the cicadas, telling them summer was almost over. In fall, they trekked into the hills to the north of their city to oversee the colour changes. George feels that he can remember them dragooning the blushing, self-bonsai-ed sumacs into ragged lines along the ridges. He dreams they held tuning forks aloft to trigger the sky-slide of golden poplar leaves in crisp afternoons where the frost still defied the sun under the trees

Occasionally George's four maiden aunts would travel considerable distances to babysit nature somewhere else. They drove, with plaid car rugs in a 1952 Chev, to discipline the tides of Maine and the autumn hillsides of Vermont. On liners, and later in airplanes, they journeyed to supervise the white cliffs of Dover, the Alps and at least one coral island. They tried Florida once, but gave up on it. You only got palms and sand organized when hurricanes blew them away, and there didn't seem to be any proper progression of seasons. The aunts were devoutly deciduous. They also said the fruit was overrated.

"I'd have given my eyeteeth for a nice Mac apple," one said, dismissing Florida for all time.

It's not just by the ocean or on the fall hills that George remembers the magic proprietorship of the aunts. Aunt Louise looms largest, as she did in the flesh. She comes to him sometimes at the mall. Aunt Louise taught him about artefacts. She was the family keeper of photos, pressed flowers and old dance cards. Shrunken heads and scalps would have been her department too, if they'd had any.

A sign on the booths near the food court seems to bark. "Photos! Four poses! Three minutes! Two dollars!" Next to it, another sign offers full colour in four-and-a-half minutes for just a dollar more. The curtains on the photo booths are cut short so you can't pop in and run off porn-to-go unless you can levitate or Yogic-fly above the hem of the short curtain. Either that or you don't mind having your oeuvre, your style and your anatomy critiqued by the coffee drinkers in the food court.

Years ago, he went with Aunt Louise to the photo booth at the old railway station in his hometown. The pictures are much more expensive now than they used to be. He seems to remember them being a quarter, although you only got one picture. That picture came out of a slot, newborn-wet with vinegar-smelling chemical, in a little chromium frame. When the cardboard backing dried, you pried out a prop-piece to stand your portrait up, or a cardboard loop to hang it. The picture was supposed to be art. Today's pictures are more utilitarian. They come in strips and can be cut up to put on licences and ID's or mailed to friends or stuck on the washroom wall.

Next to the photo booth of fifty years ago stood a machine like a one-arm bandit. It had the alphabet and the numbers, zero to nine around its face. It had a pointer like a single clock hand and the bandit lever on one side. If you put in money and moved the pointer around, you could print letters on a metal disk, pierced with a star-shaped cut-out and stamped with a four-leaf clover and a crown. You could identify your luggage and purchase good luck for a quarter.

George believed the machine actually transformed the quarter. He didn't think of it paying for the disk. He thought of it being widened, pierced, and engraved as a sort of free magic service. The silver of the quarter returned to you in the talisman.

It's been fifty years since Aunt Louise and George made a talisman or had a picture clink down into the slot of the photo booth. The impossible-to-understand station loudspeakers intoned echoingly over their heads. George was about six, tagging along with the big woman in the tweed coat with the brooch of painted leather oak leaves and trillium that felt the way dried mushrooms feel now. Aunt Louise understood magic and history. She saw the sense of crossing the gypsy's palm with silver. She provided the money. History was frozen for a quarter while you waited and the loudspeakers made liturgical announcements about arrivals and departures. Their voices were underwater Latin in the big, echoing, Victorian temple of a railway station. They sounded like history: "Ancestral voices prophesying…trains."

When Gerry cleaned out the family home he found an old railway station picture. The photo had turned almost khaki with chemical discolouration. His face was very low down in the khaki picture. The spinning swivel seat did not go high enough to bring his six-year-old face to the frame. His mother also gave him a metal baggage tag.

Why had she saved something like a gaudy aluminium washer for forty years?

Why does Gerry have it in his wallet as he sits in the Honda and watches the wind buffet the garbage container, high above the sea?

seven

FEBRUARY 2004

Gerry has never been quite able to figure out what sort of dynamic exists between his present wife Vivian and his former wife Patricia. From time to time Patricia seems to surface between them like an uncharted, derelict wreck, drifting through their day-to-day sea lanes. Most often, she breaks the surface when they are arguing, as they are on this early Sunday morning. They have just come home from a Valentine's party that Gerry found dull and endless. It was thrown by a woman Vivian works with. At some point in the evening, there had been nearly two hours of charades.

"We're a wild bunch, aren't we?" a lacquered-looking woman asked Gerry as they sat in a furnished basement watching a fat man in his sixties in a sweatshirt with a picture of a timber wolf on it. He was trying to act out the phrase "positive Pap smear result." His hands fluttered vaguely between his crotch and his mouth.

Gerry looked at the woman to see if she was being sarcastic. She had an uncommunicative face. Possibly she couldn't move it for fear of cracking.

"Aren't we just a wild bunch?" he said. "I dare say the orgy will start right after our friend there has a stroke and we all get through yelling 'tits' and giggling."

He said it with more brightness than he felt, but apparently not enough. It wasn't the right answer. She immediately suspected he wasn't a good sport.

"He's quiet," she said, turning to Vivian and speaking in front of him. It was as if Gerry were unconscious and "quiet" were a fatal medical condition. She was the long-suffering nurse, breaking the bad news.

Patricia looms between them as they bicker in the car going home.

"I suppose you liked all *her* friends," Vivian snaps. Gerry has just observed that hell is probably endless charades with the same herd of self-satisfied people.

"She had the honesty to admit that some of them weren't everybody's idea of an exciting evening," he tosses back.

"You should have stayed together," Vivian sniffs. "You're always thinking about her."

At home, she pours herself a stiff nightcap but drinks only half of it before she goes to bed in silence. Gerry is left to contemplate what she said.

Patricia and her new husband, Brian, moved back to town some years ago. Brian teaches in the university's faculty of education. They have twins with the everything-old-is-new-again names of Charles and Charlotte. The twins were born a year after Patricia and Brian got married, a year and a half after she and Gerry broke up. They were in Winnipeg at the time. Brian was on some kind of academic exchange. In the world series of breeding, Patricia had slid home, just out of reach of her biological clock.

"Fertility drugs, probably," Vivian muttered.

However they were conceived, the twins are nearly eighteen now and tower over their parents. Gerry and Vivian have run into them with Patricia and Brian at the mall. Charles looks at him with well-bred, dumb distaste. It's as if he feels that Gerry had ignored a "reserved" sign stuck on his mother. Charlotte is friendlier and more curious. She seems to be weighing him up, wondering about the decisions her mother made. For Gerry to exist, neither her mother nor her father can be as straightforward and uncomplicated as they appear. Perhaps she's storing Gerry up for some future argument on choices, mistakes or fidelity.

Gerry would have to admit that he was interested to see Patricia when she first re-appeared, but he's sure there was no real stirring of desire.

"You had to feel something," Vivian insisted at the time. She still does, occasionally, when they're bickering.

Actually, there was less of a pang than a deeply personal curiosity. He compares it to a kid with his tonsils in a bottle of formaldehyde, or a baby tooth in his pocket. It was morbidly fascinating to see someone you had been attached to floating free and untouchable in the pickle of a new existence. It's intriguing to find that old tooth feels alien if you slip it back into your mouth. It can't be made to fit the healed gap where something else is pushing in.

Gerry sits at the computer and pushes his characters, George and Paula, around the stage of his marriage to Patricia. Actually, he just pushes George around. Paula is off-stage and George is acting out Gerry's old indiscretions.

Fragment: Jane Doe

In the mid '70s, they had lived for a summer and fall in another city. George had got a job writing features for a plump and prosperous little weekly paper. Paula was away, finishing a summer course and going on to visit her mother and sisters in Toronto.

George met the woman in a bar where not-very-successful journalists and business people hung out together. The mixture made the business people feel raffish. It gave the journalists the opportunity to cadge drinks. It was a Friday afternoon, Happy Hour, and her name was Jane.

Jane was older than George, close to forty. She was divorced and normally hung out with an architect. George had even interviewed him once about something or other. He and Paula had met Jane and the architect in this bar as couples, but on this night, they were both alone.

It was early summer and they drank gin and tonics and sang around a piano with an aluminium top to put drinks on. Talking about drinks, they got onto quinine in tonic and tonic in India and curry.

"I make a very respectable beef vindaloo," George said. "I can do goat too, but it's hard to get goat."

"Show me," Jane had said and they left the bar and went hand-in-hand into a warm early evening. She giggled as they got into her car in a parking lot.

"What?" George asked.

"I was thinking about goats playing hard-to-get," she said. She kissed him in the car the same way she drank gin, a long, determined draught of him, eyes open, appraising.

They stopped at a downtown grocery store and a liquor store on their way to his apartment.

"My daughter's at my place. She's seventeen," she said. "I was twenty when she was born."

She tossed this out, letting him do the math, perhaps as a last warning, a token attempt to see if he would back off.

George had the wit not to remark that he was twenty-seven. He was ten years older than her daughter, ten years younger than she was.

At his apartment, they were clumsy with bags of meat, rice and spices, a bottle of gin and tins of tonic. They felt they had to buy everything new. They played at unpacking their purchases together. They got in each other's way in the kitchen and by the time the curry was simmering they were leaned against the sink, necking, his knee forward and clutched between her thighs.

"This isn't going to happen often," Jane said as they fell apart briefly, like near-sighted fighters, refocusing on each other before they tangled again. "We're both other people, real people. This is just because we're pals tonight."

George felt himself soar in the freedom that implied. He wanted to just be her pal. They made it as far as the dubious oriental carpet that Paula had found at a second-hand store. By then they had eroded each other's clothes away. They fitted themselves into each other, a deck of flesh cards being shuffled. A tin mobile George had made from old cans hung over them. The balcony doors were open and the asphalt breath of the summer street made the tin clink weakly.

George remembered Jane now, as feeling fragile under a mushroom-soft skin. She felt like a bird or a Siamese cat, intimately woven to her own anatomy, with a small-animal heat and rapidity of pulse or teeth. Her coming cry was like the distant scream of a hurt rabbit, unreal, inconceivable until you heard it.

Afterwards they took a tepid bath together and sat wrapped in towels, eating their curry and drinking gin.

"Stupid hard-to-get goats," she said, leaning against him.

They repeated their love-making a couple of times over the next six months. As she had predicted, they didn't do it often, although she broke up with the architect and took a new apartment for her and her daughter.

Once, George went to her after some sort of spat with Paula. Her daughter was away with her father. They drank a lot and made cozy, sloppy love until long after the buses had stopped running. George had wanted to stay.

"No. Go home, you're married," Jane said. "We're pals. Remember?"

She had had too much to drink to risk driving. Neither of them had enough money for him to take a cab. He walked home and, on the way, broke the heel off one of the cowboy boots he was wearing. He cursed her as he hobbled home to make his peace with Paula, but he thanked her later.

The last time he met Jane was sometime in the early '80s. He was visiting her city for some sort of workshop. They got together for lunch and she told him she was getting married to somebody who ran a travel agency. She'd met him on a cruise. They argued like old friends over the bill and when they said goodbye, George repeated the old navy toast that he'd quoted to her once and made her laugh.

"Wives and sweethearts, may they never meet."

She laughed and the last time he saw her, she was striding past the ice cream sellers of a green city square to go back to work.

Gerry scrolls through the four or five pages that are Jane on the computer screen. Vivian is out and the house is quiet. When the furnace cuts in with its soft, sibilant roar it seems intimate and close, a breath in the ear.

I'm having an affair with the damn furnace, Gerry thinks. Wait until Viv gets out the door and push up the thermostat. I'll be naked with the vacuum cleaner next.

Gerry sometimes wonders why he's been faithful to Vivian for nearly twenty years while he found Patricia fairly easy to cheat on. He wonders if it has anything to do with having split up once and knowing that it's possible. He and Patricia had seemed so very permanent when they were married. Other people felt trapped and destroyed by the minutiae of houses and kids and lack of time for each other. They were trapped by their freedom from all of that. When they'd been married for ten years or so, people pointed them out as indestructible, a perfect couple. It took half as long again before they could bring themselves to admit out loud that, with everything in their favour, they had failed. On both sides of the family, their in-laws loved the people they had married.

"Who gets custody of the parents?" they had asked each other ruefully on the phone. Each was in somebody else's apartment. They were choreographing their last steps by long distance from cities miles apart. "Maybe we can just swap them."

Sometimes he feels he had almost been set up to fall away from Patricia, or maybe that's just what he wants to believe to make himself look better. He recalls the time a university friend of hers visited them. He converts her into a George and Paula episode.

Fragment: Poor Old George

She came to stay with them for two weeks at the end of August while she looked for a new apartment. She had broken up with her husband the previous spring and was going to be a language specialist at Paula's school. Her name was Rachel.

It was a warm August that year, a sweet, lingering end of summer. Paula and Rachel had nothing much to do before school started. They apartment-hunted. They bummed around the apartment or lounged in the tiny backyard in swimsuit bottoms and T-shirts. When they came to the supper table, they brought the smell of warm skin and suntan oil. There seemed to be a lot of bare legs in the apartment. Rachel kidded George about his household of partially clad women.

"Poor old George," she would say when she and Paula giggled and mimicked the cheerleaders at their university, bouncing around the kitchen. "You've got a disorderly house full of lewd women."

"It's a burden," George would say with a sigh and they'd all laugh.

It was almost Labour Day when Paula had a car accident. She was driving their ancient Volkswagen from the supermarket when a kid in his dad's big Buick ran a stop sign. The Volks was whipped sideways. The other car cut its front half-off, just in front of Paula's legs. She was taken to hospital on a stretcher, in a plastic collar. George and Rachel raced to the hospital by cab and spent the late afternoon in waiting rooms and corridors. By nightfall, the X-rays showed that, amazingly, Paula had nothing broken, but she had two black eyes and was painfully bruised and stiff. A sleepy resident told them they'd keep her overnight. He gave her something for the pain and she fell asleep with George and Rachel at her bedside.

They walked up the hill from the hospital to the apartment through the pools of streetlights' glow. They felt strangely companionable as they talked about Paula's close call. Back at the apartment they drank a bottle of white wine that was supposed to have gone with the supper Paula was bringing.

"Jeez, I guess the fish is still in the car, wherever they took it."

"Poor old George," Rachel said.

Later he was lying in bed when she came into the room. She was wearing a long man's T-shirt, one of her ex's.

"My loot," she said, tugging at the tail and sitting on the bed. "How are you doing in here, poor old George?"

She pulled the sheet aside. The curtains blew briefly into the room as a breeze moved outside. Rachel administered herself like first aid. Her hands, her hair and her mouth washed down the front of him. Finally she settled herself, astride, on top of him with a pre-occupied little grunt, like someone finding that they've remembered the sequence of CPR properly and the patient is responding. George looked up at her and realized he'd been willing this to happen.

Rachel went back to her own room at dawn. Later that day they went and got Paula in a taxi, fussing over her and making a special *supper. On the Labour Day weekend, against all expectations, Rachel found the perfect apartment.*

For some months after, George visited her occasionally. Paula had signed up for a dress-making class at the Y. Rachel always seemed abstractly glad to see him, but along about Christmas, she gently told him she was busy when he called from a bar to see if he could come over.

"I'm seeing this wildlife biologist. We met when I was escorting a field trip," she said. "I think maybe it's serious, like you and Paula."

Which is why I'm calling you, George thought wryly. That's like Paula and me.

Not long after that, she moved in with the biologist whose name was Mark. Later they got married.

Paula was Rachel's matron of honour. George got drunk with the groom and said he was a nice guy. They went to Labrador afterwards and sent a letter to say they had been living in a tent on the barrens all summer. They tried to conceive when Mark wasn't busy putting radio-collars on caribou.

Gerry and Patricia were godparents for the real Rachel's son. It was one of the things they did in what he thinks of as their polite period when they were both working in Labrador and got back together with the couple he now calls Mark and Rachel.

They had stopped fighting about things by then. Patricia had become a specialist in art and language curriculum and did more work in school board offices than in the classroom. She moved around more.

"I'm going to St. John's for six weeks. It's an exchange."

"That's nice, I'll see if I can't get down a couple of weekends."

He was working in local television then. The shifts were arranged so that you worked for ten days and got four off. A northern town in winter is ideal if you want to be idle. Seasonal workers lie-up for the winter. When Patricia was away, Gerry spent whole days in a bar just down the road from the radio and TV station.

They were aware that their special-ness was dead and they were nice to each other in their bereavement. Eventually, though, it was spring and time to get on with their lives.

Gerry remembers an unseasonably warm May night with the smell of burning. They were at a barbecue on the lawn of an air force mess and there was a forest fire burning on the crowns of the hills across the valley. As the dusk came on, it made an orange-red necklace on the green-black skyline and threw a red glow on the bottom of the smoke clouds. The smoke of meat and the smoke of burning forest mixed. It made the barbecue feel momentous and yet heedless, like Drake's game of bowls, or Wellington's ball before Waterloo.

"Drink, love?"

"Those pitchers of Sangria look good."

"I've got our names on a couple of steaks."

Now he remembers that they seemed to circulate through the party with different clumps of people, getting together only for polite practicalities. Occasionally they'd lob badminton serves of banter to each other from the safety of their separation. They waved across the grill like a couple who had consented to crew in different sailboats in some trivial regatta, smiling, but whizzing past each other, driven by different strategies and winds. They wound up at two different parties that night after the barbecue broke up.

They came home at daylight with the smell of the fire drifting through the open windows of their rented house. They slept the morning away. About lunchtime on Saturday, they found themselves taking a shower together. They touched each other tentatively, like antiques under the spray and eventually found themselves back in bed. They made practised, but slightly distant love, each sensing comparisons being made. They finished together, sweating, but strangely unmoved.

Gerry thinks of the argument he had with Vivian after the awful Valentine's party, how she had said that he and Patricia should still be together. He writes a more up-to-date scene about George and Paula and adds a Vivian character he calls Ellen.

Fragment: Explaining "Over"

They came together, but then again, they almost always did. They lay with the shades down against the afternoon glare and spoke only of things that had nothing to do with them.

"That wind's warm."

"It'll be hot work for the crews on the fire."

The distant growl of water bombers, shuttling to the fire, underlined their silences.

It is the enduring finality of that slightly mournful calm that George has never been able to convey to his wife Ellen. She seems to resent Patricia's and his unanimity in deciding they were through.

When he went to bed he found half of Ellen's drink, unfinished on the bedside table. She was asleep on her back, still wearing her sweater and underwear. She snored slightly and he could smell the rye. He lay carefully on his own side of the bed to make sure he didn't wake her and wondered about the calmness he felt.

eight

FEBRUARY 2004

D arren's Donair and Pizza is closed indefinitely and Darren has skipped town. He got up early one morning and got on a plane to Alberta to go to work for his older sister who runs a pizza joint in Fort McMurray. Gerry and Vivian and Melanie have pieced together these facts at councils of war at the kitchen table.

The business had wallowed to a halt in the post–Christmas restaurant doldrums. Darren nibbled away at the float in the cash drawer to go and play the gambling machines in the bar next door.

"He just stopped paying the bills," Melanie says. "He just took what was in the till on Friday and went on."

It turns out that Darren ran his disappearance with a lot more planning than he ever ran the business. He had managed to keep one credit card, paid-up and functioning. That bought his ticket, a new wardrobe and a suitcase at Wal-Mart. The kitchen-table war-room knows that because the bill has come in.

"He sold his car to his buddy Ryan," Melanie says. "Ryan drove him to the airport and then kept the car. He came up home to see if the summer tires were in the shed."

"I'd tell him what he can do with his summer tires," Vivian says.

"They're no good to me if I don't have a car," Melanie says philosophically.

Meanwhile, Gerry is in the process of discovering that, insofar as Darren's D&P can be said to exist as a corporate entity, Gerry is it. He signed for a loan to get the business up and running.

"I should have made him go to the mob or the triads or somebody," he says. "Somebody who'd like a set of kneecaps as a desk ornament."

It turns out that the collapse of Darren's business empire is not exactly Enron or Nortel. The suppliers had doubts about Darren for some time before he flew the coop. He hadn't been able to run up very much debt. Gerry learned that there was a local black market for cheese and that, in the age of billing-on-line, it was defiantly cash-based.

"There's just a couple of things that came in after," says the loans officer at Gerry's bank. "I don't know what the equipment is worth, you're better to sell that yourselves."

In the end, Gerry and Vivian sell a savings bond to pay off about eight thousand dollars to the bank. Vivian is incensed that one of the items on the business loan is gifts for Darren's sister's kids. He charged them to the shop just before he left. Melanie knows someone who wants the oven and the power mixers. Gerry has quixotic notions about making sure the staff gets paid. However, it turns out that the girl on the cash got paid from the till on the last night of business. The drivers only worked for beer and dope money. After they'd peered into the dark store around the "closed" sign and shaken the door a couple of times, they ran out of ideas.

The bar next door to the store called Melanie about a tab. She gave them Darren's sister's phone number in Alberta.

"Call real early in the morning," she suggested. Darren is not a noted early riser.

Vivian, the realtor, makes sure that Melanie and Diana will have a roof over their heads. She and Gerry paid off their own mortgage when his Aunt Louise of the photo booths died and his mother sold the house in Ottawa. Vivian talks to some people at the bank and she and Gerry assume Melanie's mortgage. She'll keep up the payments. To do that, Melanie dusts off her restaurant résumé and gets a waitress job at an upscale place downtown.

"With only the costly imported ketchups," Gerry kids her. "Would you like to see the ketchup list, madame?"

"You got it," Melanie says. Gerry thinks she seems tougher now, with the sapping growth of Darren removed. She goes clubbing with the other girls from work. While Vivian complains that she drinks too much, when babysitters are a problem, Diana stays with her and Gerry. They play Crazy Eights.

"You got the ace, Grampa Gerry. That's twenty-five."

"You and your grandmother are card sharks."

Outwardly, Melanie and Diana seem to take the departure of Darren pretty much in stride. Gerry doesn't remember Melanie fighting with Darren much. Darren always seemed to lack the metabolism to fight. His temperature topped-out at a sense of grievance and victimhood. Gerry wonders if that was his and Melanie's version of the polite phase he and Patricia had gone through. He vaguely remembers a grade-school science lesson about leaves falling. Cells form, cutting off the connection. Maybe Darren and he had just dropped off stems that had invisibly scabbed over.

He wonders if Darren ever found Melanie's right-ness squeezing him out. He could remember that feeling. Patricia was eminently more sensible than he was. She had an instinct for the reasonable. He was a cowardly nihilist.

"Talk to me about what you want," she said. The walls closed in.

Gerry punched holes in walls. He broke his little finger when he inadvertently found a stud behind the plaster. He found it a relief to slide away for an affair that had no redeeming social merit, where *wrong* was the given. Still, he had generally wanted to come back in a day or two. Low-metabolism Darren was braver. He burned his bridges.

"It's ironic," Gerry says to Vivian while they're having supper one night.

"What is?"

"When I punched holes in walls I broke my finger on the stud. Now when I want to hang a picture, I can't find the damn stud."

"Jack used to punch the walls, "Vivian says. "He used to beat the place up."

It occurs to Gerry that if Vivian started writing vignettes from her past, they would be the mirror-image of his own musings.

Heroes and villains are where you find them, he thinks, and wonders
if he's a change in quality from Vivian's first life, or just a fluke of better
timing: post-wall-smashing, post-sulking-with-a-one-night-stand.

It's an early morning and Gerry is the only one up, sitting at the
computer trying to write. The sky is starting to lighten outside. The days
are getting longer.

He looks at the last bit he wrote about Vivian as Ellen, but doesn't
feel courageous about the present this morning. He dodges back into
the past. He settles on a pile of jottings that deal with a time in the
mid-'80s, after Patricia and before Vivian, between Paula and Ellen in his
recycled chronicle.

Fragment: Weasel Lodge

They called themselves The Loyal Order of Weasels at the bar. They
said Weasel was an acronym. It stood for "Week-End-Adventurers-
Sans-Ethical-Luggage." What they mostly did was drink and wait for
bars to fill up so they could complain about them being too crowded and
go somewhere else.

Today the Weasels are meeting in a place that justifies being a bar
by having pretensions as a restaurant. It isn't anywhere near noon yet
and only thirsty Weasels are there. There is nothing less trendy than an
empty trendy restaurant. It will be an hour or two before the place can
pretend to be either a restaurant or trendy. It's almost entirely in its
loser-bar incarnation, except that it smells of old mussel shells. There was
a dirty clot of blood on the sidewalk outside. One of last night's
lined-up trendies must have smacked another as they waited to get in.
Courage must have failed the victim. He had decided to stay in one spot
and bleed a quiescent pool on the pavement rather than snort a red froth
in the face of his attacker and charge.

Today the Weasels consist of a broker named Simon and Lem who
owns a greasy spoon where the group can get beer at breakfast time. Then
there's Chuck who works for a collection agent but says he used to be a
pilot in the air force. The other members are George and a woman called
Fiona and the obnoxious FM disc jockey she's been going out with. He

goes by his on-air name of Lance, but Fiona says he was christened Heber. Currently she is auditioning George as the DJ's replacement. Lance/Heber has made the mistake of demonstrating how easy Fiona is to boss around in social situations. George doesn't boss her around and, because he's between jobs, has lots of time to drink with her. Fiona was divorced from a dentist and hasn't bothered to go back to work yet. They have already been to bed when Lance was doing an all-night shift and are toying with becoming an item.

On this day, Lance is elsewhere. Fiona has brought her ex's camera to the bar.

"I want to get some pictures for my friend in Calgary," she says. Fiona went to university out west.

It's a mild day with winter cautiously trying on spring. There's actually a bit of heat in the sun as they walk around the town. They take pictures of fish stalls and the court house and the Anglican graveyard.

"Taking pictures. It's like George Formby, 'Washing windows.' It ought to be a music hall song," George says. He is wondering if this afternoon's walk is going to end up in bed. He hums the Formby song for her. She's too young to have heard it.

"When I'm taking pictures," she sings along with him then.

George keeps his questions about where the afternoon is leading to himself, tucked, like their hands, in their pockets.

"Wanna go downtown and look for answers?"

"No, let's just sling our questions over our shoulders and go take pictures."

When there are no pictures to take and Lance is in the ascendant, George fills the lulls in his love-life with drinking and people-watching. He looks for hidden messages and portents in the mundane.

Over breakfast beers, he talked to Lem at the greasy spoon about his grandmother's shroud.

"Gran had it all made and put away," Lem said. "She showed it to the wife and told her to try it on."

"Like you would," George said. In a world that drank India Beer at seven in the morning, why wouldn't people try on each other's shrouds?

"It had a flap down the front," Lem continued. He was the perfect witness, no emphasis, just detail and pure chronology. "The wife asked her, 'What's that? What's that flap there for?' The old lady says, 'They pull that up over your face before they closes the coffin.' The wife got the shivers then."

When he wasn't gathering Lem stories, George threw himself into the various silly diversions that the Weasels held dear. It became enormously important to buy the most horrendous greeting card, the chamber pot with the smoke alarm or bicycle bell. They became members of "The Cruise Club." They paid ten cents extra on drinks and filled in little cards. When the cards were full after twenty-four drinks, they went in a big jar behind the bar. The draw was to be on St. Patrick's Day.

On Paddy's Day we're sending our snakes on a vacation, George wrote in his notebook. Somehow, though, he wasn't there for the draw.

Gerry sits and sifts through some of his old notebooks and bits he's tried to write before about those times. A dozen pages after the Weasels in a notebook, he finds the first jottings that refer to Vivian and Tanya, a first Saturday, waking up at her house:

I'd not given a lot of thought to hopscotch in recent years, but that doesn't mean I wouldn't have considered playing the other morning. It was Saturday and the sun was emotional Alka-Seltzer. A few bubbles in your psyche will get you thinking about hopscotch if you're asked by someone who is either nine or a leprechaun, with her hair in elastics with neon plastic balls on them and earrings to match.

There are worse things than to listen to someone run a bath. The shuffle of bare feet in a kitchen goes well with the morning kettle sounds and the smell of sleep-tangled hair blends with the toast smell.

Thank God it's not a race. I'm not up to racing. However, if asked by blasé, neon-eared leprechauns, I could probably play a passable game of Hopscotch.

Underneath he had jotted down a bit of Chuang Tzu:

The white fish are swimming at ease. This is the happiness of fish.

nine

MARCH 2004

It's snowing gently as Vivian drives Gerry to the airport on a Friday evening. They're in an armed truce. She complained about having to drive in the snow, but when he said he'd just as soon take a taxi she accused him of being extravagant. He's going to Ottawa to see his mother. It's one of those emergencies that may, or may not, be an emergency.

"Could you come up?" she'd asked on the phone. "I think I've had a stroke."

"She's been a little agitated," the nurse at the home said. "The doctor was in to see her. She gets a little depressed. I'm sure if you came she'd love to see you, but there doesn't seem to be anything much wrong."

It is part of the guilt-price that Gerry pays for living far away that he has to over-respond. It's two days since the call and he's on his way.

Vivian parks aggressively at the departures gate, but leans across the car and kisses him.

"You be good now," she says. "Your mom will be fine."

"I know, but when you're ninety odd…"

"I know."

He grabs his elderly folding suitcase and his shoulder bag from the backseat and waves from the pavement. Vivian, not looking, cuts off a taxi and pulls away through the big soft flakes of snow.

Gerry knows he's on a sober, grown-up mission, but feels an out-of-school lightness as she drives away. He humps his bag to the check-in. The flimsy computer print-out they give you now instead of a fat ticket folder adds to the feeling. It's like a typewritten hall pass. He feels compelled to joke with the women at the counter.

"The bag's going to Ottawa. You might as well send me with it."

"Would you like window or aisle?"

"Window if you've got it and I'm large and speak English, so if you have one by an emergency door..." Gerry angles for a bit of spare legroom.

"You'll be forty-five minutes in Halifax. Change there for Ottawa."

"Marvellous," says Gerry who almost never says marvellous out loud.

It's the end-of-the-week, Friday rush-hour flight and security is jammed. Fat bald boys with goatees and rectangular women with blazers and rubber gloves poke through the carry-ons. They seem to be universal types now, varying in complexion, but not in shape, wherever you go.

Gerry, the seasoned traveller, opens his belt buckle and shows the inside without being asked, gets a tired smile, and is waved ahead. He feels hermetically sealed away from the normal now, an airline monk, cut off from the world behind. The logic of the slaughterhouse applies. The only way out is ahead. He feels like somebody else when he buys *Harper's* at the magazine stand.

When his flight boards he greets the attendants and goes to his emergency door seat with its extra inches of space. One of the attendants comes to tell him about the door.

"You pull that down, but only when you're told, and then you push the door out and it just falls away."

"Seems simple enough," Gerry says. The door ritual makes him feel at home. It's like being an old camper at summer camp. You know the chants and the shortcuts through the woods. He settles down and starts to make surprisingly good progress with the *Harper's* crossword, which is diabolical and normally beyond him.

Gerry even gets a pleasant seat-mate for the leg to Halifax. She is a tall woman with short dark hair. They nod to each other when she stops by the seat to check the number. She has a carry-on that pushes the size limit. Gerry helps her put it in the rack. A bit later, she smiles when he looks up from his puzzle and says, "This is evil."

"I only do the find-a-word, sometimes," she says. She tells him that she travels for a company that sells women's sportswear. She's been visiting stores in Newfoundland and she's going home to Halifax. Her name is Carole with an "e." She says she has just turned in a rent-a-car and hates driving on the island because of the moose.

"Speed bumps with antlers," Gerry says. "You can get a poster."

"I hit a deer driving up to Amherst," she tells him as they drink bottled water. "He came right through the windshield. I got this."

Gerry looks at a scar she points to, a three-or-four-inch Zorro slash below the knee. He can't picture how a deer would make the wound. A deer with a mask and sword? He decides it must have been the windshield, but windshields are supposed to crumble now.

"You were lucky." It's not unpleasant looking at her leg.

"I used to figure skate. It's stiff since the accident. My daughter tells me I'm old and crippled."

They compare daughters. He tells her he's going to see his mother who thinks she's had a stroke. Gerry shares his packet of wintergreen Certs. He remembers the copy of *Emmanuelle* that kicked around his and Patricia's various apartments in the '70s. He can remember the name of the plane where Emmanuelle got it on with her fellow passengers. It was *The Flying Unicorn*. The twenty-first-century unicorn is a no-frills beast. Its horn docked, it's more of a flying Shetland pony gelding. The sharing of bottled water and breath mints is the new erotica.

Gerry helps Carole with her over-sized bag at Halifax. They say goodbye in the terminal.

"Watch out for deer."

"I hope your mother's okay."

He stretches his legs around the terminal, buys an over-priced coffee and boards his flight for Ottawa. On this leg he sits next to a morose man from federal public works. The man had booked at the last minute to get home for some family emergency. He isn't saying what the emergency is, just that he has to be there. He had paid the top ticket price. When the cabin crew serves a snack he looks sadly at the big chocolate chip cookie they give him.

"This is a fifteen-hundred-dollar cookie," he says. Then he fires up his laptop and plays solitaire.

Gerry returns to his puzzle for a while over the darkness of the Maine and Vermont mountains and woods. When the lights below thicken into clusters for Montreal and its suburbs, he puts the magazine away in his shoulder bag. For the last half hour he watches the lit lines of roads come up to meet him. The geography is neater than that of Newfoundland. The rows of headlights and streetlights follow surveys of old farmland that's been cleared and harrowed flat. When the plane descends low enough for trees to show against the snow, they're in separate woodlots and groves in the fields, like clumps of hair in warts. The intercom tells him it's five-past-ten, local time, if he'd like to set his watch.

Gerry meets his friend Doc for a late Chinese dinner. He has picked up a rental car and checked into a motel near the old-age home where his mother lives. Duane and Gretchen had offered to put him up. So had Doc. He pleaded distance and unfamiliar country roads with Duane and Gretchen. With Doc he had pointed out that if things got worse Vivian would be coming up and he couldn't put them both up. In fact, he just felt like being alone.

It's an old motel. He remembers the family driving past it when it was still in a semi-rural area. It was a farmhouse converted to a guest-home then. Now the original house stands far back from the road with its front lawn covered by a parking lot for the modern two-storey "convenience units" that hem it in on two sides. It's halfway out a long divided street that used to be a main route west out of town. Now the street is ten miles of strip malls, motels and ice-cube office buildings for tech companies with two-syllable names.

Dadoo, Ronron, Gerry thinks when he drives by them. He sings the old Crystals' song and drums on the steering wheel at the stop lights. Da doo ron ron ron /Da doo ron ron.

The restaurant they go to is called The Jade Gate and is a time capsule of the '60s.

"Because, after all, the '60s were just like the '50s until '67," they will argue as they try to pin down the chronology and horoscopy of their lives.

"No. '63. Beatles. We were in grade eleven. It was different after The Beatles."

The restaurant is still busy when Gerry and Doc meet there shortly after eleven. Gerry can't remember it ever not being busy and they've been coming here since Doc got his driver's licence in '63. Maybe it was that driver's licence that made the '50s turn into the '60s.

"It's the same waiter," Doc hisses in a stage whisper, standing up at the table to greet Gerry. "You're going to have to show him ID."

"For soda water? I think I'm old enough to handle soda water."

"Maybe. Don't get rowdy though. You sing and they'll throw us out of here. They probably remember you."

Doc is tall, thin and wears dusty, Work Warehouse work clothes. He's a contractor who specializes in restoring old houses and lives nearby in a loft full of tools and old newel posts and tin ceiling rosettes. He got into the trade after a stint as a theatre set designer and carpenter, but twenty-five years ago he was married and needed something steadier. Yuppification was sweeping old neighbourhoods then and work was plentiful. He knew where to get old bits and pieces from dressing sets. Doc collected a following of customers, and although he's not married anymore, he's still at it.

Gerry remembers passing through town in the '80s, as he was breaking up with Patricia. He had gone to supper with Doc and his wife Hilary and Hilary's kid, Timothy. It was the first time he'd been anywhere as anything but half of a couple for years. He remembered how odd it felt. It seems hard to believe that Doc has been split-up for as long as Gerry's been married.

"Timothy's the manager at a computer store," Doc says. "We get together for a beer every couple of months. We helped Hilary move down to Ganonoque last summer. She's got a glass studio there now."

"Still civil?"

"Oh yeah."

They sit under an ornate ceiling of gilt dragons and flowers with tasselled Chinese lanterns. The décor hasn't changed in forty years. A dozen elderly waiters in black trousers and short red mess-jackets rush in a sore-footed way with heaping trays.

"You order," Doc says. "You're braver than me. I buy TV dinners."

"God, do they still make them?" Gerry asks. "Why don't you cook something?"

"Too much like work. Besides, I like TV dinners."

This Chinese feast has become a tradition whenever Gerry hits town, usually every six months or so. It's part of the legend of the tradition that Gerry is deprived of the benefits of The Jade Gate, marooned as he is supposed to be, in Newfoundland. Still, Doc lives practically around the corner and lives on pre-cooked cardboard turkey and the waiter acts as if he recognizes Gerry.

He expects to be almost-recognized, like a kid expects Mickey to wave to him or her at Disneyland. Gerry finds his former hometown has a Disney-feel to it now, not quite real. Gerry had read somewhere that Disneyland buildings are five-eighths scale.

Welcome to Soo guy Land, he thinks, looking around the restaurant. Only the reason for being here is full-size.

"So you're going to see your mom tomorrow?"

"Yeah, I told her I was getting in early in the morning. They put them to bed about eight at the home. I told her I'd see her in the morning."

They order too much food, eat too much of it, and still have a doggy-bag full for Doc to take home.

"A nice change from the TV dinners," Gerry says. "But doggy-bag can't be politically correct, can it?"

"Companion-animal container, maybe?"

It's late when Gerry parks his rental car outside his motel room. The parking lot is like an empty hockey arena under the cold sodium lights. He had turned up the heat before he went for supper. The room breathes warmth at him when he opens the door,

A hotel room can be a retreat. The simplicity of living between a bed and a suitcase appeals. Gerry gets into bed and flicks the TV remote through its channels. There seem to be more here, more languages, and what appears to be a soft-porn channel.

Is your porn soft? Gerry muses. Get Viagra and jump over hydrants in commercials: hydrant humping, the new metaphor for sex.

When he awakes hours later it is the weather channel he's dozed off in front of.

The Disneyland feel of the city is with Gerry again the next morning as he walks around a shopping mall near his mother's nursing home. He has learned from bitter experience that it's hard to get a parking spot at the home on a weekend. He parks at the mall a couple of blocks away and walks.

Gerry is up early, still running on Newfoundland time. He is waiting outside a restaurant in the mall when it opens at seven. This neighbourhood around the mall is peppered with retirement homes, seniors' apartments and condos. The restaurant is like a halfway house on his pilgrimage to see his mother, a warm-up. There are specials with fruit and bran and prunes and the tables fill up with old people who seem to be regulars. Plastic pill boxes are produced from the pockets of bright jogging suits or golfy-looking cardigans. Tables fill up by ones and twos. The old people greet each other in a congratulatory way. They're Disney-bright automatons. They've survived another night.

At the nursing home, music is frozen in the 1940s. Glenn Miller plays over the sound system. Presumably somebody has done the demographics. The '40s are the decade where the greatest number of residents' musical tastes solidified. Presumably in another decade or so, the music from the speakers will be Elvis. Give it twenty years and it will be Doors and Jefferson Airplane.

Gerry signs in at the desk. The woman behind it scans the signature and who he's seeing and sort of remembers him.

"You're visiting from…Is it Nova Scotia?"

"Newfoundland."

"That's right, I remember. Your mother will be so glad to see you."

Upstairs, he supposes she is glad to see him. At least she clutches his hand and smiles in a bemused way when he wakes her in her chair in the day-room. For a year now, she's been on a floor where she can't operate the elevator buttons herself. She still goes down to the dining room, but she's taken.

"You're here," she says, sounding surprised.

"Yes, dear, I told you I was coming, remember?"

"Is Patricia…no…I'm all balled-up…I mean is Vivian with you?"

"No, Mom. She's home."

"That's nice."

It sometimes seems to Gerry that his mother awards some kind of brownie points for knowing who he's married to at the moment and where she is. There are times when he suspects she thinks Patricia was mislaid through some negligence on his part. At other times she seems to think that he's a bigamist. However, she's diplomatic about this and waits to take his conversational lead as to who's the spouse of the moment.

They have gone past conversation. She goes nowhere. He does little that has any meaning here in the warm limbo of the home. He gives quick updates on what the kids are doing. She actually asks about Tanya. She knew her better than the other kids. Gerry and Vivian had brought her with them when they first came to visit before they were married. She and Gerry's Aunt Louise had babysat while they went out in the evenings. Gerry's mother sent Tanya birthday cards with cheques in them until fairly recently. Now Gerry wonders just how recent it was. Tanya's been in Alberta for more than a year and away from home for longer than that. He mentions the grandchildren but they don't seem to register. His mother's posterity cuts off at Viv's kids. She doesn't seem able to fathom that they have children now. The last time she visited them in Newfoundland was the year Diana was born.

They sit, side-by-side, in two armchairs that Gerry remembers from the living room at home. She was allowed to bring some furniture to the home. He tries to get her involved in a conversation that is more than a monologue from him.

"How's Carmen? Does she call you?" He asks after her younger sister.

"Not so much. I don't know if there's something the matter."

"Let's call her."

He phones his Aunt Carmen and confirms what he suspected. She calls, but his mother often doesn't answer. She doesn't hear the phone. He puts her on the phone to chat with Carmen and roots in the dresser for hearing-aid batteries. When she gets off the phone he changes the battery in her hearing aid.

He looks at the clock radio on the bedside table. He has been here a little over an hour and has virtually run out of things to talk about. Grasping, he throws out that he'll be glad to get back to sailing when the spring comes.

"Just be careful, dear."

And if you're careful you'll end up here, Gerry thinks. This is the prize for being careful for ninety years.

They go down to lunch together, leaving the room at exactly twenty to twelve.

"You have to go down early. The elevator gets crowded."

It does too. Even twenty minutes early, they have to wait while old people and their attendants untangle legs of walking frames and back an electric scooter into the rear corner of the elevator. Mrs. Adamson has vetoed any suggestion that a walker or even a cane might help her be steadier on her feet.

"When I need that, I'll just sit."

Lunch is a pale cream-of-something soup, a slice of quiche and a salad. Gerry's mother doesn't care for the quiche. They send it back and get her a chicken salad sandwich instead. She eats only half. Dessert is a strawberry sundae which she devours. Gerry has a second cup of coffee which she seems to consider daring. When they finish and go back to the elevator, they have to wait while the early arrivals for the one o'clock sitting untangle their walkers.

After lunch, the home's doctor drops in. He's British, professionally cheerful, and has his volume control pitched to the elderly. He gets Gerry's mother to do some hand movements and asks her questions about the date and if she remembers his last visit.

"She's not in bad shape, all things considered," he says chattily, talking to the two of them. Gerry finds this talking about his mother in front of her off-putting. He follows the doctor into the hall when he leaves.

"She thought she might have had a stroke."

"Yeah, well, she might have, a little one, but there's not much change in her awareness. She's not doing all that badly for what, ninety-five?" The doctor looks at Gerry. "You don't get in much, do you?"

"I live in Newfoundland," Gerry says, defensive now.

"Well there you are then. You'd see a bigger difference because you don't see her day-to-day. She's not doing all that badly."

Gerry's not sure if he's been reassured or put in his place. He decides to take the optimistic view.

"That's good to know, and of course you do know where to get in touch with us?"

"Oh, the lodge has all that. Not to worry."

Not to worry, Gerry thinks as he walks out in a bright winter afternoon. His mother is taking a nap and he needs to move, to get clear of the petrifying air of the home. He has contrived a few errands to run. She needs some hand cream, cough lozenges, and a battery for her watch. She wants a bottle of milk of magnesia.

"They steal it."

Gerry has heard Vivian quote the same complaint from her mother in a home in Gander.

It's a big syndicate, he thinks. The Russian mob is muscling in on the laxative black market.

He buys the things on his list at the mall and walks back to the lodge. He knows that by the end of the week he won't be so quick to buy a whole list at once. He'll split it down into quick trips for one thing as the need to move gets stronger. Today is only the first day. When he gets back, they get through the afternoon by reading the newspaper together. The inside pages yield enough news of their old neighbourhood that he can read snippets and make small talk. He lasts until it's time for her to go down to supper at five o'clock. As he signs out at the desk and steps into the gathering evening, again he feels that *school's-out* thrill. He wants to yell and run with his arms swept back like jet wings.

In the name of getting it over with, Gerry visits Duane and Gretchen and the kids for supper. He follows directions Duane has given him and drives south and west of the city. The city extends much farther than it used to and apparently plans to keep on going. Gerry arrives at a crossroad that used to be on the family's route to the cottage. It's a blank intersection in the middle of featureless fields, almost at the divide where farmland yields to cedar swamp. A harshly vertical brick church stands aloof, a quarter-mile back down the road. There are no signs of life around the church and virtually no traffic, but over the intersection a big modern stoplight hangs from a curved and polished aluminium pole. For now the light is talking to itself over an empty landscape, but if the city ever reaches this far, it's ready to take charge.

Duane and Gretchen's house is at the end of a road that straggles to a halt against the edge of some woods. It's a long, low house, somebody's country dream house from the '50s, built at the edge of the swamp. It probably seemed safe and far away from city taxes then. There is a much newer plastic-sided, two-storey shed behind with a rail-fenced paddock and a snow-covered manure pile. Gretchen's horse is tucked up for the winter. Beyond the horse shed is the winter ghost of a garden. Stakes and dry stalks push crookedly through the snow, giving the impression of an abandoned winter battlefield. A black metal satellite dish seems to have its muzzle in the air, baying silently at some electronic moon. There is a brass-plated fish symbol on the front door.

In Cod we trust, Gerry thinks as he rings the bell. He restoreth my sole.

Duane answers the door in jeans, a flannel shirt and work socks. Joshua and Natalie look around him from the hall.

"Gerry," he says. "We're glad to see you. We surely are."

The "surely" niggles Gerry. It has a soapy, southern, TV-preacherly feel to it. Duane is starting to talk like the representative of a congregation or a board of trade. It strikes Gerry as a new thing. He doesn't remember Duane sounding like this when they visited at Christmas just a couple of months back. He was earnest but not so pompous. He decides it's because Duane's in his own world here, home-field advantage. Gretchen just comes to the kitchen door and smiles shyly and waves.

Gerry had stopped in an upscale toy-store in a mall to buy presents for the kids. He's got a sort of loom for Natalie. It will make a strip of weaving that can be a belt or a narrow scarf. For Joshua he'd picked up a sort of beginner's palaeontologist kit. It had a pocket magnifier with little folding legs. There was also a packet of "real fossils" to look at: some snail-like impressions and some things that looked like earwigs and carpenters in sandy-looking stone, shaved thin. There was a book that said how many millions of years old the fossilized bugs might be. That's where Gerry gets into trouble.

"Joshua," Duane says. He never abbreviates. "You'd better give the book here, son. Dad wants to see what's in it before you read it."

Shit! Gerry thinks. Joshua doesn't mind. The book was the least interesting part of the present. He's examining things through the double, plastic lenses.

"The carpet looks like trees from a plane."

"I'm sorry, Gerry," Duane says blandly. "You've got to understand where we're coming from here. When it comes to creation, we believe in the scriptures. I don't want to confuse Joshua."

"You don't think a billion or two years of evolution is more impressive than a seven-day parlour trick?" Gerry asks. He hopes he's keeping it light, but doesn't feel like apologizing for the book. Duane purses his lips.

"The length of the days may have been much longer than what we understand now," he says. "But even scientists are finding now that mankind is much older than they originally thought."

Shorter and furrier too, Gerry thinks. Pictures of "Lucy," the hominid fossil, come to mind. The serpent probably offered them a banana or some choice beetles and grubs.

"Daddy, how do you do this?" Natalie asks from the floor where she's trying to wrap yarn onto her loom.

"Supper's on," Gretchen calls from the dining room.

The meal reminds Gerry of a spartan veggie restaurant he used to go to sometimes in his Weasel days in the '80s. Some woman he had met in a bar had suggested they go there. Gerry remembers thick soups of coarse root vegetables, not so much cooked as laundered. The way he recalls it, everything had tasted of parsnips, whether they were in the dish or not. The vegetables had all seemed old and woody. Gretchen's vegetable stew brings it all back. It's garden cuttings with a muddy background of lentils. Gerry likes lentils, but he likes them with Indian flavouring. Curry has apparently not made it into Gretchen's gospel cookbook.

"We're only eating one cooked meal a day now,"she says. "Everything else is raw."

A scrap of a high school football chant floats across Gerry's mind. Rah, rah, eat 'em raw!

"Good for you," Gerry says. He feels he'll owe himself another debauch at The Jade Gate for this. He thinks of a Garfield the Cat cartoon he saw once. Garfield is asked how he'd like a head of lettuce prepared. Deep fry that little sucker, Gerry remembers.

There is no coffee in the house and dessert is a bowl of raw fruit, so the meal seems unfinished. There is some sort of herbal tea that has a tang of catnip about it.

After supper Gerry plays the good and interested guest. He and Natalie manage to load her loom. He is taken out to the shed to meet the horse. It's a pony really, a stocky pinto gelding, getting fat on bought hay. It appears to be exempt from the family's dietary laws. No one says anything when he brings out the cube sugar he took from the nursing home dining room and wrapped in a paper napkin as a horse offering. He offers it on his flat palm, a skill learned with milkmen's and bakers' horses fifty years ago. He remembers that reaching up a back-arched hand to the big teeth and prehensile leather lips had been his six-year-old equivalent of putting your head in the lion's mouth. The bored horse deigns to accept his sacrificial offering. The big sausage tongue snakes the sugar wetly away. Gerry breathes the smell of horse and thumps the beast chummily on the withers. He finds he's surprised he knows the word "withers." It slips into his mind automatically. His mother and father both had country backgrounds. He'd been taught the right words. He thinks he must tell his mother about visiting the horse when he sees her tomorrow. It may be more real than the great-grandchildren.

When the kids go to bed, Gerry, Duane and Gretchen sit in the living room and drink another cup of the catnip-flavoured tea. The room strikes Gerry as too bright. Gretchen is proud of her hardwood floor under a high-gloss urethane. It reminds Gerry of a high school basketball court, too big and too bright. He recalls that a million years ago, in the early '60s, there was such a thing as a basketball dance. You went to the game. When it was over, the lights were dimmed; borax was spread on the floor and a DJ set up his turntables. Red and blue spotlights were clamped to the basketball hoops.

You could use some borax and sexy lighting, Gretchen, he thinks.

There is a huge, flat-screen TV in the room. It bubbles on, just below the pain threshold. The programming has lots of sparkly animation interspersed with pastoral scenes that have scriptural texts superimposed.

Thou shalt not spice thy lentils, Gerry thinks. He watches over-dressed people with floppy, phone-book-style bibles urging him to call the numbers below. The women look plasticized, too-bright and urethane-sealed like Gretchen's floor. The men remind him of the boys who ran high school clubs, earnest-jovial with a streak of dumb and mean just below the surface, the little crazy glint of "conform or else."

"We've got satellite," Duane says. "Maybe you saw the dish. We get all the American channels, stuff you can watch, family viewing, family values."

"Whose family?" Gerry asks. "Take a tribe like ours. You've got a zoo with Mom and me and you and Melanie's Darren. You'll have trouble finding common ground for our lot."

Duane just looks disapproving. The television continues to mutter. Gretchen offers a bowl of fruit. As they sit and talk, she works at hooking some kind of throw or afghan. It's in a brightly white synthetic yarn. Similar yarn appears in wall hangings and a covering on a sideboard. Gerry suspects she's practising to knit a polyester angel.

He finds the room simultaneously too big and bright and claustrophobic. There are no books. The only picture is a dawn seascape, poster-sized.

And the Spirit of God moved upon the face of the waters is written in greeting-card script across the picture. Gerry knows a bit about the sea. The inscription seems pretentious and superfluous.

Gerry pleads middle-aged eyes and night driving to get away by ten o'clock. Gretchen and Duane are polite but don't press him.

They're probably relieved, he thinks. They've got time for the exorcism before bed.

"We'll get together before I go back," he says, but knows it's unlikely as he says it. They probably don't want to and where is he going to find a locusts-and-honey restaurant to take them to return their hospitality?

Gerry drives slowly, retracing his route back onto bigger, busier, better-lit urban roads. He's glad to get back where the street lights mean he isn't dazzled by the oncoming headlights. He realizes he's gripping the wheel hard and that he's unaccountably weary. He's glad to pull up in the time-warp courtyard of his motel. When he enters his room, the phone is blinking. There's a message from Vivian. She's called to see how he's getting on. Gerry decides to call, although it's late her time.

"Were you asleep?"

"Not really, just dozing."

"I saw the kids tonight. I'm in trouble, I think. I took them some fossils that were created before last Tuesday."

"How foolish. How's you mother?"

"About what you'd expect, I guess. Not much spinnier than the rest of us."

The lampshades in the room are dark, metallic material. They throw the light down in low warm circles at the sides of the over-size hotel bed. Transient couples have probably found them seductive at some time or other. Tonight Gerry finds them comfortably home-like with Viv's voice, sleepy at the other end of the phone line. At a distance, it strikes him that he prefers Viv sleepy. It slows her down and makes her less abrasive.

"How long did you spend at the home?"

"A couple of hours in the morning and about three in the afternoon. I ran over to the mall for a bit. I had to get out and stretch."

"You're good. You know that?"

Gerry doubts it. He knows the time he spends visiting is guilty quantity, not quality. Still, he's grateful to her for saying he's good.

"I'd better let you go to sleep, kid."

"Goodnight. Love you."

"Love you too."

When they hang up, Gerry spreads himself, a-sprawl in the too-big, two-hooker bed and falls asleep quickly.

As the week goes on, Gerry finds visits with his mother get better. In large part, it's because he found the photo album. He was looking in a bottom drawer for some papers she thought she'd lost and came upon the fat, black album. It's a compilation album really, belonging to no particular time, although the book itself is one that started off as a record of a trip to Vancouver in 1946, a year before he was born.

The trip only lasted three weeks and film cost money so it had come nowhere near filling the album with its dimpled cover, made to look like the tanned skin of extinct reptiles. After the last dinner menu and picture of women in hats around tables, there is a compressed version of Gerry's life from birth to about halfway through his life with Vivian. It gives them fifty years of starting points for conversations. Oddly enough, Gerry also feels he remembers his parents' trip west. Looking at photo albums had been a childhood thing. The Capilano Canyon Bridge and Pauline Johnson's grave have been shown to him time and time again. He feels he owns their legend. He has never seen the Alberta dinosaur park, where his mother pats a plaster brontosaurus. She squints into the sun but manages to be jaunty in a '40s hat with a long pheasant feather taking off like the oblique slash sign on a typewriter keyboard or possibly, a quill pen sticking out of an inkwell.

"That's Dad with Bill Brown on the ferry to Victoria."

He knows this. It's been told to him when he was sick and allowed to spend the day in his parents' bed, given the photo album to keep him amused.

"That's you." His mother points and smiles triumphantly, as though she's managed to win a difficult trick at cards. It's a joke for her to point him out in a nightgown in his father's arms. His father's head is inclined sideways towards him. It's as if he's listening to hear if Gerry is ticking.

"A fine-looking infant," Gerry says, kidding her along. "You must have been very proud."

In the course of the week, Gerry figures out that long visits tire her, so he drops in for an hour or two several times a day. They leave the album out and dole it out to themselves when they need a topic of conversation.

"There you are with your steamroller and that's the time you and your father made a boat out of the glider swing."

Gerry looks at a picture of a lawn swing with a piece of tarpaulin tied, sail-fashion, to its frame.

"That was a great steamroller," he says. "And the swing looks really shipshape."

The album gives them digestible bites of themselves.

"That's Aunt Louise's new car, the Lark. That was 1960, the spring before I went to high school."

"There's your dad's retirement party."

The pictures become more jumbled as they near the present.

Just like real life, Gerry thinks. There are pictures of Patricia and him and his father in their first apartment in St. John's, from a visit just after they were married. There's a picture of Patricia and her mother in a later apartment. There's a newspaper clipping of an advertisement with a picture of Gerry as part of the radio coverage team for a provincial election long past.

Towards the end of the album, pictures are just piled in between the pages, often in the envelopes they came in. There's a picture of Vivian and Tanya and him on their first visit to Ottawa together. There's Melanie in a strapless dress going to her graduation. Her date wears white socks with a suit. Gerry can't remember his name.

There are also mystery pictures, children neither of them can name. They're kids of contemporaries of his: cousins, children of friends' children. In some cases there are cryptic first names written on the backs and they can work out the identifications. These pictures seem to run from the mid-'70s to the mid-'90s. In one case, Gerry holds two pictures of somebody called Barbara. The pictures are paper-clipped together. In one, Barbara is a baby in a Jolly Jumper. In the next she's graduating from the University of Toronto. This is all Gerry knows about Barbara. He suspects it's all he'll ever know. Still, the Barbara pictures and the snaps of Gerry, on a horse-drawn hay rake, in rowboats, or in his first dinner jacket, get them through the week.

Towards the end of the week, Gerry and Doc get together with two other old school mates, Bob and Mort. Bob is arguably Gerry's oldest school friend. They went to kindergarten together.

"But you were an Elf and I was a Brownie," Gerry says as they settle into a restaurant of Bob's choosing.

"And you got to play the triangle while I was stuck with the stupid rhythm sticks. My God, what could you do with rhythm sticks?" Bob demands. "For the first God-knows-how-many-weeks you could only scratch them together and it was just before Christmas when you got to click them together."

Bob is a partner in a law firm now, the estate side of the firm. He's a Q.C. but says he hasn't been in court in years. His partner handles the litigation and they have a herd of young lawyers doing the criminal work. Of all of them, Bob has changed least since high school. He was a widow's son. A friend of his father's had kept an avuncular eye on him growing up, and had passed on some middle-aged mannerisms. At twenty-something he could kid Gerry about being "a pot-smoking goddamn hippy."

In fact, Gerry in his twenties was more of a hard drinker than a pot smoker and the kidding was always good-natured. Bob seemed to be one of those rare and wonderful people who knew stereotypes were inaccurate but useful. He didn't take himself any more seriously as a pillar of the community.

"I'll probably wind up disbarred or in jail," he says. "I'll get senile and take somebody's trust fund across the river to the casino."

Bob has grown into his mannerisms. Tonight his wife Mavis is out of town. Mavis is an ex-pat Brit. She runs a decorating consultancy and she's in Indonesia buying prints or something. Bob is enjoying slumming. He's picked a place that offers big steaks and ribs and peanuts in the shell that you can shuck onto the floor. He's shelling peanuts with a vengeance.

Mort, in his way, probably has the most in common with Gerry. He's a consultant or a lobbyist, depending on your point of view or prejudices. He skidded through journalism and into public relations as a photographer thirty years ago. He worked his way onto a couple of election campaigns and became a minor image and polling guru. Like Gerry, he sells ephemerals: spin, trends or information. He works out of his house and does "projects" for bigger consultants.

"So how are things in Newfoundland?" Mort asks while Bob is fussing with the waitress over what kinds of imported beer the restaurant has on tap.

"Damned if I know," Gerry says. "I'm so far out of the loop these days it's not even funny."

Mort looks at him appraisingly. It seems to be a look he's practised. "Yeah, but you'd know though."

Gerry feels he's being discreetly flattered with the implication that he's being modest about what he knows. He's glad Mort is a school buddy and not somebody he has to deal with at work. Of all of them he's the most subtle. He's not married but has been seeing the same professor of Celtic archaeology for more than twenty years. Her five-year marriage fit somewhere about the middle of that relationship. They keep separate houses but take long holidays together. They've spent several summers in various European marshes. She's written a book on sacrificial pools.

"When she wants to go to the bog, she really wants to go to the bog," Gerry had quipped once.

"Stella Artois for you, Mr. Snerd?" Bob asks. Mortimer Snerd as a nickname for Mort is as old as their friendship. In fact Mort is from his middle name, Morton. It was his mother's maiden name. He's actually Patrick Morton Bowes. His mother and sisters call him Patrick. His father, who has been dead for a decade, called him Paddy.

It dates them that they know who Mortimer Snerd was. They were raised on re-runs of '30s and '40s movies on television. They watched Edgar Bergen on *Ed Sullivan*, long after he should have stopped appearing.

"A great ventriloquist on the radio," Doc says.

"Come, my little man, and I'll take you for a nice ride on a buzz saw," Gerry says, doing his best W.C. Fields voice.

"It was Charlie McCarthy he said that to."

"I always carry a little alcohol with me in case I see a snake." He pauses. "Which I also carry with me."

The waitress stares at them and waits for some cumulative punch-line. She's probably only old enough to have seen *Cheers* in re-runs. It occurs to Gerry that *Cheers* was probably the first TV series he almost totally ignored. He's pretty sure he never watched a single show all the way through. Even when he and Patricia hadn't owned a TV in the mid-'70s, they watched shows at other people's houses.

Why would I have needed to watch *Cheers*? he wonders. He was living in bars in 1984 when it came on. Drinking wasn't the least bit funny. That's my religion you're making fun of there.

There have been lots of shows he's missed since *Cheers*, but he sees it as some sort of milestone.

"Three Stella Artois, pints, and a pint of soda water."

The waitress decides that they are a sufficiently humanoid life form that she can go into her hospitality *shtick*. She takes a crayon from a plastic basket in the middle of the table and writes her name upside down on the brown wrapping paper that serves as a cloth.

"I'm your server, Alison,"

Not servant, Gerry thinks. I remain, sirs, your humble and obedient server, Alison Upside-Down.

Alison lists the oversized steaks and racks of ribs, giant burgers and trendy pizza toppings. She skips away to get the drinks.

"That's a really good trick, writing upside-down like that."

"I wonder what else she can do upside-down."

"Bob, you can tell you don't work in a progressive workplace."

"Bullshit. I'll get my partner to collect little Alison a nice little fortune if she ever finds herself in an un-progressive workplace and wants to do something about it. I was simply speculating about her spatial perception."

The restaurant is one of those that are happy enough to be a bar after the supper-hour rush. After they've polished off over-sized steaks and a dessert that Gerry wanted, they sit.

"I never used to eat dessert until I quit drinking," Gerry says. "I had no sweet tooth at all. In the old days, Patricia used to make me a birthday meatloaf and ice it with mashed potatoes."

"Alcohol turns to sugar. You were running at the equivalent of a nice steady three Black Forest cakes a day."

"But look at all the chewing and tooth decay I spared myself."

Bob is back on kindergarten trivia. "Do you remember going down to the inlet to catch tadpoles and Denny Menchetti fell in?"

Gerry wonders if he's got incipient Alzheimer's. He can remember Denny Menchetti's name and he can see his running shoes. They were scuffed black with round white labels on the sides of the ankle. Gerry wasn't allowed to wear that kind yet because his father didn't think they gave you any support. However, he can't remember the greater context, the earth-shattering fact of Denny having fallen in.

"Stepped in, actually," Bob says. "To about the knees."

"I must have missed it."

They are all arguing about scandalous cases of favouritism in the allocation of rhythm band drums and cymbals when Alison brings their bill. Bob and Gerry are arguing that the primary school they went to was far more corrupt than the ones Mort and Doc attended.

"This is the geezer equivalent of having a life," Doc tells Alison, "fighting about what you did in kindergarten while you wait for your pension."

"I hope we haven't been too much of a bore," Mort says.

"Gee, no. I mean, I'm studying early childhood development and it's just so neat, the stuff you guys remember."

"She means…" Gerry says, as they fluff up Alison's tip for being so nice, "that, up until now, she had no idea what power she'll have to warp the young when she passes out the modelling clay and the toilet paper tubes. I dare say we're the basis of a thesis on rhythm band pathology or the latent effects of eating white paste."

Later, Gerry drops everybody off in his rental car, the automatic designated driver. Back at the motel he finds he's not sleepy. He's been swilling coffee while the others drank beer and he's probably wired from the killer-cheesecake he ate for dessert. He sits at the desk in his room and tries to be literary. He writes a poem he calls "Boys' Night Out."

Our waitress Alison
Writes her name in crayon
On the brown paper tablecloth,
Upside-down;
Pretty and pleasant.
They happen, it seems, now,
Or are we now invisible,
Just not there?
Our waitress Alison
Plays the manners game well,

Like someone with perspective sense,
Dealing with elves;
If she can't see us,
Alison pretends well,
Looks at the place she thinks
Our voices come from;
Our waitress Alison
Sits down and chats awhile,
Bright to either side of her,
As if we're there;
If she has kids some day,
She'll be convincing,
Conversing with the penguins
Or invisible blue bears.

Bob has been Gerry's mother's lawyer for some time now. She hadn't been crazy about the idea at first, but Gerry had persisted and had paraded Bob to show how thoroughly he'd grown into his middle-aged mannerisms, and she had come around. Today is the last day of Gerry's visit and he is meeting Bob in his office. The office had a lot to with convincing her. Bob has furnished it with his father's desk, brought from the family home when it was sold off. His wife, Mavis the designer, helped him capture 1950s respectability. There is a silver inkwell and a dark leather couch and matching chairs. There are old survey maps and deeds in copperplate handwriting on the walls. Gerry always feels that it looks like a film set, but it's a well-done film set. The furniture is real and not Bombay Company knock-offs.

A nice degree of wear around the escutcheons, generally good patination, Gerry thinks in an *Antiques Roadshow* voice. He's sitting in one of the big chairs, wondering at himself and Bob doing grown-up things. Bob's secretary brings in Gerry's mother's file. Gerry guesses she must be close to seventy. He wonders if Mavis found her somewhere. She wears a charcoal-grey suit and fusses over Bob in a well-bred way. Bob has told him that she's active in amateur theatre. She plays aristocrats in drawing room farces. Her husband is in the late stages of Alzheimer's.

"So how is your mom getting along?" Bob asks.

"You tell me," Gerry says. "Should I be picking her out some garbage bags and a heating vent to sleep on?"

"No, no she's fine financially for now." Bob has full power of attorney. He pays the bills and does the taxes or at least his firm does. "Though we're not living on interest anymore, you know. We're starting to take a little bite out of capital."

"So how's she doing?"

"Well, let's say three, or more like four, thousand a month for the care she gets now at the home. That's forty-eight a year from a pot of what, three-hundred-odd thousand, depending on the market.

And what happens when that goes? Gerry wonders. Money from the house and from Aunt Louise has allowed him to be quite comfortable, even with occasional gaps in the freelance business.

What happens if I have to start being responsible at sixty?

"So you're talking six years or so if things stay as they are now," Bob is saying, putting a deadline on it. "Prices go up of course, but then again we haven't been making any very big amount on the interest."

They have scheduled their meeting for late in the morning so they can go to lunch. Bob takes Gerry to his club. He's even gracious about having "a club."

"After the fire, when they were rebuilding, they'd let anyone in, even me."

But the fire was twenty-five years ago, Gerry thinks. Bob was a member here when the old man died. Bob has been a grown-up for a very long time.

The lunch tastes homemade, almost school-lunchy: soup and sandwiches to order.

"So you fat cats gather up here and eat '50s comfort food," Gerry kids Bob. "What's for dessert, animal crackers?"

"I always try to go a little light at lunch," Bob says.

They talk about their fathers over lunch. Each was at the funeral of the other's father.

Bob's father died when he was still in university. Gerry's lived on until the year he was breaking up with Patricia.

"I remember we went over to your place the week I was home from school for the funeral," Bob says. "Your dad gave me a huge Manhattan."

"That's because it was still April," Gerry says. "If it had been after the twenty-fourth of May you'd have got a gin and tonic. You could set your clock by him."

The summer Gerry's father died, he went out to Bob and Mavis's for dinner. They had bought trendy, authentic Chinese take-out. Their eldest son was about four at the time. Bob had showed Gerry the kids' programs you could get for the new computer. Bob was the first person he knew to have a computer at home. After Mavis went to bed they drank a bottle of Glen Livet, or at least Gerry did. His father was eighty-seven, ten years older than his mother at the time. Now he'd be well over a hundred.

"You've got great genes, you know," Bob says. "You'll go on forever."

Gerry and his great genes drive straight to the nursing home after lunch. He tells his mother about his meeting with Bob.

"You're in good shape," he says. "Anything you need, just call Bob or call me and I'll call him."

They spend the rest of the afternoon with the photo album. They put names to various cats that have been photographed, squirming in people's arms or in other uncooperative poses.

"That's Misty."

"He got run over."

He looks at a picture of himself on a rocking horse in a front room with a Christmas tree. There are doilies on the backs of chairs. The right word, *antimacassars*, floats into his head. The room comes from a 1920s movie although the picture is from about 1950. The Depression and war rationing froze time, so Gerry could be born into an earlier decade.

He leaves as the time for her supper approaches.

"I'll walk you down," he says. "I'll take you down to supper and then go on to the airport."

She's confused.

"But I'm not packed."

"You don't need to be packed, dear. You're staying here."

"I'm staying here?" She digests this, unsure.

"Yes, love, you're staying here."

Gerry drives to the airport through the late rush-hour traffic and returns his rented car. Once again he feels himself getting lighter, freer. It's the same sense of freedom he felt leaving St. John's to come here a week ago. He's glad to be heading home, but he's not sure that's what's elating him. Perhaps it's the untouchable limbo of the flight itself. The time when the wheel is spinning, no new bets can be made and nothing changes. He wonders if "Limbo" had occurred to the airlines as a name when they were looking for short snappy names for their cut-rate subsidiaries.

When the plane takes off he watches the motorway tracery of Ottawa and then Montreal slide below him. He dozes off with his head tipped to the window.

ten

G erry and Philip are sitting in the over-stuffed chairs of The Coffee Shop of the Space Debutantes. It's a Saturday morning and Gerry is explaining that spring is an alien concept to St. John's.

"You disappear into the fog in March and have a few blizzards to keep you edgy until about the twenty-fourth of May and then, if you're lucky, you pop out into summer in July." Gerry feels fussy and old as he says it. When did he start caring about the weather?

"At least the sidewalks are clear again," Philip says. "Snow clearing here doesn't make any allowance for people who don't drive."

"It's Dickens season," Gerry says. "The best of times and the worst of times."

That's the way he has felt since he came back from visiting his mother. He feels weighed down by the smallness of his problems. He remembers what he thinks was an old *Reader's Digest* joke about the priest who said that hearing nuns' confessions was like being stoned to death with popcorn. Orville Redenbacher winds up for the pitch.

The writing group has come to an end and Gerry has been busy filling-in at the radio station again. Somebody slipped a disc shovelling and he's found himself with a month or more of steady work. It's evening work. He goes to work at four in the afternoon and works until midnight, so he tends to goof off in the mornings. His characters, George, Paula and Ellen, seem too heavy to push around. It's easier to write about scenery in his Chinese notebook.

"Maybe I'm a landscape writer," Gerry says to Philip. "Maybe I shouldn't do portraits."

Philip fetches a bagel with vegetarian cream cheese and shovels three spoons of sugar into his coffee.

"Maybe you should write non-fiction. Most Canadian novels I read are just people whining."

"He whined," Gerry says.

"Point taken," Philip says. "But remember, I like Marcus Aurelius. You don't see him trying to write novels."

"No. Just 'Poor old me. I'm emperor of Rome and I have to meet a lot of people with bad breath. Roll on death.'"

Later in the day, Gerry sits at his computer and transcribes notebook pages. He's reverted to putting down random jottings in the hope that they'll gel into something significant. His muse skids wildly. The phrase "like a pig on ice" floats into his head. To pretend that he's not just rambling, he dusts off "George" and writes in the third person, but he can't fool himself into getting George to take off on his own.

Fragment: Only George

George has a short attention span, or maybe an only-kid self-satisfaction with one's own doings. When he was a child, people used to ask him if he didn't wish he had a brother or sister. It was an alien concept. They might as well have asked if he wished he had a truss or a cream separator. He needed neither, although both had a certain robotic allure as pictures in the Eaton's catalogue.

Paul Simon may have got it right in "Kodachrome." People often don't match one's sweet imagination.

Easter is coming, fertility feast of horny rabbits and over-stuffed eggs; call it Spring, if you'd rather. The idea of a religion from Wind in the Willows occurs to George as it has before. He thinks about Rat and

Mole meeting their god when they go looking for Otter's lost son. Worship Pan in the island glades without knowing about it afterwards. George thinks Kenneth Grahame knew a thing or two. He came up with a religion with no hangover. Spend the rest of your time feasting in badger banqueting halls.

Gerry can't bring it off the page. He thinks about a party they were at a week or so before. Vivian had complained that he faded into the wallpaper.

"You were like somebody dead. You might as well have stayed home."

"I wasn't rude to anybody," Gerry said. Vivian sniffed.

He's been thinking about manners as a substitute for morals lately. In some ways they seem to work better. He thinks eastern religion has a grasp on this. The mannered universe is easier to take. However, he knows he doesn't work like that. He dives into despondency and dithers and snarls at the drop of a hat.

Perhaps the ability to dither inwardly is enough, he thinks. Absence of visible dither is enlightenment.

Partway through the party, as the talk swept by him, Gerry had envisaged himself alone in his boat with a middling sea running. The boat was sailing as it does sometimes when he's alone, like a giant perfect sailboard, with a fulcrum right under his feet when he stands at the forward end of the cockpit. The vision of the boat was devoid of any practicalities about how he'd stop or survive, how he'd eat, keep warm or leave the helm to go for a shit. Instead it is just a screen-saver vision of the sea rising to the boat and the boat splitting it and raising itself on the swell. This was the Rat and Mole after-life perhaps, an open, endless sea and no bodily functions. Maybe Mole would like something a bit more confined though, an infinite summer hedgerow with a companionable pub around the corner.

Gerry had talked about *Wind in the Willows* at the party. He talked about the interaction between the animal characters and the humans. Animals slide like shadows through winter villages or give them a wide berth. On the other hand, they sue, go to court, land in jail and carry out the social duties of the landed gentry.

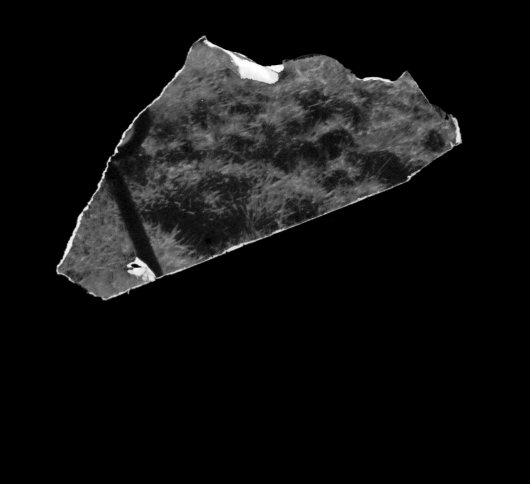

"Is the lesson to remember that you're an animal, as you do the social thing?" Gerry asked somebody who'd backed him against a mantelpiece.

The man had just done a hiring board for a promotion. They'd asked him what kind of an animal he'd like to be.

"That's the worst kind of anthropomorphism," Gerry said. "Eagles and lions aren't proud. They're just unaware of any values but their own. Hyenas and sculpins and crab lice are probably just as proud."

The man said he'd told the board he'd like to be an otter because they played creatively. He got the job.

Gerry is still thinking about it. He decides foxes aren't sly. They're just good at being foxes. They just fit perfectly into the blind spots of their enemies or their prey. The mouse that gets eaten probably isn't much concerned with slyness. The person hit by an asteroid or a falling piano isn't thinking about astronomy or music, except by chance. Foxes look smart because they work along an adjacent set of premises that are magic to us.

Gerry rehearses things he could say to a suit on a hiring board who asked him what kind of animal he'd like to be.

Why would I want to be another animal?

Would it not be better to just be good at being the animal I am?

Why do you distinguish between us and the other animals?

Gerry's hypothetical questioner suggests that it's an exercise in "imagination."

Have you ever tried using your imagination to get the best out of the species you can claim membership in?

In Gerry's imagination, the board members flee like startled weasels and he's guest of honour at a bash at Toad Hall for that one.

On another spring Saturday morning, Mr. Dickens gets it right. It is the best of times. Gerry wakes up early to a completely silent house. When they went to bed, it had been raining and they had been arguing about the need to paint the kitchen. They went to bed a half hour apart and silently, and the mouse-foot skittering of the rain on the vinyl siding had put them to sleep. At least, it also seems to have eroded their fight.

As first light creeps into their bedroom it has a watercolour pallor. Gerry gets up and pads down the hall to the bathroom in his ancient terry-cloth robe. Then he goes to the kitchen and puts on a pot of coffee, looking out at the morning. The rain has cut the snow. Almost the whole lawn is visible, with only a spine of thawed and refrozen slush down the middle. Around the foot of a tree, their half-dozen crocuses aren't in bloom but are visible, pushing up like lurid, cheap ballpoint pens through the winter-kill beige of dead grass. Gerry goes back down the hall to the bedroom. Vivian has the covers pulled way up. Only the tousled top of her head shows.

"Boat day, I think, kid," Gerry says, tentatively, checking that peace has really broken out. "Have you got any open houses?"

The blankets stir. "No. The one I've got is tomorrow."

"No viewings?" Gerry thinks the jargon of her business sounds like undertakers' euphemisms, but sometimes he finds himself using them.

"No. Nothing today."

"Are you up for the first injection of boat for the year? It looks like it's going to be a nice day." Gerry is feeling benign. Sometimes he just sneaks away to do boat stuff. Vivian doesn't particularly mind. The preparation part of boating doesn't interest her much, but this morning she senses that some sort of private Easter is on offer. The winter's dead are being offered a day out of the tomb to go and play.

"I'm not going to do much work," Gerry says. "Just uncover and air her out. We can take a picnic."

"I guess so, but later. I want to sleep."

"Don't sleep too long. It'll probably blow up a blizzard by lunchtime."

Gerry gets dressed and goes back to the kitchen. He finishes his coffee. Then he goes to the basement and drags up a tool box, an electric drill and a couple of coils of orange extension cord. There is still no noise from the bedroom. The sun outside becomes more assertive, angling into the kitchen. Gerry feels he has to be moving. He shifts into picnic-planning mode and heads out into the day.

He stops at a Tim Hortons to plan his picnic and make lists. Chinese notebooks are excellent for making lists in. Sometimes it worries him that the stir-fry ingredients and to-do lists are threatening to swamp the journal entries. Today it doesn't bother him. He's feeling efficient.

Polish sausage, he writes. *Cheese, French bread, margarine from home, olives, Pinesol, WD-40, J-cloths, garbage bags.* Gerry can never recall, from fall lift-out to spring, what he left on the boat. Vivian says it's going to sink under the weight of carefully hoarded, virginal, economy-size packages of garbage bags.

Gerry eats a cinnamon-raisin bagel and works on his list at one of several tables where a group of regulars gathers on Saturday mornings. They're a collection of first names and single identifying facts. There's Wayne who paints houses, Clyde who works at the mental hospital, and Harry who is retired and keeps beagles. Vern sells cars and Wally repossesses them. Gerry imagines he's "Gerry who's got the sailboat."

"It's a great day out there."

"You don't have your boat in the water yet, do you?"

"I've got to get over to Wal-Mart. They've got a special on the big bags of dog kibble."

Their days organize themselves into simple tasks. Everybody wants to get out in the sun and do something.

Gerry drains his coffee and heads for the supermarket. He's got his picnic in his head, peasant stuff, sausage and gooey cheese with a skin to it, or maybe two kinds, sharp cheddar too, to break into hunks on big chunks of bread, a pagan folk sacrament.

"Kielbasa, kielbasa, kielbasa," Gerry chants under his breath as he mentally goat-dances through the deli section. He buys a crunchy, resistant stick of French bread. He buys bulk olives from a tub. They look sleek, bloated with their own importance and potential, oiled, like some sort of vegetarian ammunition. He picks up a packet of miniature cinnamon buns, tight spirals of scorched brown sugar. Shag diets. It's spring.

He is at the door of the liquor store when it opens at ten and buys a bottle of wine. He buys French. It's cheaper than the domestic now and, after fifteen years off the booze, he's out of touch and not very interested in what's supposed to be good among the new designer domestic wines.

Gerry stops for yet another coffee and reads the *Globe* books magazine at a chain coffee shop in a mall. He collects Viv at home at eleven on the dot.

Gerry had never expected to have a boat, although he has always bought boating magazines. They pile up in the bottom of closets and on basement shelves. When he drank, there was no money for a boat, although for a number of years in the late '70s and early '80s he had real jobs. Now, thanks mostly to Aunt Louise and the house in Ottawa, he seems to have the money, although he doesn't have a real job.

Gerry wonders what his father would have made of the boat. The Old Man saved a 1927 Buick engine in the back of the garage for years. It was a big, old twelve-cylinder out of what used to be called a touring car. Gerry's father said he was going to build a boat and convert the engine to power it. The boat was going to be a cabin cruiser. Each spring, magazines advertising plans for do-it-yourself boats appeared in the house. The engine stayed where it was. The garage was an old one. It had housed the car the engine came out of. When the snow broke some rafters in about 1960, it had to be replaced. Gerry's Uncle Cyril took the engine. Cyril was building a small sawmill, not far from where Duane and Gretchen live now. He was Gerry's mother's brother and he had never had a steady job.

"His nerves are bad from the war," Gerry's mother or his Aunt Carmen would say. Cyril raised a few sheep and chickens. He trapped muskrats in the winter and when Gerry was about six, he showed him how to set off a spring trap with your nose. There was nothing to it, really. You just tipped one jaw of the trap up and went in from underneath, but it looked impressive as the steel jaws clashed shut, inches from your vulnerable face. Apart from that, Cyril hung out in the Legion with some other bad-nerve victims. His wife Enid worked in a cheese factory down the road to keep them going. It was decided the sawmill might steady Cyril down. After a few years, it settled him down completely. He passed out drunk in his sawmill shed and somehow managed to set the whole thing on fire. Enid was at work and Cyril's sawmill wasn't close to any neighbours. It was a while before the fire was spotted.

About the time Gerry was starting university, Enid married a reliable Dutchman who had a small dairy herd and did business with the cheese factory. Gerry's father never built his cabin cruiser.

"Your Uncle Cyril was a damn fool," he would say. "But when he was sober, there wasn't a better man to walk in the woods with."

Gerry thinks the Old Man would have liked the boat.

Gerry would be the first to admit he's not the world's keenest sailor. Often in the summer, he just potters. He'll spend an afternoon doing small things, like re-sewing the sun-rotted stitching of the zipper on the sail cover. He'll fuss with wear on the plastic covering of the lifelines. In places, it's wrapped with white tape like a cartoon character's sore foot or a vinyl mummy.

Gerry has spent afternoons hemming the Power Squadron pennant or the club burgee that beat themselves to nylon fluff against the shrouds. On a rainy day he knelt in front of the plywood cover that folds down over the marine toilet and makes a chart table of sorts. There he plotted positions in handy places around the bay and punched them into the hand-held GPS. He punched in the middle of approaches and safe-distance-off spots and various obstructions. The rain drummed on the fibreglass over his head as Gerry constructed the boundaries of his little marine universe.

Sometimes he just goes aboard and takes naps.

Lately, Viv humours him with the boat although she used to complain that they never went anywhere. Now they agree that she's not happy to be left at the helm to spell him off, so short cruises are their best bet.

Gerry has tried to teach the rest of the family to sail. Early on, when she was still in high school, Tanya had brought out several boyfriends and had looked on as Gerry tried to be polite to them and let them steer. Melanie had sailed with other people before she married Darren and had been useful as crew. Darren was only moveable ballast.

The last couple of seasons, they have cut their losses.

Vivian spends a weekend or two on short, overnight trips to nearby places. She's come to terms with the heel of the boat and is sufficiently at ease to take a nap or read below if she gets tired of just watching the water roll by. On weekend trips they have made love in the V-berth, which is arguably the roomiest part of the boat.

"If the boat is rocking, don't come knocking," people joke over drinks at the club or at weekend anchorages. Mostly though, Gerry day-sails single-handed or rounds up a few buddies to race on the weekends.

Gerry hasn't planned a very busy day at the boat. As they drive to the sailing club, a patch of overcast sidles across the sky and seems to threaten rain, but it blows by when they get to the boatyard. A pale sun skims across the yard like spotlights at a skating show as the wind parts the clouds. Then it clears again.

The boat is on its cradle and they have to un-padlock the chained-on ladder and scramble up into the cockpit. Gerry guides Vivian up first and then passes up the tool box and the lunch and the various bags and bundles he's brought along. They find a piece of frozen snow in a corner of the cockpit and throw it over the side to smash on the boatyard gravel. They fiddle companionably with little things. He takes off the winter covering he screws over the hatch every fall. Vivian passes him tools as he wrestles the screws out of the damp plywood. The sun heats the wood and it gives off a faint forest smell. When they get the plywood off, they unlock and open the hatch. Vivian sniffs the crypt-cold air of the cabin.

"It's not too musty."

"It shouldn't be. I put pie plates of Kitty Litter around to absorb some of the damp," Gerry says. "All the cushions and cloth stuff went home so there's not much to mould."

"It's probably bad in the cupboard under the sink."

"Locker," he corrects her. "Besides, I've got to have a major clean-up in there anyway. I'll hit it with the Pinesol and the Murphy Oil when she's in the water."

Opening lockers is like unpacking Christmas decorations. You forget what you have and familiar things become surprises. Salt-crusted sunglasses at the back of shelves and plastic bottles with dregs of sunscreen are artefacts.

The cabin is bare without its cushions, but the boom and a lot of the fenders are stored inside. They move stuff out to the cockpit lockers to make room in the cabin.

"Last year Darren helped you get ready," Vivian says.

"For what it was worth," Gerry says. "I mean he poodled away with a scraper for a bit, but he got tiresome to listen to."

"He respected you," Vivian says.

"I doubt it," Gerry replies. "Are you ready for lunch?"

Vivian has always been impressed with Gerry's ability to make picnics. They were not a feature of her previous existence. Gerry has his picnic-prone aunts in his genes and he and Patricia had spent a good deal of time out of doors. He sometimes feels he has scored some easy points with picnics.

They use the boat's emergency knife to cut up chunks of cheese and spicy sausage and slices of crusty bread. He opens the wine with the corkscrew on his Swiss Army jackknife. He's brought a big thermos of coffee for himself.

The wind is cool, but the sun comes more than it goes and the day is almost warm if you stay out of the breeze. Gerry sits on a cockpit seat and leans on the cabin. Vivian leans back against him. The boatyard is spread out below their ladder.

"We're like kids in a tree-house," she says.

More people arrive as the afternoon ripens. Orange and yellow extension cords snake around the yard. The whir of sanders and drills emerges from under boats, and here and there, there's the iron flatulence of a winterized diesel being turned over for the first time.

Vivian's hair is against Gerry's chin. It smells lightly of herbal shampoo but seems to have additional scents of warming wood and clean new rope.

"How are you doing there, sport?"

"Great. How about you?"

This is how things might endure, Gerry thinks, scented moments of nothing. Think too hard and you'll destroy them.

eleven

JUNE 2004

G ood weather arrives the way parcels from faraway places did when Gerry was a child: slowly, unbelievably, tightly wrapped and hard to get into.

His wandering aunts once shipped a cuckoo clock from the Black Forest. There was no way they could carry the thing. They were coming back by ship, the *Empress of Britain* to Montreal. They sent the clock by what used to be called "surface mail."

Does "surface mail" exist anymore? Gerry wonders.

Some German clockmaker shipped the clock in a huge, stiff box, wrapped with hairy cord. He had wrapped the clock in layers of what seemed to be lint sandwiched between paper. The lint was grey like the German uniforms in the movies. Perhaps it was those uniforms, shredded by the late '50s. The pine cone weights of the clock were rolled in cocoons of the stuff. They felt like hand grenades dressed for winter. Every space in the box was stuffed with shavings.

"There can't be much of the Black Forest left," Gerry's father said, surveying the mess of packing on the kitchen floor.

In the end, Gerry's aunts had found the clock kept them awake. When his parents bought a cottage in the '60s, the clock was banished. Its tick and cuckoo seemed less annoying when you were already listening to nighthawks, frogs and whip-poor-wills.

"Is there still surface mail?" Gerry asks Philip. Perhaps Philip knows. He's still mailing books to Toronto so maybe he has inside information. They're sitting at a table outside the coffee shop. So far this year, there have been very few days when you could do this.

"I suppose. I mean if you mailed an anvil overseas, I guess they'd put in on a ship."

"You know you can't get airmail forms anymore?" Gerry says. He found this out a couple of weeks ago when he got a sudden urge to write to a former flat-mate in the U.K. He felt saddened by the loss. When he'd gone abroad for a year in 1969, little blue airmail forms had seemed the perfect amount of news to send or receive.

"I think I knew that," Philip says. "I think they've been gone for a couple of years."

Philip will soon be gone. He's bought a plane ticket for the end of June. He says the call centre is getting too crazy for him. A couple of weeks ago, one of his California crazies called about her website. Something was wrong with it. Philip connected to her site and found a gallery of nude photos.

"Do you think I ought to get my other nipple pierced?" the woman asked.

"This was not an unattractive woman," Philip says. "She did not need to be doing this."

"You both probably brightened your supervisor's night. I assume you still have the random monitoring of calls."

"Anyway, this is not what I came to Newfoundland to do. I thought I'd sit by the ocean and read."

"You do read and the ocean is, verifiably, out there. Maybe you missed it. It's the big wet thing I took you sailing on a couple of times. I'm pretty sure I pointed it out though."

It occurs to Gerry that he, himself, is supposed to be living beside the ocean and writing. This morning's notebook entry, written before Philip came along, started as a description of his ball cap with the sailing-club crest and goes downhill fast.

My sailing hat is looking a bit the worse for wear after launch a month ago: bottom scrapings and crud blended with a dust of blue anti-fouling. It has a sort of a Danish navy-blue cheese look.

Pretty much resolved to quit work although I wonder if that's just sublimation of a desire to quit altogether. I think I may go fishing this week or just hang out on the boat and eat Chinese noodles and canned tuna. It's been a year or more since I drove across the island. Then again, how long is long enough?

Gerry and Philip go inside to fetch refills. In the line, they're behind a loud twit who seems convinced the world needs to know how he feels.

"...just totally blown away, you know?"

He has one of those stand-up haircuts which have come back into fashion from Gerry's childhood. He's professionally boyish like a '50s peanut-butter ad. He wants elaborate sprinkles on some kind of boiled-milk coffee.

"Please, Mom, can I have some more?" Gerry says. "Can I lick the bowl? God, I'm getting sour and old."

"Or you just want a second cup of coffee," Philip says.

They return to their table on the street. Philip brings one of the coffee shop's complimentary newspapers. It's full of federal election.

"I'm going to have to vote in an advance poll here," he says. "I won't be able to vote when I get to Toronto."

"The perfect moral situation," Gerry says. "You can vote for whoever you like here and not have to live with the result. Then you get to complain about your member in Toronto because you had no say in picking the beast."

"It all seems to be coming down to kiddie porn," Philip says, shaking out the paper. Stephen Harper looks out of one picture like a politely interested android. Paul Martin appears to be experiencing convulsive cramps in a facing one. "Harper seems to think the Liberals are in favour of it."

"I think Mr. Harper is on shaky ground there," Gerry says, "Turn out the sock drawers of all your candidates and I suspect the neat and tidy Sunday school types will come off worst. Who's the obnoxious ex-cop MP who went down for molesting Indian kids? People with a sense of sin are more likely to commit them."

"You have no sense of sin then?"

"Being mean is the only sin. I commit that all the time. Manners are better than morals most of the time. The world's full of Gladstones and Mackenzie Kings ready to give those naughty hookers a stern talking-to. There's lots of creepy uncles and daddies out there."

"Vote Adamson, for an end to meanness. I like it, but it doesn't seem to have much of a platform to go with it."

"When I was in university, somebody ran for student council on a platform of 'A return to the golden age, an end to menstrual cramp and a tail for everyone.'"

"That's the Conservatives this time, except I think they're *for* menstrual cramp."

"I'd like a tail. Tails are great. Wouldn't *you* like a tail?"

It is the time of year for Gerry to be lining up his summer work. Summer is his busiest time as people take vacations and his apparent suitability for responsible work increases. He meets with producers and they find that perhaps a few weeks of him working on their show won't quite end western civilization as we know it. This year, his talk with Bob, rhythm band sticks player and family lawyer, hangs over these chats. *We're getting through four thousand a month or so, out of a pot of three hundred.*

"I mean the money's got to run out in a few years," Gerry says to Vivian after supper. "I don't mind not inheriting anything. We did okay off the house and Aunt Louise, but what about looking after the old dear? She seems to be planning to outlive me."

"I've always said she could live with us," Vivian says.

She has too, usually when they are fighting. They sometimes propose escalating martyrdoms they say they'd endure for each other, one-upping each other into slammed doors or angry silences.

Gerry pictures the frozen-in-amber atmosphere of the nursing home moved to their house. How much longer would the drives and walks and sails have to get to avoid death by osmosis? What new things would it bring to have fights or silences about?

"It's something to think about," he says. That's true anyway.
He thinks about it, talking to a producer. Gerry is trying to be an adult and get a real job.

"There are a couple of jobs you'll be filling when everybody gets back in the fall," he suggests.

"Oh my God, I haven't even been able to look at them yet," she says.

"One of these days I might just apply for a real grown-up job."

They're drinking coffee in the break room. He tries to keep it light and bantering, fishing for any encouragement.

"Really? You'd be interested?" The producer's tone implies that he's suggested he'd like to take up brain surgery in middle-age: an interesting concept, but not very practical. "I mean, Gerry, would you really want the day-to-day? Weren't you working on a book? You really *should* write a book."

"Yeah. Really."

That night, while Vivian is out showing a townhouse somewhere, he pushes the laundry off the desk in the basement and tries to kick George and Ellen into gear.

Fragment: Argument

"Why do you keep that damn office?" Ellen asks.

"To deny I'm dead," George says bleakly. "To deny I'm dead, to deny that I don't care anymore, to deny that I have nothing to say and that all I've learned is that you should shut up and worry about your house!"

"Why are you so angry?"

"To deny you've got no one to talk to but people who tell you to walk on your hardwood floors in your socks," he says. "To deny that you have to be buried for years before you die."

To deny the rage you inflicted on yourself in good faith, George thinks. The world isn't unfair. The seating arrangements for viewing it are.

On a shelf over the desk is a handful of paperbacks Philip has given Gerry. Philip's clearing out his duplicates, getting ready for his big Toronto move. Marcus Aurelius is on top of the pile. Gerry thumbs through the book. It's thin, more scholarly notes than musing emperor.

"No one loses any other life than the one he is living nor does he have any other life than the one he loses."

You should get out of the emperor racket, Marcus, Gerry thinks. You should write a book.

Summer finally seems to be taking hold. Vivian is busy because people use the long evenings to look at houses after work. On the other hand, she gets some that aren't likely to buy and wastes a good deal of time.

"Not a pot to piss in," she says, setting out to meet a young couple somewhere. They'd left a grunted message on the answering machine and wanted to see a house in a pricey new subdivision. "They can't afford that neighbourhood. I feel like Miss Jane on *The Beverly Hillbillies* showing some of these goofs around."

"Push 'em in the cee-ment pond," Gerry says. "But be nice, maybe they won the lottery."

The evening is warm and Gerry decides he'll take in one of his rare AA meetings. He's going for all the wrong reasons: nostalgia for another set of problems that have faded, *schadenfreude*, voyeurism or the fact it's a nice night. He decides a walk would do him good and leaves the Honda home. The first lawn mowers of the season are out and doing. They make a bumblebee background to the shushing of the sprinklers as he walks to his meeting.

Gerry gets the reception he expects as someone who doesn't attend very often. There are the caring people who ask how you've been, in case you'd had a slip and been drinking and need support to come back. Then there are the others, the competitive losers, who want to know that your roll ended, that you fell off the wagon. Then, however brief the sober time they've got in, they've got more than you have.

Gerry supposes he was a bit that way himself when he first came to AA fifteen years ago. There were a lot of people with more sobriety who pissed him off.

I wanted to get sober to have a life and they thought getting sober was life, Gerry thinks.

In those days, somebody talking about seven years of sobriety sounded like a description of a hundred-mile tightrope walk with an egg balanced on the end of your nose.

Yes, it was an achievement of sorts, but why a tightrope and why the egg? Couldn't you just do what you did before, but sober?

It seemed to Gerry that if you decided it was a tightrope you had to keep concentrating on, you were setting yourself up for a long drop and a nose full of scrambled egg. There were times he secretly willed banana skins onto the tightrope.

Let the poor bastard have a life and not a substitute religion so I can learn to do the same, Gerry would think. In my worst moments I've tried to worship the drink and I've believed in vengeance and the whole nine yards. Now let's see something sustainable.

At tonight's meeting "Johnny" comes over to talk to Gerry while people are still milling around getting coffees and finding chairs with their buddies. He's always "Johnny," never John.

He's one of us, Gerry thinks. One of the people with a built-in diminutive.

When Gerry first went to AA, Johnny had a year in. He got a medallion at the second or third meeting Gerry was at. Since then his luck hasn't been good. He has a collection of three-month medallions and probably a dozen years of sobriety in total, but he can't seem to string it together. It's made him bitter, although he keeps coming around.

"I haven't seen you around," Johnny says,

"I've been busy. No rest for the wicked," Gerry says. He's aware of his equivocal reasons for being here tonight. He suspects that Johnny hopes he's been out, that his world's a mess. Then he could regain some of that magic time he had when he had a year's sober ascendancy and Gerry thought a day without a drink was magic that only wizards could do.

"I'm suing those bastards where I used to work," Johnny tells Gerry. Gerry recalls that he had some sort of tangled unfair dismissal case that had dragged on for several years. Building scrap had gone astray. No charges were brought but Johnny got fired. He claimed his union hadn't taken his part. At one point, when Gerry was trying to be a keen reporter, they had talked about him doing something on the story. However, the union and Johnny's sometime lawyer had both shied away. They stopped just short of saying that he'd got himself fired and that was all there was to it.

"It's a big fucking swindle, you know. Honest-to-God, sometimes I think you'd be better just going out to Red Cliff and jumping over."

Or wait until the blood donor people send you a letter with a surprise in it, Gerry thinks, remembering his own reminder of mortality. Be careful what you wish for.

Gerry has never been able to find pat answers for people who talk about killing themselves. It's not something he considers for himself any more. He's not sure that he ever did, but he used to threaten. Once, in an empty house, he had stretched a toe to the trigger of a shotgun, a morbid rehearsal. Despite the fact he knew the gun was empty, it took every muscle straining to make the trigger click. He'd decided that the drunk's slower suicide was better suited to his more cowardly, lazier style.

Gerry knows he's a disappointment to Johnny. He wants the church-conditioned response: "You can't. You mustn't." Gerry is afraid he's a bit more pragmatic than that. It's more a question of how much pain, or prospect of pain, you can take. It's like taking aspirin. Some people resist medication and do acetylsalicylic martyrdoms. Others pop a pill at the first twinge. Who's right?

People who talk about suicide get on Gerry's nerves a bit. They want him to be responsible for their life or death, to be their advocate in the capital case they're trying in their heads. Gerry suspects they would not be happy to be told to look at how they fit into the world and then do what they think best.

The meeting finally gets started.

"God grant me the serenity…"

Gerry looks out the window at the thickening dusk. The meeting is in an upstairs room so he's looking at a skyline. The trees are plump, frozen explosions of dark green against his horizon. He remembers summer dusks in early childhood, when the trees in the backyard seemed to draw closer to his bedroom windows as the sky purpled and the murmur of grown-up voices on the lawn swing replaced the last roulette-wheel whirr of the hand-pushed lawn mower.

A few late gulls flap purposefully across his patch of window. A droning small plane, its lights already gem-bright, bumbles across the sunset to get down before dark.

Gerry declines to speak tonight.

"No thanks. It's great to be here, but I'm just going to listen tonight."

The deepening evening quiets him.

On his walk home he picks up chocolate ice cream drumsticks. Vivian is home when he gets there. They sit on the steps of their backyard deck and eat the dripping waffle trumpets in what is still a warm darkness.

According to the sun, it is just past mid-summer when Gerry and Vivian have Philip around for his farewell dinner. Gerry has never found mid-summer works very well in large parts of Canada, in Newfoundland in particular. The days may be long but the water is still cold and the fog can lie in. It's not as warm as it's going to be yet.

"What is so rare as a day in June? Then, if ever, come perfect days," Gerry recites from a '50s memory work assignment. "There ought to be a scale of correction for where you are. Add one month for mainland Canada. Add two for St. John's."

Despite Gerry's grumbling, it is a pleasant summer evening. He has picked up Philip and his luggage and brought him home. He's not working this week. Summer relief work will start in earnest in a week or so with the July 1st weekend. Vivian is working until almost six so Gerry has been cooking, pork tenderloin and roast potatoes. Vivian will buy a trifle for dessert on her way home. Philip sits at the kitchen table with a large glass of white wine. Gerry is fussing with salad makings.

"I'm going to miss dinners here," Philip says. "I like your family."

"That's because you only come a couple of times a year. We'd wear a bit thin if you spent more time with us."

Gerry is feeling petulant because Darren has been in touch from Alberta.

"He misses Melanie and Diana," Vivian had told Gerry earlier that week. "He *wants* to come home."

"Jesus, he's like the cat, "Gerry said. "When he's in, he wants out. When he's out, he wants back in."

"He called them the other night," Vivian said. "He really misses them. He's stopped playing the machines."

"His sister's smart enough not to let him near the till."

"I told Melanie I'd pay for a ticket. I put it on Visa."

"You were the woman who wanted the little weasel dismembered a couple of months ago."

"He wants to come home. Diana's all excited."

"We could buy her a pony cheaper and she'd still be excited. We'd only have to feed that," Gerry had said.

"I keep telling you your family is pretty normal," Philip says now.

"They get on top of you," Gerry says. "The other day I was in the liquor store and they were giving out ugly cloth smiley faces or some damn thing for Father's Day. The girl asked me if I was a dad. I said no without thinking. I think I meant it."

Vivian rolls in with the trifle. Gerry pours her a wine and himself a soda water. They sit down to dinner.

"I hear your son-in-law is coming home," Philip says.

"Yes, we'll see how that goes."

"He's probably quite worried about coming back. I know I'm wondering if I'm doing the right thing going back to Ontario."

"Well, I'm sure you miss the place," Vivian says.

"No, actually I dread the thought of going back. Toronto has changed from the city I grew up in," Philip says. "I like the size of things here but I'm afraid I'll never move. It's addictive."

"What's your point, caller?" Gerry asks. "I just dropped in for the weekend thirty years ago."

After dinner Vivian clears away, putting plates in the dishwasher.

"You boys cooked," she says. "I'll clean up."

"I'd hardly say I contributed anything," Philip says. "I just sat around and watched your husband."

"That's what made it art," Gerry says. "You were the audience."

After dinner Gerry and Philip go for a walk. One of the things Gerry likes about their neighbourhood is that the country intrudes into the town and comes up against it. On a summer night, a wooded hillside looms over the end of their street and it's possible to imagine you're in a more rural and a smaller place. A conservation group has run a network of trails close to his and Vivian's house. Gerry liked the hillside better when the trails were old ones and less frequented by joggers and up-market dogs, but there are still good walks to be had.

Gerry and Philip climb on a gravelled path through moss-hung fir.

"Snotty var," Gerry says.

"That's it, is it?" Philip asks. "I've heard the term. Var just means fir, I guess."

"It's var and it's snotty all right," Gerry says.

The path switchbacks up through the trees, with pressure-treated wooden steps up the steep bits. The woods smell like a mouldy apothecary shop.

"Vivian runs up this," Gerry says. "There are five hundred and some steps,"

"I'll take her word for it."

The evening is warm and they're both short of breath and sweating when they come out into a clearing on top of the hill. The town is spread out below them. At their feet are a brook, some ponds, the parkway and Gerry's subdivision. His Honda is visible, parked in the street, a sesame seed in the tree-and-pavement salad of the neighbourhood.

South and east, the older parts of town hold the ridges. The Basilica and the new art gallery stick up and bite into the belly of the sky. Beyond them, the Southside Hills and Signal Hill rear up, as high as where they're standing now. Beyond that is the sea, like silver paper now in the flat light. Far off, the fog lurks, waiting to come to land with the evening's cool.

"I'm going to miss this place," Philip says.

"I know," Gerry tells him. "I go to Ontario now and the ocean is missing. Even if I don't go near it for days at a time, I want it around."

They walk home down a road that still has an outpost of country in the city. A tiny pasture and a cow barn occupy a rural island in the subdivisions that climb the slopes of the hill.

"I do like the smell of cows," Gerry says.

"It's an acquired taste, I guess."

"An affinity for bullshit is no bad thing for a journalist."

When they get back to the house, Vivian has finished the dishes. She's on the phone to some client or other. Gerry gets Philip a beer and makes himself a coffee and they sit on the back deck. When Viv finishes her call she brings a beer and joins them.

Gerry has given some thought to a going-away present for Philip.

He's settled on a tiny collection of Whitman poems. They were part of an anniversary set that Penguin put out a dozen years or so ago.

"I have said that the soul is not more than the body,/And I have said that the body is not more than the soul,/And nothing, not God, is greater to one than one's self is," Gerry reads. "And whoever walks a furlong without sympathy walks to his own funeral drest in his shroud…"

"That's beautiful," Viv says.

"That's some barbaric yawp," Philip says. "Thank you, Gerry."

Trees overhang, and alders enclose the darkening yard. Beyond their leaves, the traffic whooshes by, tires sibilant. They watch the night fall and then go to bed. Philip has booked a bargain flight that leaves before five in the morning. Gerry sets double alarm clocks, the way he does to go to an early shift at work.

Gerry phases his alarms. First there is a little battery-powered travelling clock that makes a monotonous bird-like piping, an idiot nestling calling insistently to be fed. The back-up is the clock radio set to "alarm" with its chainsaw buzz, but this morning the idiot chick is enough. Gerry reaches out and stifles it before Viv has a chance to do more than roll over and mutter in her sleep.

Philip, it appears, hasn't slept. Gerry raps on his door as he goes down the hall to the kitchen to put on coffee. There's already a line of light from under the door.

"I got interested in some of your books," Philip explains as they drink the coffee at the kitchen table. "Then it got to two-thirty or so and there just didn't seem to be much point to going to sleep. I'll sleep on the plane."

The fog that was offshore when they took their walk the evening before is on the land now as they load Philip's stuff aboard Gerry's wagon and set out for the airport. The headlights make long, narrow white cones in the mist. There is virtually no traffic. They're more than halfway to the airport when a taxi passes them, heading the same way. A few others join the convoy as they make their way along the main road to the airport.

The car radio is politely murmuring the latest news from sub-Saharan Africa on one of the overseas broadcasts the CBC runs late at night. Two announcers, one with an Afrikaans voice, the other, Oxbridge-African, are talking about Zimbabwe. Gerry flashes to an early apartment with Patricia. It was the time of the Rhodesia war. They used to listen to Barbara Frum on the radio, talking on the phone to white Rhodesians in a bar. The Rhodesians would talk and Gerry and Patricia would cook and eat their supper. Gerry was a local current affairs producer then. They always listened to *As It Happens* and *Sunday Morning*. They hoped that national radio might be contagious.

The airport looks like the final scene of *Casablanca*. The lights are ringed in haze. Water jewels the chain-link fences. The planes poke into the terminal like shiny, dark piglets around an aluminium and glass sow. However, the mist is growing greyer. Somewhere the sun is trying to come up.

Gerry helps Philip carry his bags into the terminal. The TV screens say that his flight is scheduled to depart on time.

"They can take off into it," Gerry observes. "It's landing they're not fussy about."

"You don't need to wait around," Philip says. "I'll check in and just wait for my flight."

They shake hands.

"Give my best to Ontario."

"Don't run into anything with the boat."

The sky is lighter still when Gerry goes outside to the parking lot. Philip will get away just fine. Driving away from the airport, he turns away from town and drives in a wide loop through some of the communities on the outskirts of St. John's. Sometimes he drives on winding roads by the sea. Then he drives through wooded roads where suburbs are just starting to take hold. In one of the new suburbs he spots a tall figure farther down the road. It stands in the middle of the lane he's in. It grows improbably tall as he nears it. It seems to want to block his passage. Gerry slows down. As he nears it, the gawky shape resolves itself into a moose. It looks at him as he stops in the road. The big ears semaphore. The new bungalows along the road look on with blind windows. Gerry taps the horn, a short Bronx cheer of a beep. The moose startles sideways slightly, offended more than frightened. It clacks up somebody's newly paved driveway, walks through a breezeway and disappears across a newly sodded backyard. The big hooves cut up the new sod.

"Go moose," Gerry says and continues his drive. The fog is burning off. The radio plays the national anthem and the "Ode to Newfoundland" and resumes local broadcasting. The weather report says it will be a sunny day.

twelve

The theme for the mid-day news gallops from the speakers around the radio station. Gerry's work for another day of early-morning shift is ending. He listens to hear the voice report he just recorded over the telephone. Like him, the reporter who did the report is a summer relief, but a brand new summer relief. She was sent to a spectacular road crash that has blocked the Trans-Canada Highway. Something had caught fire and somebody was dead and somebody else had to be cut out of a wreck with the "Jaws of Life." Gerry has never cared for the term. He supposes somebody was being clever with "Charge of the Light Brigade." "Into the jaws of death..." On the other hand he's never been able to come up with a handy shorthand for the big power scissors that cut the tops and doors off crushed cars. "Hydraulic shears" doesn't exactly roll of the tongue. Still, Gerry says that "Jaws of Life" sounds like a porn title.

"It's the sequel to *Deep Throat*," he says. "Or maybe a soap opera about orthodontists."

The reporter's name is Kayla and she has had a hard morning. She'd been sick in the ditch once and made a lot of false starts and stops in her report. Gerry had to edit them out. He finished just in time for the news. He hopes he got them all. He didn't have time to play the piece through.

"No sweat," he'd told her. "You're good down to there. Just take a breath and start again. I'm still rolling here."

He remembers when he and Patricia were in Labrador and he did a lot of military flying stories. He remembers being flown in a helicopter to look at a ring of sheared trees and a sandy crater in the bush. The ground still stank of burning and jet fuel. It seemed to Gerry that there was no wreckage bigger than the burned wheels of the undercarriage. The RAF pilot had been a cheerful kid from somewhere in Scotland. His name was Duncan. They'd met him at a mess do a couple of nights before. He wanted to meet Canadian girls and urged Patricia to bring some of the other teachers to a toga party his squadron was planning.

"It'll be magic," he said. "Like *Animal House*. To-ga! To-ga! To-ga!"

Duncan had tapped wings with somebody else. The other pilot wrestled his plane back towards the base and ejected. He came down just outside the perimeter fence. Duncan had apparently spun straight down. If he tried to eject, it hadn't worked.

To-ga, to-ga, Gerry thinks and flops back and bounces in an ergonomic swivel chair that is adjusted for somebody else. The girl's report is fine. The strain in her voice makes it real. He shuts down his computer, collects his thermos bottle and waves to the day shift, just halfway through their day. He takes his sailing ball-cap from the top of the computer, steals one of the office *Globe and Mail*s and heads down the stairs to the summer street.

It's a Friday and Gerry has no particular place to go. Vivian has gone to Gander to visit her mother and one of her sisters. She had hardly stirred when he left the house at four this morning to go to work. He wonders if the accident on the highway will affect her trip. It shouldn't. It's beyond Gander but Vivian is cautious on the highway. She could have heard the early reports of the accident and taken it as an omen and cancelled her visit. Gerry hopes she hasn't done that. He feels anti-social or at least hungry for a bit of solitude. He heads for home to see if she's left.

The last several weeks have been full of Darren and Melanie. Darren came home and moved back in with Melanie. Vivian and Gerry have taken Diana for a couple of weekends while they get re-acquainted.

"That's like taking her when Melanie has to change a light bulb," Gerry complains. "Old Darren or new Darren, he's still an asshole."

Still, they'd played Crazy Eights and prowled the malls and, on one civil weekend, taken an overnight trip to Brigus and back on the boat.

Darren seems to have no ideas about what to do now that the pizza and donair business is gone. He manages to exude an aura of mild victimhood. He says nothing about his sojourn working for his sister in Alberta. Gerry thinks he's like a war veteran, implying that nobody who hadn't been there could possibly understand the horror. He seems to have some money. He sets off in the morning, supposedly to go to the employment office. Then he meets up with his former delivery drivers and they hang out at a pool hall. They seem to have forgotten that he owes them money. Darren talks vaguely about joining them and delivering pizzas for a chain. Unfortunately he hasn't got a car anymore. Hints are dropped that he could use one and would be prepared to put up some of the money.

Gerry hasn't forgotten Darren owes him money.

"Oh yes, he needs a car now! Why the hell didn't he buy his own ticket if he's got money?" Gerry demands. "Anytime he'd like to start squaring up what we paid off on the take-out, I'm not too proud to take cash."

"Why are you so angry?" Vivian asks. "You hold it against me that he owes you that money."

"Well, as I recall, it didn't come to me in a dream to sign for the damn loan," Gerry says.

"You're so angry."

Vivian's car is gone when Gerry gets home. The house already feels closed. In case of rain, she'd shut the windows before she left. Gerry doesn't open them. He stuffs a sweatshirt, a pair of jeans, and his travelling washing kit into a small duffel bag. He loots some canned goods, a few onions and potatoes and the end of a bag of bean sprouts. He fills two jars, one with sugar and the other with tea bags. They go in double plastic bags from the supermarket. Then he's on his way.

A few hundred yards down the block, Gerry tries to remember if he rattled the door to make sure it was locked. He does this more often than he'd care to admit. Most of the time it doesn't matter if Viv is home, but today she's not. He drives around the block and leaves the Honda running while he trots up to check the doors. He has, in fact, remembered to lock them.

Gerry always says his blood pressure drops below the scale when he reaches the community where he keeps the boat.

"You come over the hill by the Chinese restaurant and mellow right out," he says.

Today, as usual, he's quietly delighted, slowing to drive through the easy curves of the road past the white-painted houses and down to the pin-cushion of masts in the marina. It's too early on a Friday afternoon for many people to be around. People with normal jobs will turn up in late afternoon. Gerry parks his Honda and carries his duffel bag and groceries down to the dock. He puts the boarding ladder across to the bow of the boat and swings his stuff onto the foredeck, one-handed. Then he pushes the ladder back past the point of balance onto the dock. He carries on moving his supplies along the boat to the cockpit and, after some fiddling with the lock, into the cabin.

Today is a day for sloth. Gerry has no make-work projects to do. He brings a cushion up from the cabin, positions it in a corner of the cockpit seat. Pulling his cap over his eyes, he stretches out and lets the sun and the light breeze play over him.

He's been dozing when voices on the dock bring him back across the border of consciousness. A man and a woman are walking along the dock, chattering about boats. *The Wind in the Willows* Water Rat in him warms to them. He lifts his cap off his eyes and cranes from his cushion, squinting into the sun to see them. The man is dapper, late fifties, about Gerry's age. The woman is much younger. He'd put her somewhere between Tanya and Melanie, thirty-ish tops.

"Nice afternoon," he says. You should always be nice to sightseers. They get hooked and turn into new boaters and buy yours when you want to move up. "You looking at boats?"

"Looking at boats," the man says. "Not looking for a boat. Just driving around and stopped for a look."

He points vaguely to a hulking Mercedes four-by-four parked at the end of the dock.

Gerry realizes he knows the man. His name is Roger and years ago, he was in the advertising department when Gerry worked at a newspaper. When local ad agencies bloomed, he went to work for one of those until a particularly gruesome cabinet minister took him on as a handler. Gerry and other reporters had referred to him as "Roger Wilco," making fun of his yes-man job. He had weathered that and run unsuccessfully as a candidate once. Then he floated around government and business until it seemed to be forgotten that he had started off as a writer of news releases. Now he sat on a couple of boards and was a *consultant*.

"How's it going, Roger?"

"Gerry, Gerry Adamson." Roger got where he is, at least partially, by having a good memory for names. "I didn't know you had a boat."

"Well. She's an elderly lady now but she's still afloat. Like most of us. Would you like to come aboard and have a drink?"

"Vanessa Honey, have we got time?"

"I suppose, Roger."

Gerry goes to the bow and pulls his boarding ladder down to the deck. He makes helpful noises about staying in the middle and not looking down and grabbing the forestay. Roger is cautious, edging down the plank, lingering in the riskier middle, while he reaches for the stay. The girl comes aboard like a pirate, barely aware of where she puts her feet. Gerry ushers them back to the cockpit. He fetches them beers out of the starboard locker that is always colder than any portable fridge he's been able to find. He opens himself a Fresca and looks at his guests sitting in the stern sheets of the boat.

They are dressed for nothing that Gerry can see himself doing. Vanessa, abbreviated to Nessa, wears a striped pink-and-white tube top and a short white skirt like a tennis skirt. She has on a pair of the fashionable pastel rubber thongs that look like they come from the dollar store but are probably quite expensive. Gerry sometimes skims the style section of the weekend *Globe*. He thinks he recalls that these thongs are imported from Brazil. Nessa has an even tan and a dusty vinyl smoothness. The few gold hairs on her arms seem to be applied like sparkles to compliment a gold chain. She has semi-big hair that falls around her shoulders. Her eyes, when she takes off her big sunglasses, are round. The whites seem to show all the way around the corneas, giving her a slightly surprised look. Her lips are full and pout a little. With the startled eyes, they suggest a child in the split second before deciding a tantrum may be called for. Still, she smiles at Gerry in an abstracted way and makes polite small talk.

"This is nice," she says, stretching her legs along one cockpit bench.

Roger Wilco looks as if he's dressed for a sport that has yet to be invented, but will be exclusive when it is. His white shirt, with open collar and little pilot shoulder straps, vaguely suggests boats or planes. He wears high-end sneakers and white socks that don't droop. His white shorts are tennis-length over legs that are tanned and bulged with muscle at the calves, but hairless. Gerry wonders if this hairlessness is old age or the new androgyny. He can't tell if Roger has been shedding or waxed.

Roger's face and neck aren't as tight as the skin on his legs. He's got a tan and his hair is beach-boy bleached, but his skin looks finely creased, like paper that has been wet and dried. He seems to keep his lips pursed to hold his jaw up. Gerry recalls that Roger never had a great chin. He's got the beginnings of an iguana neck flap, just above a flat gold chain.

Gerry gives them the one-minute tour of his twenty-four-foot kingdom. Roger follows him around to look in lockers and bounce a bit on the cushions in their original '70s tweed.

"They must have looked everywhere for a fabric that could swallow mildew and puke and anything else and just blend it in," Gerry says. Roger pays polite attention. He hasn't had much to do with Gerry for the last ten-or-more years. He remembers Gerry from his tab-running, drinking-reporter days. The Fresca-sipping boat owner is a new incarnation and Roger is taking it all in.

Vanessa doesn't leave the cockpit. She just leans into the cabin and makes approving noises about the little brass oil-lamp over the galley table. She's like a mother or older sister humouring a little boy who has found something mildly slimy in a tide pool. Gerry wonders when Vanessa came on the scene. Twenty years ago, when Roger took his stab at elected politics, he remembers a wife and a couple of kids. They were in a picture in a pamphlet with a dog at their feet by a fireplace. They all wore matching hand-knit Newfoundland sweaters. Gerry used to say there was an agency that rented presentable kids and stuffed Labrador retrievers for politicians' PR photos and Christmas cards.

"For a little extra you can get the kids stuffed too," Gerry would say. Until Patricia threw them out, he kept a collection of Christmas cards in which, he swore, the dog was the same and stuffed.

The boat is too small for confidential asides and he doesn't really know Roger well enough anyway to ask when he'd warped back a generation in the spouse department. Vanessa actually answers his question for him, making nautical chit-chat.

"We were on this neat catamaran in Tahiti five years ago. It was our third anniversary. We got soaked, didn't we, Roger?"

They sit and chat as the marina gets busier. People roll in from work and go aboard their boats. Engines are turned over and some head out of the little harbour and head down the bay. They yell destinations and meeting places over puttering engines.

"We'll be in Middle Arm."

"We'll go to Brigus tonight. We'll be in Carbonear tomorrow."

Gerry waves to the departing boats and calls across the yacht basin to those who are flashing up their barbecues.

Roger and Vanessa tell him they have a four-year-old daughter and a three-year-old son. They imply the daughter was conceived on the Tahiti trip. The kids are at home with a nanny. Roger and Vanessa are expected at a barbecue nearby. They had the afternoon to themselves and they were just driving around, killing time.

"Of course, Roger's first family are all grown-up now," Vanessa says. She's bloodthirsty with collective nouns.

"Yeah, young Roger's a doctor in Markham, and Tiffany is articling with Peters and Peet downtown," says Roger.

Gerry figures Roger Wilco is at least his age or a year or two older. He remembers moving in with Vivian when Tanya was eight or nine and he was just turning forty. That had seemed a shock, but Roger is going to be dealing with childhood and adolescence until he's seventy. If he's not careful he'll be dealing with the Darren's Pizza and Donair stage of his life when he's in a walker.

Maybe he can get his first lot of kids to raise his second lot.

Roger and Vanessa leave about six. Gerry is not going anywhere tonight. What wind there was dies completely in the slanting, late afternoon sun. Noises from across the harbour seem extremely distinct. Kids yelling and a trail-bike winding up through its gears aren't loud, but crystal clear. A screen door slams somewhere.

Roger goes over the boarding ladder more easily this time. A couple of beers must have relaxed him. Vanessa swings off as easily as she swung on. Gerry walks them up the dock and waves to them as they drive away in their tall, brooding German car with the smoked windows.

Gerry gathers the empty beer cans and puts them in the plastic garbage bag after holding them over the side upside-down to drain. He goes below and flashes up his alcohol stove for what he calls "fission" cooking.

"It's like fusion cooking only not so safe," Gerry jokes. "You have to eat it off lead plates."

"Only masochists, Brits and lunatics like alcohol stoves," people kid Gerry. "Which are you?"

Gerry doesn't mind. He finds the two alcohol burners enough for any cooking he does. Tonight he boils some oriental noodles, fries some onions and a handful of bean sprouts and tosses in a can of tuna. Stirred together it hits the spot. He saves the noodle water and adds detergent to wash his few dishes.

After his humble meal, Gerry goes for a walk along the railway right-of-way that hugs the long gravel beach at the head of the bay. There is no wind now, but the remainder of the swell still makes a soft gravely hiss beside him as he walks. He thinks about Roger and Vanessa and himself and Vivian.

"If I died would you get married again?" Vivian asks him sometimes. Sometimes it's not a casual question. It can be a ranging shot in an incipient argument.

"I think I'd just have affairs," Gerry says. "I've been domesticated twice. A third time would be too much."

"You'd probably shack up with some young one," Vivian says.

"Only if she had some sort of grandfather complex," Gerry says. "Besides, I was never a cradle-robber. Some of my old girlfriends are collecting pensions by now."

He's telling the truth. When he fooled around on Patricia it had been pretty much a perverse point of honour to find women older than she was. It was as if he didn't want it said he was looking for a younger or prettier woman. It also helped if they made it quite clear, early on, that they were just out for a fling themselves. Patricia had no such rules. Brian, when she found him, was six or seven years younger and obviously in it for the long haul. Gerry wonders if Brian was playing a modified version of *his* rules and got caught.

Only in his inter-regnum, between marriages, did Gerry date younger women. Fiona of his Weasel jottings was still in her twenties. Walking along the beach he does some mental math.

She was twenty-six and I was just about forty, so she was born about the time I was in the tenth grade. She heard "The Twist" in the womb. She listened to the Beatles in her playpen. The Beatles broke up when she was eight and I was in England after graduation.

Gerry imagines 1960s playpens, or tries to. He thinks they'd stopped being wooden by then, although the wooden ones were still around. He suspects that the folding, plastic-netting type had arrived.

In the mid-'80s they had been drinking in one of the bigger hotels. There was a piano player. Gerry had requested "As Time Goes By." Fiona didn't realize that he only knew it from *Casablanca* on TV and from childhood, pre-TV radio. There was a program called *Make Believe Ballroom*. Fiona thought it was something he really knew. Dancing with her, he felt she was right.

"It's 'Play it, Sam. You played it for her. You can play it for me,'" he told her. "It's not 'Play it again, Sam.'"

Fiona, in bed, had made him aware of their different ages too. She hung out in the same bars he did and her body had an indoor pallor. Her body hair was unobtrusive and her nipples pale and pink. Naked, she looked wispy, immature, ready to be given a bath and tucked in. Patricia had read *The Female Eunuch*, and alternated between letting her bush grow and then clipping it with nail scissors when swimsuit season rolled around. She suspected the clipping made it grow back with an increased vigour. Not long before they split up, she went for bikini-line electrolysis.

Gerry had enjoyed going to bed with Fiona but the cliché about age difference proved true. They had little to talk about when they finished. They were good-enough company out somewhere, where they could talk about their surroundings and other people, or flirt with each other. After that had played itself out, though, they tended to drop off to sleep silently. Although they had apartments near each other, neither suggested moving in together, and one or the other usually walked home in the early morning. Gerry remembers feeling slightly relieved by the solitude of those walks.

He wonders what Roger and Vanessa Wilco talk about in the early mornings while the two kids and the nanny are asleep.

It is nearly dusk when Gerry gets back to the marina. He visits along the dock for a bit, chatting with other people who haven't gone anywhere. The evening gathers around them.

"The nights are starting to draw in," somebody says. "It was only a couple of weeks ago we had the longest day."

A small bunch of people sit in somebody's cockpit and chat until it is fully dark. Then Gerry ambles back to his own boat and crawls into his sleeping bag without bothering to light the oil-lamp. The hull makes little contented, clucking water noises. The halyards in the mast make a soft brushing as the boat rocks. The marina lights shine through the scratch-hazed plexiglass in the portholes, and everything in the boat is dimly visible. Gerry falls asleep quickly. Tomorrow, if the weather is decent, he may go for a sail somewhere. On Sunday, he'll try and round up a crew and race.

thirteen

SEPTEMBER 2004

O n the Tuesday after Labour Day, Gerry sits in a coffee shop and thumbs back through his Chinese notebook. He finds he has not made an entry since a day or two after Philip left at the end of June. When he made it, he was poking through the last of the books that Philip had left him, the discards from the humanist funeral project. One was a collection of haiku. He'd copied down the one by Issa about a puppy. Without fooling around with the syllables to be faithful to the form, he'd written: *The puppy who doesn't know it's autumn is a Buddha.* After that there were shopping lists and sketches of boat race courses with a couple of times and positions scribbled down.

Why am I surprised? he wonders. He has drawers full of notebooks with similar gaps.

Gerry finds himself hanging on at work past Labour Day this year. The reason is that a bunch of people have been taken off their regular jobs to do an anniversary special on 9/11. They're busily calling people who were stranded in Newfoundland. They head out to interview people who billeted other people from all over the world. Several on-air reunions are arranged.

Gerry suggests they interview Vivian's older sister Nellie. She still lives in the tiny community of Burleigh, where Vivian's family resettled in the '50s. Nellie is on her church's flower committee. When marooned travellers were billeted in town, she went into the church one day and found a man from Kenya stretched out in the back pew.

"Scared the life out of me," Nellie says. "Black as the ace of spades, with a three-piece suit on and his shoes off and a six-pack of beer. I don't suppose he knew where he was, no more than a child."

Nellie and her husband Plemon took the man home. He was a government agronomist from Nairobi. They took him berry-picking. They still exchange Christmas cards.

Outside of Nellie, Plemon and the agronomist, Gerry has little to add to the local 9/11 remembrances. He and Vivian were on a holiday cruise in mid-Atlantic when it happened. With little else to do, he decides to get back to his writing and convert the cruise into a George and Ellen story.

Fragment: For Those in Peril on the Sea

The napkin-folding class was cancelled when they learned the planes had hit the towers.

George had taken the galley tour that morning and had been waiting by the pool for napkin-folding to start as the cruise ship steamed west, a day out of the Azores. While he and Ellen were not exactly fighting, they had had a minor row over souvenir shopping in Punta del Gada the day before and were giving each other some space. George had gone napkin-folding because he thought it might be silly enough to write about some day. Ellen had gone to lunch with a school friend from Burleigh she'd only just encountered, between Lisbon and the Azores. George and Ellen had been walking off lunch when they overheard three women walking behind them.

"They're Newfoundlanders," Ellen said. She stopped, turned and smiled at the three. "Excuse me, aren't you from Newfoundland?"

The reunion followed. Ellen and her classmate, a woman called

Velma, recognized each other. Velma introduced the other two women with her. They were her sisters-in-law. They'd all had their bangs corn-row beaded at the ship's beauty salon. No one in Burleigh had beaded corn-rows and they were on vacation.

"We married three brothers," Velma said. "They're here somewhere."

Presently the brothers had appeared. They were short grizzled men who ran a carpentry business together. They kept to themselves and walked the deck in a way which suggested they were measuring it and might build a cruise liner from memory later on.

"They're hobbits," George said to Ellen. "They've got furry feet, I bet you."

They had been on the cruise for ten days. It was what the agency called a repositioning cruise, one where the ship crossed the Atlantic to be back in its winter cruising grounds. They got a spectacularly good rate by booking a September cruise the preceding winter.

"We could die before then," George told the girl in the travel agency. "We're ancient, you know."

However, they had paid for cancellation insurance, kept their fingers crossed, and now had cruised from Italy to the Azores with only Boston left on the itinerary. Now the announcements were saying that on this repositioning cruise, more than the ship was being repositioned.

The ship's PA speakers extinguished the afternoon like a sprinkler system. Activities were cancelled. Horse racing was postponed. Passengers were asked to please be patient trying to call the States. An ecumenical prayer service would be held in the Aloha Room. The ship's closed-circuit TV channel would give news as it became available.

The pool deck cleared like a rained-on garden party. George wandered down into the central atrium of the ship. He found Ellen and Velma coming out of the dining room.

"Should we try to call the kids?"

"Not much point. Besides, what do we tell them? There's nothing wrong here. If they're dropping planes on people, the middle of the ocean on a moving target's a pretty good place to be."

Gerry sits at his computer and looks at the notebook he used for a travel diary on the trip.

Early internet news is garbled and poor. CNN wire stuff is better after supper, but still no attempt at casualty figures. We played a guess-the-word game with a bunch of comedy fatalists, then attended a sock hop, complete with Twist and hula-hoop competitions.

Gerry remembers the hula-hoop competition. It was won by a sparrow-like British granny who managed to twirl eight hoops around her neck. She wore a floral-print summer dress and peeked out of the wreath of bright plastic hoops as if from a nest. Gerry guesses she'd have been a teenager in the Blitz. No sky-borne terrorist was going to stop her carousing with her grandkids.

The next morning he and Vivian had shared a table with a retired marine biologist and his wife. Gerry works them into his narrative.

Fragment: Armageddon Breakfast

They came from Mobile, Alabama, and their name was Hickson. Dr. Hickson had a sad-basset-hound air and a polite southern slowness of speech. He had done research on farmed shrimp. Work with tiny crustaceans had made him comfortable with big numbers. He had heard there might be forty-thousand dead in New York

Mrs. Hickson was at ease with big numbers because of her work with the Book of Revelation.

"It's all prophesied," she told George. "We are in the end times. We should all pray."

In fact, Gerry's travel diary shows they did not pray. In the final days of the cruise, he recorded menus, weather – as the ship skirted the edges of a hurricane – and the scarcity of world news. He chronicled fights with the tour company reps as rumours spread that the ship was going to be diverted to any number of places. Finally, he noted that the almost-famous doo-wop group that was the final night's show was holding up pretty well, despite not having had a hit since 1966. The three grey-haired men and one bald man in Italian suits sang well. Like the hula-hooping granny, they were indomitable. Gerry's last entry says he went to the show alone. The hurricane was nearby and Vivian was feeling seasick. She stayed in the cabin and started packing.

Gerry and Vivian had come most of the way back from their cruise on a bus to Halifax. The airline had arranged it. The planes were still not flying when their ship got to Boston. They called Tanya from a phone booth during a rest stop somewhere in Maine. She was house-sitting for them. She seemed to have trouble with them being on an un-planned activity.

"Where are you?" she demanded. "I was worried."

"I don't know," Vivian told her. "We're in some kind of public washroom. The sign says it's maintained by the blind. If you smelled it, you'd wonder if they're only just blind."

The bus dropped them at Halifax Airport. After all night in the terminal, they got on a flight back to Newfoundland.

Having been insulated from the initial events, Gerry followed the run-up to the Afghanistan invasion closely. Work was slow. The budget for freelancers had been spent covering the stranded air passengers. Gerry was restless.

One day he called the local naval reserve unit. He talked to the commander, a woman he'd known for years.

"Just in case you needed an elderly sub-lieutenant to count the paper clips or answer the phone or something. Free up some of the younger ones. I did have a commission, years ago."

"You're over the age, Gerry," she told him. "It's all different now. They don't let people hang around like they used to. You're not the first I've had a call from. Thanks anyway."

"Apparently my reserve status is somewhere just after nuns and just before Cubs and Beavers," Gerry told Vivian. Still, he felt old that fall.

On a fine September day, Gerry meets his ex, Patricia, in the parking lot of the Family Life Centre of the Roman Catholic Archdiocese. He is there because of a phone call from a man he used to work with at the newspaper in the '70s. The man's name is Michael. Michael and his wife Maureen were friends of Patricia's and Gerry's. They used to go to clubs together and invite each other for meals. Then everybody had changed jobs and moved a few times and Patricia and Gerry split up. So had Michael and Maureen, but later on. Gerry recalls that he and Vivian had encountered them somewhere in the mid-'90s and they were still a couple, but barely. They'd had dinner together and promised to do it again and hadn't. He heard they'd separated not long after that. Michael had moved to Vancouver. Now, it seems Michael wants to remarry. His new bride, like Maureen, is a Catholic.

"We're going for an annulment," Michael told Gerry on the phone. "They'll want to talk to people who knew us when we were just married. You can give a deposition there. Somebody from the church will be in touch."

To say what? Gerry wondered at the time. To prove what? However, here he is today in the family centre parking lot. He's early because he left himself lots of time to find the place. It's a beautiful day, with bright sun and big, towering clouds. Gerry lounges in the warm seat of his wagon. Every city sound seems muted and remote. He's been sitting listening to Mozart on Radio Two when Patricia pulls in.

She drives a minivan these days. Gerry reflects that she must be emerging from the kids'-chauffeur period of the twins' development. She pulls into a space a couple away from where he's parked and gets out of her van. Gerry turns off the radio and gets out too.

"Hey, kid. How are you doing?"

"Gerry, I haven't seen you for ages. How's Vivian?"

They press cheeks, movie-star air-kissing, distant though touching and civil. Gerry wonders if she remembers she once slipped a pair of lurid knickers with cats on them into his suit pocket before a job interview.

"For inspiration," she said afterwards.

Patricia has had her off-the-shoulder hair done a silver grey. It looks surprisingly good over a face that has stayed youngish looking. She is wearing a khaki-coloured skirt and a Madras blouse. She has a blue blazer on. Her shoes are brown suede.

"We're fine," Gerry says, circling the wagons in the plural.

"You're here for this thing with Michael?"

"Yeah. I guess you got a call too."

"I don't know what I'm going to say. I mean they split up. It's over right? What do these people want to hear?"

"I guess we'll just have go in and see what they have to say."

"God, I'm glad we didn't have to do all this bullshit."

They climb the steps and Gerry opens the door for her. "After you, madam."

"I'll see you out here after. We'll compare notes."

The Family Life Centre is like a '50s Russian trade show. It is full of ugly chemical colours and lotion-bottle shapes. Perhaps it's been furnished by donations from parish attics, but the stuff looks too new. They tell an elderly secretary why they're there and she tells them that Sister Angela will be taking their depositions.

Sister Angela looks sixty-something, with steel-grey hair and the eyes of a jaded loans officer. She wears a navy suit and a white blouse. There's a brassy brooch with a black cross at her throat.

"Mrs. Pearce, come in please. Mr. Adamson, you're very punctual, early in fact."

"I know," Gerry says apologetically. "I left myself time to get lost and then didn't. I'll just wait right here."

Sister Angela nods and takes Patricia into an inner office. Gerry picks up an old issue of *Canadian Living* and reads about all the great things you can do with pinto beans. The elderly secretary answers her phone once and goes to a sideboard where there's an electric urn of hot water. She makes an instant coffee in a plastic cup in an orange holder and takes it in to where Patricia is doing her thing. The air has a waxy smell. Gerry is almost dozing when his turn comes.

Sister Angela and Patricia emerge from the office with a discreet clatter. They shake hands solemnly. Turning away, Patricia rolls her eyes and mouths "outside." Her suede shoes click down the shiny tile of a corridor and Gerry is being ushered into the office. Sister Angela is hitting her stride. She asks straight off if he'd like the instant coffee.

They sit at a boardroom table with a tape recorder on it. Gerry notices it because it's a good make and looks new. On the other hand, it's a model that has been replaced by digital in Gerry's work.

The volume of annulment depositions mustn't be burning out the equipment, he thinks. Either that, or nuns take better care of their gear than reporters do.

The interview, from Gerry's point of view anyway, has an *Alice-in-Wonderland* feel.

"What religion would you be, Mr. Adamson?"

"Nothing formal, sort of Taoist, I suppose."

"That must be foreign."

We smile like sick cats, Gerry thinks, mentally writing this. *We talk about the people who made the vows so long ago, the matches that are broken or are being broken now.*

"Did Michael and Maureen's separation surprise you?"

"Probably no more than mine surprised me."

"Was there a lot of drinking?"

As compared to what, he thinks.

"Not that I remember, but then again I was drinking heavily in those days."

"Did you see anything that made you think there may have been abuse?"

"No. No, I don't think so."

The questions and answers succeed each other. Gerry continues to write a poem in his head.

> *I remember a day:*
> *Two couples and Volkswagen,*
> *With a 410 shotgun,*
> *Looking for birds;*
> *There's a photo of us*
> *In a weed-bright gravel pit,*
> *Laughing in big sweaters,*
> *On a day like this;*
> *One of us, (we're saying now) was crazy;*
> *Another was a drunk,*
> *But we didn't care;*
> *The two normal ones have got out, or want out,*
> *But it was still a nice day*
> *And nice days still come;*
> *We shot no birds;*
> *I don't believe we saw one;*
> *As I recall, we went home to cook*
> *Pasta and red wine*

In a mobile-hung walk-up,
With old-time ads stuck
On the kitchen wall;
I hope the question
Isn't if that time was bad;
It wasn't then
And it doesn't seem so now.

"Thank you for your help, Mr. Adamson," Sister Angela says, the end of the interview recalling him to reality.

"I don't know that I've been very much help."

"These things are difficult. I'm sure Michael and Maureen appreciate what you're doing."

Gerry isn't sure that Patricia will have waited in the parking lot. His watch tells him the interview has taken less than twenty minutes but he's lost track of time. She has waited though. She's sitting in her van reading a paperback novel. It's *Catcher in the Rye*.

"One of the kids left it in the car," she says. "I haven't read it for years. I think we had it when we lived on top of Frankie's."

They drive to a Tim Hortons, diplomatically about mid-way between their respective homes.

"That was pretty awful," Patricia says when they've bought coffees and sat down at a table.

"I kept wondering if I was doing them any good," Gerry says. "It's like maybe we should have been saying they were unconscious drunk at the wedding and never consummated it and spent the rest of their time beating each other up and having perverted sex with wombats."

"Wombats?"

"You never found out about the wombats in leather? God, there I was, thinking that's what drove you into Brian's arms."

"Fool." She smiles.

"And here it turns out you were just embittered by having to carry me over the threshold drunk."

"You weren't drunk then."

"No, I guess I wasn't. I was later on, though."

"Do you ever wonder why?"

"Christ, you do harder ones than Sister Angela."

"No really, I mean you've been sober for years now. You go to meetings and stuff. Did you ever figure out why?"

"Well," Gerry says, "I always liked that old line that I drank to make other people more interesting."

"You did always say that, usually to guests."

"But I think maybe I was trying to make me more interesting."

"How do you mean?" Patricia asks.

"I mean sober I was way too uncomplicated," Gerry says, cradling his coffee mug in both hands. "Booze was my religion, something I could be the guru of. I wasn't just drunk. I was declaring a new reality."

"You were pretty real. I didn't like phonies."

"Worst sin you could commit back then, being phoney. Now how phoney would we look?"

"When I said I wanted to come down here on the bus to live, you just asked when we were leaving. That wasn't phoney."

Gerry looks at the face framed in the silver hair. He looks for and finds the eyes that floated in candlelight as they'd sat up, naked in two sleeping bags zipped together, talking about taking off to Newfoundland.

"I just wanted to be as cool as you. You were so damned grown-up. I figured I had to be some kind of Byronic wild-man or you'd throw me back in the pool."

"I really believed in your writing, the poems, the novels. Do you still write?...Outside of work I mean."

"Yeah, I do, but a lot more slowly. I know I've got to work for it now. The booze-muse doesn't dictate whole chapters anymore. Do you still paint?"

"Touché," Patricia says, "You know, Gerry, apart from the drinking you were never a bad guy. You were drunk when you fucked around."

"You knew then."

"Some of those perverted wombats were friends of mine."

"I never wanted to hurt you, Pat."

"I know that now. We didn't hurt each other much. I mean, hey, we're nice people."

"Yeah, pretty civilized."

The autumn afternoon is turning to orange and gold when they walk to their cars.

"See you, Gerry. Say hello to Vivian." She gives him a hug. He returns it and finds there's no muscle memory of her. They embrace like strangers, unsure of the fit, the pressure to exert. He remembers when they fitted each other's fronts like hot poultices. Still, the unfamiliarity is comforting in a way. They're immune now.

"See you around, Pat. Say hi to Brian and your mob too."

Civilized, Gerry thinks as he drives home. That's what we are, civilized.

It is an October day and Gerry is waiting for a bus in the early morning. The rain in the night has changed to mostly drizzle and fog, but with occasional hard showers, like parting shots in an ice-cold argument, sneaky, over-the-shoulder afterthoughts which sting if they don't kill. The mist skirmishes through the spruce trees on the hill above Gerry's neighbourhood, a guerrilla army of diagonal, wet ghosts, angling down the slope to invest the day.

Gerry turns his back to the clammy drift and turns his raincoat collar up. He's riding the bus today because the truck is in the shop for its umpty-seven-hundred-kilometre check-up. He has to go downtown and it's too wet to walk all the way. He's consulted the bus schedule he and Vivian keep stuck to the fridge for car-less emergencies. If they haven't changed the schedule he should be able to ambush a bus without being out in the wet too long.

As he waits under the dripping bus-stop sign, a string of ducks scrambles up the sky. Hitting it running, they hurtle up from the furtive muskrat stream that subverts the tameness of the neighbourhood. The stream lurks in the alders and reeds, stalking the tame horticulture of gardens and lawns. Gerry remembers the old Dorothy Parker tag on horticulture: You can lead a whore-to-culture, but you can't make her think.

The ducks gain frantic height. They cut through the wet grey over the morning traffic on the parkway. They level off and fly fast and straight over the oiled-looking shopping mall parking lot.

There's an asthmatic, diesel bulldog snuffling from a side street. The bus snorts around the corner and fusses damply to a halt at Gerry's stop. The pneumatic doors give an iron-lung slurp and gather him in.

The bus pulls away, a window-steamy rolling community. Cheek-by-jowl, its residents are morning loud or quiet, depending on their natures. Gerry is quiet. He digs in an inside pocket for his notebook and pen. He looks out and sees a crow on a wet post and thinks of the rhyme for magpies and crows. One for sadness, two for joy, three for a girl and four for a boy.

Gerry reflects that you don't often see just one crow. He suspects the old rhyme-maker was hedging his bets. He'd have been more likely to see two crows or magpies or ravens or whatever. He'd be more likely to get "two for joy" because crows are social.

Maybe the old rhymester wanted a son who wouldn't cost him a dowry, Gerry jots. *Maybe he wanted somebody to help out with the heavy work around the smallholding. Four crows are probably just as likely as three, maybe even more likely. Make it three for a girl and four for a boy. From a peasant perspective, the deck of crows is stacked for optimism, but can there be too many crows for luck?*

Gerry remembers his father's stories of the First World War. He said he'd seen the sky black with crows after Passchendaele. They flew in from all over Flanders to gorge on the dead. What would the old peasant make of that in his couplet, assuming a passing army didn't loot or shell him out of his contemplation?

Four million crows for Armageddon, Gerry writes.

The bus turns another corner. On the Kiwanis ball field is another crow. This one is on the ground with a flock of seagulls. They're eating the suicidal autumn worms the rain has driven up into the cold.

Do crows, separated by a couple of minutes of bus ride and mixed with gulls, count as "two for joy"? Do gulls count?

The bus goes on through the fog as Gerry tries to do the math.

The woman sitting next to him has a newspaper open to the local arts section. The paper flops into his line of sight. He sees a picture of someone he knows. It's Nish from his writing workshop.

"Coastal boat steward serves up salty treat," the headline reads. "*This Bucket Here*, a must-read!"

But I've got the crows counted, Gerry thinks. Right here in this notebook.

fourteen

NOVEMBER 2004

I
t's not quite four on a Friday morning and Gerry stands at his kitchen
counter, drinking coffee with his raincoat on, staring out the window.
He's waiting for a taxi to take him to the airport, and his old folding
suitcase and shoulder bag are slumped together by the door, like old
dogs waiting patiently for a walk. Only the reading lamp on the small
desk in the kitchen is turned on. Its downward glow makes the kitchen
shadowed and cozy.

He hears the bedroom door open down the hall. Then the bathroom
door shuts. A minute later the toilet flushes. Vivian shuffles into the
kitchen in flannel pyjamas with snowmen on them. They were a gift
from Melanie, picked out by Diana, last Christmas.

"Did I wake you?"

"No, I never heard you. I just got up to go. You're all ready then?"

"Cab's on his way, or says he is."

"Call me when you know how your mother is. Did you take that
calling card we had on the boat? It's good for a couple more months."

"I did. Right here. You'd better go back to bed." Gerry hugs Vivian.
She seems shorter, barefoot and smaller, as if she was slightly compacted

for sleep and has not completely unfolded.

"Call me," she says and shuffles back along the hall.

After supper the night before, they had said they meant to go to bed together, but they didn't. Gerry had turned in early because he has an early flight. Vivian had a house-showing that ran late. Gerry knows the feel of the snowman pyjamas and now wants to run his hands under them but it's too late. The cab is called. Car lights flash on the kitchen window. He picks up his bags and lets himself out the kitchen door, locking it behind him.

There's been frost. The steps are slippery under his desert boots. The grass of the lawn is glazed under the street lamps and feels like frozen vegetables when he pauses, humping his bags down the driveway, and tests it with his foot. He throws the bags in the back seat of the cab and climbs in beside the driver.

"Airport, please."

On the ride through the empty streets he reviews what is happening. The retirement home in Ottawa has called. His mother had a fall.

"She must have got up in the night. One of the girls found her on the bathroom floor."

There had been a trip to hospital and X-rays. Now there's apparently a broken arm and pneumonia. She isn't eating. She's been sent to hospital.

The night before, Gerry had spoken to a doctor who sounded about fifteen.

"She's not eating and she's very disoriented and she's a bit dehydrated. I think we may be looking at tube feeding. For the moment we're just giving her electrolytes and something for the pain."

"I've got a ticket bought," Gerry had said. "I'll be there tomorrow."

"Business or pleasure?" the cab driver asks, breaking in on him.

"Family," Gerry says. None of the above.

Gerry balances a Hortons coffee through security, shoving his corduroy jacket, raincoat and shoulder bag through the scanning machine. He took the trouble to empty his pockets of pennies before he left home. He manages not to swamp the change and key tray as he often does and goes by the sweeping wands virtually beep-less.

In the departure lounge little tribes form around the various gates. At his, he runs into Kayla, the girl who did the voice report on the car crash back in the summer. She's been moved from a regional station into St. John's.

"Good morning, Kayla. Where are you off to?"

"Oh hi, Gerry. Toronto. They're sending me on the radio skills course."

She wears jeans and a sweater and a short suede coat. She has a Kool-Aid orange streak in her short hair and carries a tiny knapsack. Gerry is reminded of the teddy bear and puppy knapsacks that were in vogue a few years back. Tanya had a floppy-eared beagle.

"That's a good course," Gerry says. "Someday, I ought to take it and acquire a few radio skills myself. There've been a few changes since I started with carrier pigeons."

She realizes he's joking and guffaws. It's gratifying. She has a nice big laugh, unaffected. It's a nice balance to her serious workplace manner.

"Where are you going?"

"Ottawa. My mom's not very well. She's ninety-six."

"Wow! That's too bad."

"Well, she's a pretty old lady. You've got to expect…"

Gerry wonders what ninety-six means to Kayla: A bargain-price for a pair of sneakers, or a number of beer bottles in a kid's song, or do they even sing the beer-bottle song anymore?

Gerry thinks of the headache commercial with the singing kids and the woman in the car. It is the song that has no end. It goes on and on my friend…

Once he web-searched "Song That Has No End" on the computer and found that Shari Lewis wrote it. Shari Lewis has been dead for half a dozen years. Gerry remembers her and her puppets on *Ed Sullivan* a billion years ago.

Their flight is called. Kayla and Gerry walk together through the zigzag accordion walkway and board the plane. "I change in Halifax," she says, tossing her little knapsack into the bin. Her seat's far ahead of his.

"See you when we get back."

Gerry goes to his own seat and for most of the flight snoozes or looks at the daylight growing stronger as they fly west, a milk-run, delivering the morning.

Inland weather always comes as a bit of a surprise to Gerry now. He's lived beside the ocean too long. The apparent stability of a bright, late fall day in Ontario catches him off guard as he drives to the hospital. The sky seems curiously empty and static.

If the sky is empty, the parking lot is not. Gerry gets a reminder he's not on his home turf where he knows the best hidden parking places. The lot is full and two lanky Somalis tell him to just leave his car in the middle of the lot's traffic lane, blocking at least two cars into their spots, and leave the keys with them.

The Somalis are swaddled in marshmallow-pile jackets and fake-fur bomber hats although there's only a degree or two of frost.

"Nobody is going to steal your car, mister," the shorter of the two tells Gerry. He has an aquiline face with a spatter of pock marks on his cheekbones. He seems to be senior in the hierarchy of the parking lot. "Just leave your keys here on this board, with a tag on them."

Gerry hesitates for a moment and then thinks, Hick! Why should you care if some secret organization of Somalis decides to take your rent-a-car for a drive, show your luggage the sights?

The board is full of keys with tags. All sorts of cars are blocking off all sorts of other cars. The system apparently works. He leaves the rental agency keys, with their unfamiliar electric door-opener-cum-horn-blower attached, and walks away, feeling strangely conscious of not having their weight in his pocket.

His early morning flight has brought him here too early for regular visiting hours. When Gerry goes to the floor his mother is on, it is in its full mid-morning internal routine. People in pastel uniforms push high-tech floor cleaners around the halls. Posses of doctors and medical students roam the wards. Because Gerry has come so far, the nurses at the nursing station tell him he can look in on his mother.

She is asleep when he goes to the room. She looks small. Her head is thrown back on the pillow, and under a clear plastic oxygen mask, her mouth, with her dentures out, is open. With her eyes tight shut she looks like she's breathing for a sprint in slow motion. Her breathing gurgles. Her injured arm is in a plastic sleeve, like an elongated archer's wrist brace with Velcro straps. It strikes Gerry that plaster casts seem to have gone out of fashion. He touches her hand but she does not wake.

There are two other women in the room. One moans softly but persistently. Two nurses come in and rattle a curtain around her bed. Inside it, they begin some procedure that makes the moaning louder. When they finish, Gerry sits and holds his mother's hand for a bit. Then he goes downstairs for something to eat. The airlines don't feed you breakfast any more. On his way past the nursing station, a podgy man in a mauve sweater over green scrubs tells him that the *real* visiting hours start at one.

The hospital is old with wedding-cake pillars and stone railings, but the cafeteria is in a newer section, big and modern. It seems to be driven into an angle of the old building like some mountaineer's wedge, made of space-age material forced into the ancient rock. It is big and busy and timeless. People order whatever meal is appropriate to where they are in their staggered days. Gerry buys bacon and eggs but walks past an iced counter of sushi in plastic containers. Sushi has been in the supermarkets of St. John's for only a year or two. Gerry is impressed that, here, you can buy it in a hospital canteen. The coffee comes in a California confusion of canisters, flavours and levels of caffeine, but when Gerry tracks down French Blend among the hazelnut and vanilla oddities, it's tasty. He takes his breakfast to one end of a long table. A clutch of hospital workers are taking their break at the other end. They're rehashing a reality TV show that was on the night before. Outside a plate-glass wall are little round, street café tables, bolted to a patio. The chairs have been removed in preparation for winter. As Gerry finishes his coffee, a man with a gas-powered leaf-blower chases leaves into lines among the tables. His partner rakes them into plastic bags. The blower makes a cocky, outboard-motor sound. The men's breath makes clouds in the bright November air. Cramped from his plane ride and the unnatural stillness of sitting in his mother's room, Gerry decides he needs to be outside.

Across six lanes of traffic, in front of the hospital, is the old federal experimental farm. Now the experimental plots and the animals have been mostly moved to other research facilities, but years ago, when he was in university, Gerry worked there. He strides down the hospital walk, past the flowerbeds winterized with evergreen branches, and punches the buttons on the traffic light at the road crossing. The farm is mostly greenbelt parkland now. There are few fences. In a minute he's hiking over slightly frosty fields.

Gerry figures that at some point in the centennial summer of 1967, he probably hoed this field. Before the war, his parents had worked at the farm. His mother had spoken to someone she used to know and Gerry had got a summer job as a labourer at the plant research division. Now he walks briskly but aimlessly across the crisp fields, swinging his arms to shake out the kinks. Fields away, traffic growls around the edges of the farm, a distant accompaniment to the crunch of his feet on frosty turf.

In early afternoon, Gerry is back on the ward at the hospital. His mother is awake but doesn't seem to know him. The top of her hospital gown is stained with the spatters of an attempt to feed her, and she tosses and feebly fights the mask, the saline drip in the back of one hand and the weight of the plastic on her arm. A nurse comes and gives her an injection and she lapses into quiet with only occasional moans and whimpers. Gerry sits and holds her hand.

Later that afternoon, a blonde woman in slacks and a shaggy sweater of earth tones comes to the door and gestures him into the hall.

"Mr. Adamson?"

"Yes, that's me." Gerry does his helpful big kid impression. "I just got in this morning."

"I'm Rosalind Fife, hospital social services," she says and presents a card. She is about Gerry's and Vivian's age and, like Vivian, looks like she works out and takes care of herself. Her only concession seems to be her feet. Her shoes are smooth walnut leather and look expensive, but they are one of those shapes that grew out of Earth Shoes and clogs thirty years ago. They have a width and bluntness that is, somehow, slightly clownish, Hobbit chic or shoes for a fat cartoon animal. Still, she's pleasant and confiding, and sitting in a corner of a ward waiting room, Gerry finds he's quite happy to have her to talk to.

"She seems pretty out-of-it," he says. "If she doesn't get better than that, I don't know about her care. She's in Laurier Lodge at the moment. We live out of town, Newfoundland."

"There is long-term care available," Rosalind Fife says. "We went to Newfoundland in 1997, the Cabot anniversary."

They talk about nursing care and visiting workers and what's available at Laurier Lodge. They agree to meet at her office on Monday and go into more detail. They shake hands and she walks silently away in her stylish/comfortable Wally Walrus shoes.

As the evening starts to draw in, Gerry meets his mother's doctor. On the telephone the night before, Gerry had thought the man's name sounded like "Oompah." It turns out to be Huta.

And he's not fifteen, Gerry thinks. He's sixteen if he's a day.

As well as being young, Dr. Huta is slight, deep-eyed and sandy-haired. He wears an Oxford-cloth shirt and khaki pants. He has a stethoscope around his neck and a Velcro pouch for some other equipment on his belt.

If you're not careful, you'll grow up to look like me on holiday, Gerry thinks. Still, Dr. Huta is sensible and practical.

"She's not eating," he tells Gerry. "She hasn't got much strength to fight the pneumonia. Her lungs don't sound good. I think we ought to tube-feed her and see if we can get her strength back."

"Is she going to be okay?"

"I'm not very happy with the pneumonia. She is quite old. Do you know what her wishes might be? Is there any sort of living will?"

This is for real, Gerry thinks. The false alarms and dry runs are over.

"There is, and I've heard her talk about it, but her lawyer has it. As far as I recall, it's just to keep her comfortable and not prolong things if she's not going to get better."

"No heroic measures," Dr. Huta says. "That's the normal thing."

Gerry feels anything but heroic. He wonders if he's coming across as ghoulish, bloodthirsty: Can't wait to get the old lady out of the way. He must call his buddy, Bob the Lawyer, and see what the living will actually does say.

"So if it's okay with you, we'll put the tube in now and start feeding her," Dr. Huta says. "But I probably should mention that if she's going, some people find it harder to ask us to stop a procedure than it is to just not start it."

"So you think she's going?"

"Not right away and the feeding may make all the difference. I would say we'll know better after the weekend."

Gerry waits on the couches by the nursing station while Dr. Huta, an intern and a nurse go into his mother's room to put the tube in. When they usher him back in, it is dark outside the windows. An overhead lamp highlights the new additions to his mother's medical hardware. A plastic bag of eggnog-looking stuff hangs from a hook. A plastic gizmo on a trolley turns a little wheel that massages the liquid down the tube that runs to his mother's nose.

"She'll probably sleep now," the doctor tells Gerry. "We're adding medication through the IV now so we don't have to keep jabbing her. She's getting something for pain in the IV."

The doctor is right. She does sleep while Gerry sits, holding her hand for a while, and later, working the crossword from an abandoned *National Post* from the waiting area. She is still sleeping when Gerry leaves about eight that night.

When Gerry goes to the parking lot, the two Somalis are gone. At a sodium-lit kiosk, he picks up his keys from a little beige man in round glasses, an astrakhan wedge hat and an army-surplus parka. His rental car now has a space of its own and much of the lot to itself. It's nosed against the fence, separating the parking lot from a backyard. Across the yard, Gerry can see into a back dining room window. There are candles and people moving around. It looks warm. He shivers, looking around the unfamiliar dashboard to turn up the car's heater and blower.

Because Gerry doesn't know how long he'll have to stay, his friend Doc is putting him up. They had made the arrangements the night before over the phone. If Gerry's mother dies and Vivian comes up to join him, they'll move to a hotel. Until then he's camped on a couch in Doc's loft.

Doc lives in the building he runs his business from. It's in a small island of commercial buildings that would have been on the edge of the city forty years ago but has been surrounded by suburbs. It's a two-storey cinderblock building that began life as a sign company when plastic signs were new. It has a tidy shop front in one front corner and warehouse doors at the back. There are double doors to the second-storey loft as well, with a jutting boom for a block and tackle. However, since he's been living upstairs, Doc has winter-sealed those with silicone goo and sheets of plastic.

Over the front-corner sales office, Doc has a neat, old-fashioned green and gold sign: Mariposa Carpentry. Doc took a long time coming up with the name. It's supposed to make boomers think of the Leacock stories in old school readers and big Victorian houses. At the time, Gerry and Mort had suggested Discreet Charm of the Bourgeoisie and There Goes the Neighbourhood.

The sales office, with its window full of bits of stained glass, antique tile and brass lamp fittings, is shut and dark when Gerry pulls up and parks in the Mariposa lot. Doc had a bit of luck finding a retired teacher and antique fan to run the retail end and answer the phones.

Next to the shop is Doc's front door, an oak and lead-glass monster with an arts-and-crafts knocker. Gerry knocks. There is a muffled clatter of feet on stairs and Doc welcomes him in.

"Young Gerald."

"Doctor. I do appreciate the place to crash. Here, a small token." Gerry has stopped off at the liquor store on his way from the hospital. He presents a bottle of something single-malt and obscure. "It's made by bi-sexual Hebridean trolls out of peat water run through a sheep dip on the Isle of Muck or somewhere. Enjoy!"

Later that evening, Gerry and Doc do their traditional Chinese meal at The Jade Gate, but it's a quiet meal.

Gerry is still running on Newfoundland time. He's wrung-out from a day of flying and hospital. Doc has spent a long day trying to make a Victorian working-class row house into what the new owners insist on calling a bijou town residence.

"It's a nice enough old house," he says. "It's between Elgin and the Driveway. Actually it was a co-op when we were in university. I remembered going to a party there when I saw it. Anyway, these people think because it was built in 1900, it's got to be fancy. She's telling me she wants wainscoting in the 'drawing room.' Whoever lived in this place originally probably drove a streetcar and called it the parlour. If the place ever had any wainscoting they probably burned it in the Depression. There's some genuine '60s psychedelic sunflowers on the back bedroom ceiling though."

Their favourite sore-footed, red-jacketed waiter brings the distinctive Jade Gate egg rolls, open at the ends and cauterized by the deep frying. This is what egg rolls were like when egg rolls were exotic. Gerry remembers eating them with Aunt Louise after being taken to a parade of streetcars. It was the last day of streetcars in Ottawa. The big red and buff cars, with big single headlamps, clanked and sparked past the corner of Sparks Street. A new diesel bus followed them.

"We were going to be modern," Gerry says. "We would ride diesel buses and eat exotic foods like egg rolls every day and Sparks Street was going to be a mall, whatever that was."

"So how's your mom?" Doc asks.

"Pretty scrambled. I don't think she knew I was there."

They order fewer dishes than they normally do and eat all of what they order. On this tired Friday evening it's as if some special discipline is in effect. Grown-up rules apply. They are back at Doc's by eleven.

"I'm going on a job early," he tells Gerry. "You've got a key. The place is yours. I'm going to bed."

Although he is tired, Gerry is not sleepy yet. He undresses and settles in his sleeping bag on the couch. A tensor-lamp throws a tight pool of light over him. He looks beyond it at Doc's world.

In a corner is the stuffed owl, a fixture in Doc's apartments and houses since university. The owl is wearing a pair of plastic safety glasses. Against a wall is the harmonium that Doc rebuilt with a vacuum-cleaner blower so you don't have to pump the pedals. Doc had once had piano lessons. Years ago, he could vamp out baroque-sounding tunes on the harmonium. Now it doesn't seem to have been played in a very long time. The cover is closed over the keyboard and a stuffed squirrel holding a cocktail umbrella sits on it. Gerry remembers the squirrel being there the last time he visited.

On a shelf is the anteater silhouette of the electric robot arm that Doc had bought for Timothy, his ex's, Hilary's, kid. The arm had been brand new in '86 when he was here to bury his father and get used to being split from Patricia. He remembers the three of them sitting at the kitchen table in another house, Doc and Hilary and Gerry. They drank beer and took turns playing with the arm after Timothy was in bed. They dumped a packet of seashell pasta on the table and had a contest to see who could pick up the most in a minute. Hilary had won. With the tip of her tongue between her teeth and her eyes squinted with concentration she had buzzed the pincer claw back and forth with unerring precision. Now the robot arm sat hunched and gathering dust.

Tomorrow I must call Duane and Gretchen, Gerry thinks. His musings about Doc's former family get him musing about his present one. Vivian, when she visited Doc with Gerry a couple of years back, found Doc's loft strange.

"That owl would give you the creeps," she said. "I wouldn't even want to touch it."

But is he any creepier than Duane and Gretchen? Gerry wonders. How does Melanie's Darren stack up against a stuffed squirrel with a parasol for general utility or artistic merit? How do we pick the tangents that define us, the stuff we choose to have hanging around or, at least, neglect to get rid of?

He puts out the light and is not conscious of having to wait for sleep.

Gerry is actually up and about when Doc goes out on Saturday morning. His Newfoundland internal clock wakes him before daylight. Twice he hears the clack and splat of Doc's newspapers coming through the mail slot downstairs. When Doc gets up for work, Gerry gets up too and makes a pot of coffee.

After Doc leaves, he sits at the computer on the desk and plays a Space Rocks game for an hour. He can't match even the lowest high scores that Doc has recorded, but the game is comfortingly cheesy. The asteroids you shoot at appear to be made of crumpled-up aluminium foil. The flying saucers and metallic mushrooms that are the enemy have the look of '50s kitchen utensils, shiny and bright, Corning Ware in space.

It's too early to phone Duane and Gretchen or his Aunt Carmen or anyone else in his sparse circle of family. He puts on a chunky pullover and a shell jacket and goes to a diner around the corner for breakfast.

An hour later, with eggs, sausages and the morning papers under his belt, Gerry returns to the loft and gets busy on the phone. He calls his Aunt Carmen first.

"I don't think I can get in to see her, Gerry. I'm just waiting here to see if I can get my other cataract done."

"That's okay, Aunt Carmen. There's nothing very much you can do. She didn't know me yesterday. I'll keep you posted."

He touches base with a handful of cousins he hasn't seen in years. They're all his age or slightly older, retired or close to it. He's strangely pleased that they all remember him, apparently kindly. They make practical offers of rides and meals. He explains that he has a car and is sticking close to the hospital. He decides his mother must have put out only the carefully edited version of his ups and downs over the years, or they were too busy with their own to notice. His presence now is accepted, whatever guilt he may feel about having kept his distance. Still, he feels warmed. It's like finding money in a pair of pants you haven't had on for a long time.

Duane and Gretchen are less warming, although he supposes they mean well.

"Mom called last night," Duane says. "Your mother's in our prayers. We'll be in."

Gerry wonders what they prayed for, what he'd pray for himself, if he prayed.

"That's fine, Duane. It's room thirty-twenty. That's the old building. I'll see you kids up there."

He returns to Space Rocks and drinks coffee and blasts asteroids until it is time to go to the hospital again.

To Gerry it seems to be a weather-less day, only temperature, no climate. He notices, as he has on other visits here, that he wants exercise, to move, to explore. He decides that the Somalis' parking lot will be blocked on a Saturday afternoon and that a walk would do him good. He trots downstairs to tell the retired teacher in Doc's shop that the car in her lot is his. Then he sets out in the general direction of the hospital, quartering along back streets and mentally giving the neighbourhoods he passes a beagle-like sniff.

He passes people raking their lawns and contemplating frost-softened pumpkins, past their best-before dates now, more than a week after Halloween. He walks through a neighbourhood of post-war veterans' bungalows. Some are now in their God-knows-how-many incarnation as somebody's first house. Others still sport the old, heavy aluminium doors with initials or deer or flying mallards that declare they're outposts, bunkers where the original inhabitants have held on and are making their retirement last stand. The air smells of damp earth and wet leaves. Broom rakes make an insect scratching on the pavement of driveways. Gerry is no great yard and garden man, but there seems to be a rightness to the careful tending to these small fall chores. He wonders if he turned off the outside tap at home so it won't freeze. He must ask Vivian when he calls.

Eventually, after zigzagging up quiet streets, he pops out on a parkway, in sight of the hospital and hugging the parkland edge of the experimental farm. He jogs across a busy intersection and passes by a statue of some early hospital benefactor, a mayor or councillor in a frock coat. Then he takes a deep breath of the fall air and goes into the hospital.

Because he has walked, Duane and Gretchen have arrived ahead of him. He hears Gretchen before he sees them. As he nears his mother's room he hears her strangely adolescent voice singing.

"Yes, we'll gather at the river, the beautiful, the beautiful river…" Gretchen sings. She's rocking to and fro in a chair with her eyes tightly shut. Duane is standing, also rocking, also with his eyes shut, a hand on the bed rail like a captain on his bridge in some heroic movie.

Oh shit, Gerry thinks. Oh sacred shit.

His mother is conscious but clearly confused. Her eyes are open, frightened, uncomprehending. Her mouth under the clear mask is a pained "O." Her breathing gurgles. The little mechanical wheel that massages her feeding tube hums quietly along with Gretchen.

Gretchen's voice isn't loud, but it is insistent. It wheedles its way into the hall. A nurse looks in quizzically but says nothing. In the bed diagonally across from his mother's, a huge old woman with a cavernous face gives a softly roaring grunt, in protest or accompaniment. Gerry can't tell which. She sounds like a distant lion cage at a zoo.

"Gretchen. Duane." He wills himself to speak softy, not to bark. He doesn't need this.

"…that flows by the throne of God." Gretchen brings herself to the end of her chorus before opening her eyes.

When the singing stops, Gerry's mother closes hers. Her breath rasps and the medical plumbing at the head of the bed bubbles.

Gretchen and Duane seem a bit put out at having been interrupted. Gerry concentrates on stroking them and defusing the prayer meeting.

"That's Gretchen and Duane, Mom," he says, squeezing the old lady's hand. "It's Vivian's boy Duane and his wife. That's who's singing for you. A nice old hymn, eh?"

After that, he keeps up relentless inquiries about Joshua and Natalie and Gretchen's horse. He blathers that his mother must meet them all when she's feeling better. Eventually he talks out the time they have to spend visiting the sick and walks them down the hall to the elevator, an arm around the shoulders of each. Gerry can't remember ever being in this pose before. It feels theatrical but theatrical seems to work for Duane and Gretchen.

"Call if anything changes."

"We're praying for her."

So you keep saying, Gerry thinks. For an easy passage, a miraculous recovery, for a few marbles left if she pulls through? What are we trying to accomplish here?

Gerry spends the rest of the afternoon just sitting with his mother. He holds her hand at times. At others, when she seems to doze, he just sits. At one point he pops down to the gift shop and gets himself a newspaper and starts the cryptic crossword but can't stay at it. Still, he feels at peace and finds it surprisingly easy to sit and be quiet. Even the laboured breathing seems bizarrely companionable.

Gerry remembers when his father died nearly twenty years ago. He hadn't felt that way then. Big ball of alcoholic empathy that he was, he couldn't handle anyone else's pain well. His father had lapsed into unconsciousness only a day or two after Gerry arrived home from Labrador. They'd spoken, but barely.

"How's that little wife of yours?"

"She's fine, Dad. She's getting things packed up in Labrador. She sends her best."

"She's a sweetheart. I don't know how you ever did so well for yourself."

Gerry has always been glad he didn't have to explain Patricia's going to the old man.

After that, he sweated through afternoons like this one he's having now. He remembers wondering if his father could possibly want to hang on. Should he press a pillow over that painful breathing?

In the end, the old man died in his sleep. The hospital called Gerry and his mother at home to tell them.

Perhaps it's because he went fairly quickly, he thinks. He was only in the hospital for about two weeks. Before that, he was pretty much the way he'd been for the last dozen years or so.

With the old man, there was never the endless slowing down of time that had come with his mother's departure to the retirement home. What bothered him about his father's death was the loss of contact. His mother and he have already dealt with that while she was in the home. While this sitting in the hospital is sad, it's got more life, more involvement, more struggle, than their last half dozen years. As a way to pass time together, this is far more real than the old photo album.

Gerry gives up on his visiting about six o'clock. In the late afternoon, a Doctor Khan, Dr. Huta's weekend replacement, drops in. She's a serious-looking woman with a *hijab* and, improbably, an East-London accent.

"Curry take-out in the Isle of Dogs," she tells Gerry when he asks. "I grew up over the shop. A real east-ender."

They walk together to the elevators.

"Do you see any improvement?" Gerry asks.

"On paper anyway, she's beating the pneumonia," Dr. Khan says, "We'll take some X-rays tomorrow. I don't see anything changing much tonight. Her vitals are pretty good."

Which means exactly what? Gerry thinks as he punches the endless calling card number and his home phone number into a pay-phone in the hospital basement. The answering machine starts to respond after four rings but Vivian cuts it off.

"I was in the basement," she says. "I've got all the boat stuff that just got dumped down there put away. How's your mother?"

"Not much change," Gerry says. "Duane and Gretchen were in for a bit. After that we just sat."

He decides not to tell her about Gretchen singing.

"So do you know when she'll get back to the home?"

"I don't know *if* she'll get back. I've got to talk to a woman from social services on Monday. The doctor says she's improving, but I don't think she knows me from Adam."

"It's hard," Vivian says.

"Sort of, but not really," Gerry says. "I mean, so far, I just sit and wait. I'll call you if anything changes."

He decides he sounds a little distant. Vivian's being supportive. He needs to add something.

"I miss you, kid."

"I miss you too. Call me."

Sunday morning is aimless. Gerry wakes up early again, still running on Newfoundland time. He's up, drinking coffee and playing Space Rocks when Doc gets up.

"What's your agenda like then?"

"Hurry up and wait, I guess," Gerry says. "I'll arse around until lunch and then go back to the hospital."

"I'm going over to Marion's," Doc says. "She has a garage-door opener she wants installed. I'll be over there for lunch." Marion is his younger sister. Up until a few years ago she'd been an actress. She was the voice of Granny Porcupine in the *Forest Families* cartoons. She was also the nosy neighbour in a successful series of toilet-cleaner ads. Then she split up with her husband and moved back to Ottawa with her daughter. She took a bunch of courses and does something with developmentally delayed adults now. Years ago, Gerry had impressed Tanya by telling her that he knew Granny Porcupine and the nosy toilet lady. Now he's intimidated by Marion's new usefulness and commitment. He remembers when she was eleven and he and Doc were sixteen and they had to sit home with her until Doc's parents came home from Friday night shopping.

Just before he met Patricia, he'd been surprised to meet her at a party, grown-up suddenly, with long legs, ankle-strap platform shoes and Sobranie Black Russian cigarettes in an old ivory holder.

"I had the biggest crush on you when I was a kid," she said. "I wrote *Mrs. Marion Adamson* in the back of my social studies book."

She left no doubt that she'd got over her infatuation.

They'd got re-acquainted when she came with Doc to have lunch with Vivian and Gerry, their last visit together. Gerry told her he'd been trading on having babysat Granny Porcupine.

"But everything changes, young rodent," she said, putting on Granny's voice and screwing up her face. "Sure as acorns, everything changes."

Gerry blows the morning away, eating at a diner and driving aimlessly around town. He heads in-town, to his old neighbourhood. He hasn't spent much time there since his mother moved into the home in what had once been the suburbs. He drives past his old house and notices that it's got a couple of pretentious urns on the front porch. The paint has been updated to a fashionable cheddar-cheese shade. The old greens, browns and riverboat whites have yielded to the yuppie palette. On previous visits, he has offered to take his mother by the house to see it. She wasn't interested.

"I've moved and I'm settled and that's all there is to it," she'd said, and apparently that was that.

The neighbourhood is full of four-way stop signs now and Gerry finds he drives through it not much quicker than he used to bicycle. He passes a horse chestnut tree, the ground under it littered with broken twigs and browning nut husks. A warning against climbing it had been read in his school when he was in third grade. He's pleased it's still attracting nut thieves fifty years on.

Gerry drives to the hospital at lunchtime and finds that parking is not a problem on a Sunday. The lot is full but parking meters along the street are not in service. He parks his rental and takes himself to lunch in the hospital cafeteria. He decides he's been overdoing The Jade Gate and diner breakfasts with home fries. He takes a bowl of soup, builds himself a salad plate and takes a pot of tea to a corner table. He has his Chinese notebook in his jacket pocket and pulls it out as he drinks his tea.

The young nurses are wolfing down poutine, he writes and runs dry. He goes back through the line for another pot of tea and takes a sticky cinnamon bun as well.

Upstairs on the ward, little seems to have changed since the day before. His mother has her eyes closed. Her breathing is noisy and laboured but regular. Her head is thrown back on the pillow. Her various support systems hum and gurgle.

Chairs are at a premium in the room today. In the night, another bed has acquired an occupant, a little stick-figure woman. A fat blonde woman in a lemon jogging suit is feeding her custard from a Tupperware container.

"Come on, Mom," she says, over and over.

A couple in matching green barn coats and Blundstone boots are visiting the big woman diagonally across the room. The man has grey, longish hair over his collar and heavy glasses. He says nothing. His wife has a scouring pad of grey curls and is upset with somebody.

"The least they could have done was call," she says at intervals. "It's not like they had to come."

The woman who was moaning the first day Gerry arrived is quiet today. He sees that she's the shrunken double of her visitor, an erect, white-haired little woman in a navy suit.

"My sister," she says, nodding politely to Gerry. "She had a stroke."

The visitors fill the room's ordinary chairs and a complicated reclining wheelchair which appears to belong to the big woman. Gerry, feeling spry and virtuous after his salad, hoists himself onto the broad, low windowsill and leans against the sash. He can reach his mother's hand on the bed. Her breath rasps regularly. Occasionally she twitches and mouths something like a distant shout.

"Hey," she breathes into the clear mask. "Hey."

The afternoon passes slowly. Gerry discovers yesterday's crossword in his jacket pocket and tackles it again.

In mid-afternoon, a couple of technicians wheel in an X-ray machine and he's sent out while they pull the curtains and position his mother for their shots. By the time they go, the rest of the visitors are starting to leave as well. Gerry now has a chair to himself.

Holding his mother's hand, he feels its chill. He remembers somebody saying an elderly relative's feet had been cold before he died. He reaches under the blankets and touches the dry, bony feet. They feel cold, but relative to what? He takes her hand again.

The window by the bed looks out across the fields of the experimental farm across the road. Gerry watches the sky get darker blue, and then redden as the shadows lengthen. In the angles of the old hospital building it is already dusk. The room has a deepening gold-red glow. He doesn't bother to turn on the light at the head of the bed. He sits and watches the dusk. He thinks that he'll have nothing to report to Vivian again tonight.

A sudden intake of his mother's breath surprises him. It's a gasp rather than the gurgle he's become accustomed to. He looks at his mother. Her eyes are open. Her head lifts from the pillow. Then she relaxes. The noise from the oxygen apparatus is gone. There is no movement of bedclothes.

Gerry places his knuckles to the side of her neck and feels nothing. He takes her wrist and feels for a pulse.

Fingers on the wrist and not the thumb, or you're taking your own pulse, he thinks, recalling some long-gone first-aid lecture. He feels nothing. He sits for a moment in the gathering twilight. He looks at the quiet forms in the other beds, gets slowly out of his chair and walks down the hall to the nursing station.

The male nurse he met on the first day is on duty when he goes to the desk. He's got his mauve sweater on. In the last day or so, Gerry has noticed that the sweater is there even when he's not. Gerry has seen it hung on the back of an ergonomic chair.

"Excuse me," Gerry says. "I think my mother has just died. She's Adamson, in thirty-twenty."

The nurse looks sceptical, as if amateurs might not know death when they see it. Still, he comes around the desk and follows him back to the room. He goes to the bed and places a hand on Gerry's mother's wrist.

"Mrs. Adamson," he says. Then, a little louder, he repeats, "Mrs. Adamson."

Gerry stands aside as the man plugs a stethoscope into his ears and moves it quickly from place to place, as though life might be hiding, playing hard to get. He gives a little sigh and straightens. His demeanour softens.

"Yes," he says. "I'm afraid you're right. She's gone. I'm very sorry."

"Thank you," Gerry says. His eyes are prickly and he feels his lip tremble. The nurse shakes his hand and then draws the curtains around their quarter of the room.

"Are you all right?" he asks. "It's always a shock, I know, even when it's expected. I know. My mom died two years ago. She was just seventy-five."

"No. No, I'm fine," Gerry says. He feels he's looking down from some vantage point on himself and the nurse having this conversation. "She was ninety-six. It's not unexpected."

The plump nurse is efficient. He explains how the body will be held and released to the undertaker. He says "funeral director."

"Do you want her rings?" he asks.

"The engagement ring, I guess," Gerry says. "I think we'll leave her wedding band with her."

"I think that's a nice idea," says the nurse and manages to get the engagement ring over the arthritic, swollen knuckle with less difficulty than Gerry would have imagined possible. He wraps the ring in tissue and tucks it in the pocket of his wallet where he normally stashes lottery tickets. The nurse assures him that the hospital will handle all the details and bustles away. Gerry stands alone inside the curtain by the bed for a minute. He finds he's holding his mother's hand again. He bends, kisses her forehead and goes down the hall and calls Vivian.

Vivian picks up on the second ring. "How are you?"

"Okay, I guess, sport, but the old lady's gone. She died about fifteen minutes ago. She just faded out with the sunset." Gerry's eyes prickle again. He hears a sniff from Vivian. Vivian is kind-hearted.

"I'm sorry, Gerry."

"I know, sport."

"So I guess I'd better come up," Vivian says. "I'll book tonight."

"Call Krista at the travel agent's. I told her you might need to travel in a hurry. She gave me her cell number. I left it on the pad on the fridge." Gerry is starting to feel efficient, glad to be doing something.

"Okay. I'll call you at Doc's later on and tell you how I get on," Viv says. "You're sure you're okay?"

"Yeah, kid, I'm fine. Call me later," Gerry says. "Love you."

Going down the elevator, Gerry feels strangely light-headed. He has rehearsed his mother's death in his head hundreds of times. He has braced himself on flights up from Newfoundland a couple of times for false alarms. The reality has been so much simpler than anything he'd imagined that he feels unreal, floating.

Shock, he thinks. Give warm sweet liquids. You're getting old. Go sit and have a cup of tea and make sure you're not going to have some kind of anxiety attack trying to drive.

He goes to the hospital cafeteria, buys a mug of tea and dumps two envelopes of sugar in it. He sits and drinks it, watching himself for shakes. Nothing happens. He wonders what should happen. A ninety-six-year epoch has passed. A chapter of his life, nearly sixty years long has closed. A guilty thought insinuates itself that he feels lighter, the way he used to when he left the retirement home at the end of a long visit. Whatever he does or doesn't do with his life now, there's one less person to answer to. He hikes his jacket collar up under his ears and walks briskly out of the hospital. He collects the rental car and drives slowly back to Doc's.

Mort is at Doc's when Gerry arrives. He and Doc are leaned back in overstuffed chairs, drinking Doc's homemade beer.

"How's the hospital?"

"It's all over. She just slipped away. I was sitting there and she just stopped."

"Oh shit, Gerry, I'm sorry," says Doc.

"Yeah. That's tough. Are you okay?"

"Yeah. I mean she just stopped. No fuss really. She wasn't a fussy sort of person, I guess. At least I was there. That's about all you can say."

"Yeah, that's something."

Mort and Doc sit and talk quietly while Gerry takes the phone to the table in the kitchen part of the loft. He's filled pages of his notebook with the family numbers. He sits down and starts punching numbers, passing the word.

Telling the bees, he thinks. I read somewhere that that's an old Irish custom. Go around to the hives and tell them so and so is gone. Hey bees, Katherine Florence Adamson is dead. She hated "Florence" or "Flo." She said it was a name for a cow. Dad always called her Kit.

It all takes a surprisingly short time. Some people volunteer to call other people. Some people aren't home and he leaves his short message on their answering machines. Duane and Gretchen are among the not-at-homes. They go to evening church. He calls his friend Bob, his mother's lawyer.

"Oh gosh, Gerry, that's a shame," Bob says. Bob is one of the very few people Gerry knows who say "gosh." "Land o' Goshen" floats into his head, but he can't remember if he ever heard anybody say it for real or if it came from a hillbilly movie. Bob says the paperwork should be straightforward. He'll get started on it. They agree to get together.

By eight o'clock he has finished. Vivian rings from St. John's to say she's booked a flight. She'll get in the next night about nine-thirty.

"I'm going to Toronto first and then coming back to Ottawa," she says. "Isn't that weird? They say it's an hour quicker than going by Halifax."

"The new geography," Gerry says. "I'll be there to meet you. I miss you."

He wonders as he says it if he's assuring her or himself. When he's away from Vivian, he finds he wants to call, but he's also guiltily glad to hang up.

When Gerry gets off the phone, he pours himself a mineral water and joins Doc and Mort.

"Is anybody hungry?" Doc asks.

Gerry realizes that he is…ravenously hungry. The hospital soup and salad didn't last. It seems days since he ate. He wonders if this is why some people binge-eat in times of stress.

Bullshit. I'm just hungry. Stop looking for symptoms.

They drive downtown to a pizza joint, legendary for the cheesiness of its pizzas. They wind up ordering a medium to back up their original large pizza. Doc complains about the general sleaziness of garage-door opener fittings. Mort provides amusing backroom political gossip. Gerry feeds his face and feels strangely light.

It's a crisp Monday morning and Gerry is busy on the phone again. He starts off with Bob. Bob is earning his money as family lawyer. He says he has the file on his desk when Gerry calls.

"It's just the way I remember it," Bob says. "Nothing complicated. You're the sole heir, so do what you like with the stuff in her room. Make any arrangements you want and send the bills to me."

"You guys have the deed for the cemetery plot?"

"Do I ever. It's a little leather-covered book that would cost you a small car to produce now. A family plot for eight in Cedar Glen Cemetery, sold to Samuel Donald Adamson in June 1935. That's your grandfather, right?"

"That's him. I never met him. He was the first tenant in '38."

"I bet those Cedar Glen guys thought they were smart, selling off un-farmable land as burial plots," Bob says. "God, if they'd held onto that land until the suburbs caught up in the '50s, they'd have made a killing. Can you imagine what that great big island of trees and dead people is worth now?"

"Anyway, we've got a spot on that island?"

"Damn right. I'll call and tell the funeral home to call Cedar Glen and they open the grave. We do it all the time. No sweat."

Gerry makes an appointment with the funeral home for that afternoon. He calls the nursing home and tells them his mother is dead. They say they'll lock the room until he and Vivian can come and sort things out.

"There's no rush. The rent is paid for a month."

Then he calls his usual time-warp motel to get a room for Vivian and him. He tells the clerk he'll check in around noon. He spends the rest of the morning doing his little bit of packing, drinking coffee and playing Space Rocks on Doc's computer. He finally manages a score that's recordable in the top ten. He checks into the motel at a quarter to twelve, dumps his luggage in the room and goes to a mall for lunch. The food court at this mall offers Greek. He dines on a kebab platter and watches people. He has his notebook out, partially to check his to-do list and partially to try to write something.

Everyone looks familiar, he writes. *But nobody is.*

Underhill Funeral Directors have been around as long as Gerry can remember.

Underhill, under valley, underground, let us bury you. Gerry remembers the jokes from public school. We're the last people to let you down. What we undertake we carry out. There was even a joke song: Under hill, under dale, we are happy when you're pale and the hearses go rolling along…

The funeral home looks much churchier than most churches do these days. It's grey stone with wrought-iron lanterns outside and high, arched windows with leaded glass. The chapel is 1920s Gothic. Only a discreet sign and the row of soberly painted garage doors for hearses and limousines betray that this is a business.

Gerry is met by an actual Underhill. He's the latest generation in the business, a man in his early thirties, with buzz-cut hair slightly at odds with the dark jacket, waistcoat and striped trousers. Underhill's is defiantly old-fashioned. His first name is Frank.

They sit in an office like a high-tech monk's cell while they work out the announcement. When it comes to the "leaving to mourn" part, Gerry realizes he's either going to have to do all sorts of homework or get his ducks in a row. They settle on him and Vivian "and family in St. John's," his Aunt Carmen "and husband Charles, Ottawa, and a large circle of relatives and friends." The hospital staff is remembered by ward number and there's a thank-you to the people at the nursing home.

Frank is good at what he does. He tells Gerry that Bob has been on the phone and the family plot is being opened. He calls the minister at the church that Gerry's mother hasn't attended in nearly two decades, sets a funeral date for the day after tomorrow and arranges a meeting for Gerry and the clergyman. They agree that Vivian will pick out clothes for his mother tomorrow and Gerry will drop them off. Then it's time to select a casket.

The display coffins are kept behind a locked door.

Do people steal them? Gerry wonders. Hey buddy, want a real deal on a hot box?

Frank stops him for a moment at the door.

"Some people find this upsetting."

"I'm fine," Gerry says. "It's really sort of looking at furniture, isn't it?"

Looking at furniture is exactly what it is and Gerry has never been very good at it. The selection ranges from a white pine box that reminds him of a magazine rack he made in seventh grade to shiny metal, mobster specials. Underhill's starchy *haute wasp-ness* slips in the casket department.

Gerry rules out the magazine rack and the godfather's mummy case.

"Something in dark wood, I think," he says.

Frank shows him a casket with interchangeable corners. They can be cherubs, flowers, or a variety of sporting images: curling brooms and fishing gear, ducks and pheasants.

"This is quite popular."

"She'd come up and choke me, Frank. Not her style, I'm afraid."

The boxes seem expensive but Gerry has a mildly drunken-sailor feeling that permits pissing money up the wall at a time like this; *within reason*. He finally settles on something that looks like it might have contained very large duelling pistols in some more fastidious age of giants. Frank makes approving noises.

"That's the 'Unknown Soldier,'" he says. Incredibly, in an alcove, there is a poster-size picture of a box like the one Gerry has picked, carried by French soldiers in kepis at some sort of re-interment.

Gerry doesn't know how the "Unknown Mother" might go over with his mother, but he thinks he remembers the coffin she picked for his father being like this one. He was drinking then, of course. He doesn't feel he can ask Frank if Underhill's has any record of what they buried the old man in.

Gerry is at the airport early for Vivian's flight. He has a need for neutral, anonymous space and the arrival hall provides it. He buys the day's newspapers and an over-priced sandwich-in-a-croissant and a coffee. He and Vivian will have something to eat later. The snack-bar is on the second floor of the terminal. He sits at a table looking down into the arrival hall, reads the papers and fiddles with the crossword puzzles. There seem to be surprisingly few arrivals. Either it's a slow time of evening for flights or the new air terminal is big enough to disperse a planeload of people and make them look sparse and insignificant. He watches Vivian's flight number slowly flicker its way to the top of the screen.

Vivian's flight via Toronto and one from somewhere in the Arctic arrive at the same time. She comes through the arrivals gate with a mixed bag of travellers. Some are in business suits, some in down parkas and improbable cowboy hats. Vivian wears her leather coat and has a self-sufficient air. Gerry feels he's seeing her for the first time. It hits him that he wants her, physically. Three days of dying and death have made him feel vibrantly alive.

This is why people are horny in wartime, he thinks. Ha ha, you missed me! The bells of hell go dingaling-aling, for you, but not for me...

He waves to Vivian and weaves through the small crowd to hug her.

It is the wrong side of midnight and Gerry and Vivian are sprawled naked in the teenager's-bedroom tangle of their motel room. The newness of place and oddness of circumstances seem to have worked for them. The room is lit only with the flicker of the TV with the sound turned to nothing. The baseboard heating hums and ticks and the room is warm. It smells funky with the scents of the love-making that ambushed them almost as soon as they walked in the door. It smells of Vivian's perfume and a medium vegetarian Greek pizza. The pizza box sits on a chair by the bed.

Vivian sits up and pours herself a glass of wine from the bottle on the night table. Gerry had picked it up that afternoon to welcome her. Her outline is indistinct in the TV lighting as she rolls on her side, glass in one hand, the other touching gingerly between her legs.

"Jesus, honey, I guess we needed that."

Gerry is drinking diet pop, delivered with the pizza. "I know I bloody did."

"Like a couple of kids," Viv says. "You don't suppose we're getting too old for this stuff?"

Gerry's hand covers her exploring one. "Doesn't feel like it at the moment, does it?"

"Get me some Kleenex. Is there any more pizza left? Now I'm starved."

"There's two chunks, a slice each, unless you want to save it for breakfast."

Later still, they lie with the light out, separate but holding hands. They're flat on their backs talking to the invisible ceiling.

"I brought your blue suit and a couple of white shirts. I put in your new black shoes,"Vivian says. There's a silence. "How are you doing?"

"Not bad, really. It's funny. You build it up in your mind and then it's just over."

"It wasn't like that with Dad,"Viv says. "He dropped down dead in the kitchen. That was a shock."

The room is very dark. It has heavy drapes to keep the parking lot lights out. Gerry rolls closer to Viv.

"You aren't still horny?"

"What can I say? Coffins and naked women rubbing themselves with pizza turn me on. Nothing odd about Adamson."

"Come here then,"Vivian says with vast patience.

She rises sleepily and invisibly around him like a tide of warm darkness, and after they've gasped and shuddered, they roll to the side and fall asleep apart.

The next morning, Gerry and Vivian are at the retirement home bright and early. Pale sun streams through bare November tree-branches outside the window as they rummage through drawers. In the home's garden below the window, black squirrels are busy. They importune residents seeking the last fall rays for food and they scrabble in flowerbeds for bulbs.

Vivian watches them from the window. Newfoundlander that she is, squirrels still have novelty value for her. For Gerry they're more nostalgia from childhood. He also knows that squirrels can be obnoxious as well as cute.

"Remember Tanya feeding the squirrels the first summer we came up here?"Vivian asks. Then she goes back to finding the right clothes for the funeral home. She purses her lips, discovering screw-ups in laundry that have been made over the years. She holds up a cotton nightgown with a teddy bear on it. "Where do you suppose that came from? It's nothing your mother ever wore."

"You never know," Gerry says. "Maybe she was a closet Care Bears fanatic."

Vivian finds the dress she says Gerry's mother told her she wanted to be buried in. Gerry drives downtown with it, to drop it off at Underhill's. He asks after a florist his parents and aunts had done business with. Frank Underhill looks blank.

"They've been closed for years," an assistant, a woman about Gerry's age, says.

Gerry thanks her. Then he gets the name of a reliable florist and orders flowers, and drives to his appointment with the minister.

The minister's name is Dr. Wallace and his office is in the basement of a church hall that Gerry still thinks of as new. It was opened the year he left the Cub Scouts. The corridor walls are covered with artwork from the daycare that inhabits a corner of the basement and rainbow emblems from the gay reading group that meets Tuesday nights. The smell, however, is familiar: a mixture of floor polish, children and dusty hymn books.

Dr. Wallace is a small, white-haired man with a ruddy face. Gerry thinks he would look at home coxing a rowing crew. His office is hung with pictures of grandchildren. There is a lumpy hand-thrown jug full of pens on the desk. It's painted in green and yellow stripes and inscribed *Grampy*. Dr. Wallace's tear-drop bicycle helmet hangs on the back of the door, and a corner of the bookshelf has back issues of *Mountain Bike* and some frayed Agatha Christies.

The minister shakes Gerry's hand and gets him a cup of very indifferent coffee. Then they sit, neither rushing to fill the silence. Gerry decides to speak first. "It must be difficult, being asked to sort of jump in here when we haven't been in touch with the church much."

"Not as much as you'd think," Wallace says. "My secretary, Mrs. Whillans, knew your mother quite well in the UCW years ago, and I've been to see Kit a couple of times."

"I'm glad you've got the name right," Gerry says, impressed. "I don't think one of your predecessors had ever met Dad when he buried him. His name was the same as mine, Gerald Edward, but everyone called him Ed, never Gerald. The poor minister never asked and we didn't think to tell him. He kept referring to him as Gerald."

"It happens," Dr. Wallace says.

In the course of half an hour, they decide that short, simple and traditional is what's called for.

"Would you like a hymn?" the minister asks as though he's offering after-dinner liqueurs. "Underhill's has quite a good little organ."

"Can we sort of pencil it in?" Gerry asks. "Mom was awfully old and the notice is only in the paper today. We may only get a handful of family. If it's you and me in duet, we might scrub around it."

"Oh, I don't mind singing," Dr. Wallace says. He seems to imply that he's been asked to do worse.

They settle on the "Twenty-Third Psalm" as very suitable. It's just as well, because Gerry can't think of many other hymn titles.

"If we've got the numbers," Dr. Wallace says, showing him out and shaking hands again. "I'll see you tomorrow a little before two."

When Gerry gets back to the retirement home Vivian has been busy. She's given away garbage bags of clothes to the home. Through Lawyer Bob, she's called a rep from a moving company for a quote on shipping the few good bits of furniture. The room is dotted with piles of stuff with sticky notes saying "ship."

The home sends up a plate of sandwiches and a pot of coffee. "Her board was paid for," says the girl who brings it.

When Gerry and Vivian go back to the motel that evening, there is a message from Duane and Gretchen.

"You don't want to see the kids tonight, do you?" Viv asks. "This is about you, this trip."

"I don't mind," Gerry says.

"We'll call them later," Vivian says. "We'll see them tomorrow anyway. I'll call after we have dinner. We'll say we came in late."

That's what they do, pleading non-existent get-togethers with long-lost Adamson relatives. In fact they go to a cozy Italian restaurant and are tucked up in bed watching a rerun of *A Night to Remember* on TV when Viv finally does call.

They fall asleep before the lovable old couple decided to stay together and drown and the ship's orchestra plays "Nearer My God to Thee."

Gerry wakes early on the day of the funeral. Vivian hardly stirs as he gets up, showers and dresses.

"I'm going out for a bit," he says. "I'll bring you a coffee when I come back."

Gerry steps out into the frosted parking lot. The motel has buildings down both sides of its parking lot. The shadows are still long on his side and the frost on the cars is heavy. However, across the lot, a golden light is working its way down the walls and across the pavement as the sun gets higher. Gerry breathes deeply, feeling the cold air in his nose.

A good day to be alive, he thinks, on this funeral day.

Gerry takes himself for a walk the way he'd walk a senile but sedate dog. He cuts out the back exit of the motel lot and wanders in residential streets, following his nose. Each intersection is a mental toss of the coin to pick the direction. The neighbourhood he walks through is brick and stone with big trees. It seems to be settling into the ground, like logs and stones into moss. Gerry realizes he misses the brazen clapboard of Newfoundland, ducked-down in the valleys or daring the wind to knock it into the sea or blow it across the bogs and barrens.

Gerry makes a zigzag progress in a big loop and eventually finds himself in a strip mall just down the street from the motel. He finds a barber shop open early and pops in for a trim. The shop is called Vito's. According to the name on his smock, the barber who cuts Gerry's hair is Vito himself. There is another barber in the shop, and he and Vito bicker like an old couple. Gerry gathers that the other barber is Vito's brother-in-law. He is reminded of his regular barber shop in the mall at home. The walls are covered with pictures of soccer teams and Grand Prix racing cars.

"Is there going to be any hockey or what?" Vito asks.

"I don't know. Are they even talking?" Gerry doesn't follow hockey but apparently he doesn't need to. Vito simply pulls isolated questions off the front page of the paper. It's like striking single notes of a xylophone.

"How about that fire in Vanier?"

With his hair cut and beard trimmed, Gerry drops into a doughnut shop next door to Vito's. It's a non-chain doughnut shop, an independent with some variety in its coffee. Gerry buys a French roast and a croissant. Spreading butter and jam on the croissant, he's surprised at how composed he feels. He feels benign, ready to be pleased by little things like strawberry jam. He orders a second croissant and takes Vivian a couple of cranberry muffins and a coffee when he returns to the motel.

The funeral is set for two o'clock and Gerry has arranged for only an hour of what Underhill's calls "visitation." Gerry and Vivian get dressed and meet Duane, Gretchen and the kids at a nearby mall where Gerry has spotted a restaurant with a lunchtime salad bar.

"They can graze," Gerry tells Viv, as they dress in their room.

"So should we," Viv says. "Pizza and muffins! This skirt is bar-tight."

They fill a corner booth in the restaurant which is big and bland.

A "family" restaurant, Gerry thinks. Well, for what it's worth, we're a family. That's why we're here.

Vivian makes a fuss over Joshua and Natalie while Duane and Gretchen commiserate with Gerry. "We're very sorry about your mom," Duane says, shaking Gerry's hand. "She's in a better place."

Gretchen just mutely hugs him with a slightly noble air, as though she's curing a leper by the laying-on of hands. She seems sadder than is appropriate for the funeral of a woman she barely knew.

At least she's not singing, Gerry thinks. Mute grief is okay.

Vivian announces she's going to do the salad bar and sweeps the kids ahead of her.

Gerry orders a club sandwich. When he's been on the road, working, he has always said that the club sandwich is the ultimate food refuge. When you can't face any more restaurant selections, the club has a taste of homemade. He's usually found that he shifts to the club-sandwich diet after about two weeks of travel. It hits him that it feels like a long time since he left St. John's.

The hour of "visitation" at Underhill's strikes Gerry as being like the beginning of some politically incorrect joke where half a dozen stereo-types have an unlikely encounter in a bar or lifeboat or public washroom: A Scotsman and a rabbi and a kangaroo go into this Turkish bath...

People from various compartments of his life gather in the dim, flower-scented room and Gerry trots about introducing them.

His Aunt Carmen is there, slim, white-haired and wearing a dark blue suit and small, neat hat. She carries a cane now, the thin metallic kind that drugstores sell. She wears thick glasses and leans on the arm of her husband, Gerry's Uncle Charles, a tall, slightly stooped man in a blue blazer. They're in their eighties now. Gerry remembers his father always referred to them as "the kids."

There are half a dozen cousins and spouses. He's kept track of some, but with others, he tries to match the solemnly smiling, almost shy faces with wedding groups from forty years ago.

Doc and Mort arrive together. Doc wears a thick tweed jacket and a tie with khaki pants and scuffed suede shoes. Mort runs to a black suit and narrow, shiny shoes. A few minutes later they are joined by Lawyer Bob and his wife Mavis. They greet Gerry and Vivian and the kids, then work the room, nodding, shaking hands and taking unofficial charge of Aunt Carmen and Uncle George. In his estate-law practice, Bob must get to a lot of funerals. Gerry is silently grateful as Bob and Mavis help stir the mix.

There are a few elderly former neighbours and some oddities. A former hair-dresser rolls in on an electric invalid scooter, accompanied by her granddaughter who drove her to the funeral.

"Your mother was always one of my regulars," she says. "She always took care of herself."

The widow of Gerry's former scoutmaster appears. She was in his mother's church group.

"We always did the scout father-and-son banquets together," she tells Vivian. Fifty years ago she'd lived down the street from Bob's parents. Bob greets her, and he and Mavis add her to their little herd of elderly guests who'd rather be sitting down.

Gerry and Vivian move from cluster to cluster of guests, occasionally keeping tabs on Gretchen and Duane. They seem a bit distant, put-off by the funeral being held in Underhill's chapel rather than a church.

Gerry finds himself seething that they are looking askance at what passes for reverence in his generation. Shag ya! he thinks. Drive into a pole going home and I'll rent a gay disco to wake you in.

Finally, Frank Underhill and Dr. Wallace appear.

"We ought to be going in now."

An organist is playing behind a carved screen as they move across a hall and into the chapel. It doesn't sound electric. Dr. Wallace was right. Underhill's organ is good.

Dr. Wallace is good himself. He tells the congregation to sit and takes them through the order of service like someone quieting a large animal. Sometimes he speaks softly and intimately. Other times he seems to thump chummily on some collective back, talking about Gerry's mother. He calls her "Kit" when he talks about her.

Listening to him, Gerry realizes that the little minister had read his silences well yesterday. The reporter in him warms to the job of interviewing Wallace had done with him.

Dr. Wallace looks at them confidingly. "I asked Gerry yesterday if he thought we should sing a hymn. He said yes, if we had enough people. I think we've got enough, don't you, Gerry?" Gerry nods. They do have the numbers and the Underhill's businesslike organist carries them along.

"The Lord's my shepherd…"

To the other side of Vivian he hears Gretchen slip half a beat out in front, used to bouncier church music than the Presbyterian rumble that Gerry grew up with.

"In pastures green, he leadeth me, the quiet waters by…"

From a couple of rows back, Gerry thinks he can hear Mort and Doc. They used to sing this psalm, drunk, rolling home from Hull in Doc's father's car.

"…and my cup o-o-overflows."

The hymn rolls to its end. The "amen" is pronounced the way Gerry remembers it from childhood church services. It's a drawn out mooing, almost plaintive *aw-men*, not *eh-men*.

Aw shucks, aw heck, aw-men, Gerry thinks. Beside him, Vivian sniffs. He looks at her and squeezes her hand and she smiles tightly. Then Dr. Wallace is standing in the aisle by the head of the casket. His arm is raised in benediction. The service is over. Duane and Gretchen look as if they want to complain about being short-changed.

"Ten minutes," Vivian says. "That's long enough."

Gerry is nervous driving behind the hearse to Cedar Glen Cemetery. He's afraid if he gets separated in traffic he won't be able to find the cemetery. The old roads that he remembers leading to it are submerged in new six-lanes. He vaguely recalls that you used to turn left at a frozen custard stand and go on past a big white barn, the first sign of the country on that edge of town.

The hearse has a flashing purple light that gives it a sort of U.F.O. air. Gerry hugs its bumper as they drive the slow lane of the Queensway. They get off the divided highway and onto smaller streets. He heaves a sigh of relief as they slide through on the yellow light at an intersection, sticking together.

Cedar Glen Cemetery does, in fact, have cedars. Gerry and Vivian drive slowly through dark clumps of them, interspersed with autumn-gaunt hardwoods on cemetery roads that regress from pavement to grass and gravel ruts like a country lane. The heater has been on in the car. Now Gerry finds he's too warm and rolls down the window. There's a country smell of wet leaves. They go to an old part of the cemetery. Most of these plots with their heavy, respectable monuments were filled long ago and haven't been touched in years. Ornamental planting has overgrown and softened the lines of obelisks and fat granite and marble dominoes. This section has a settled, natural look, with the stones seeming to emerge like some geological outcropping.

"This is beautiful," Vivian says. "It looks so old."

The mourners have thinned out here in the cemetery. Most of the frail elderly and the car-less have skipped the long haul to shiver on the edge of town in a fall afternoon. Cars crunch to a stop on the gravel path. Bob and Mavis, Doc and Mort have come. The rest are family. Cousins and their spouses get out of warm cars, button their coats and pick their way across the damp grass.

One is Barbara, the daughter of Gerry's Aunt Carmen. She's a slim, blonde woman who, Gerry figures, must be sixty-one or -two. He remembers when she was a cheerleader for one of the new high schools on the edge of town. She'd have been in her last year of high school and Gerry was in tenth grade. Barbara comes up and puts a hand on his sleeve.

"Mom and Dad have gone to my place," she says. "It's too cold for her, and, with her eyes, she's scared of walking on uneven ground."

"I'm just glad she could get to the funeral," Gerry says. "I know she's waiting to go in for treatment."

"Look," Barbara says. "I want you guys to come over to our place after. We never see you. I think you were only to the house once with your mom."

"If you're sure it's no trouble, Barb," Gerry says. Barbara pats his arm and goes off to invite other people.

Underhill's has made a slight professional miscalculation. When Gerry made the funeral arrangements, he was unsure how many healthy family members he could muster to be pallbearers. He asked Frank Underhill to provide some. Frank produced four nondescript but respectable-looking, elderly, middle-aged men, and at the funeral home, with the coffin on a trolley, they had performed fine. Now, however, they're finding the walk from the hearse to the grave heavy going.

"That little fat fellow's going to have a heart attack," Vivian says.

Barbara's husband Peter and a couple of other male cousins seem to agree. They and Gerry edge the suffering pallbearer aside and take the handles of the casket alongside the other Underhill bearers. They carry the casket to where Dr. Wallace waits by the open grave.

Gerry hears but doesn't hear the words of the committal. He hears crows, calling to each other from somewhere in the Cedar Glen cedars. He smells the damp earth and the nearby presence of the cedars. He's trying to recall the last thing he said to his mother that she might have understood. If he doesn't count having to explain Gretchen and Duane crooning at her bedside, he has to go back to short, wandering phone calls that had become shorter and more wandering in the past few weeks. If he doesn't count phone calls, he's back to his last words of his visit last winter, when she got confused and thought she was going with him.

No dear, you're staying here, Gerry thinks. That's the last thing I said. *You're staying here.* The last thing we can say to anybody or, possibly, they to us.

The crows yell in the cedars. Far off, behind the trees, the start of the rush-hour traffic growls softly.

Cousin Barbara and her husband Peter live in a tidy subdivision where every other street manages to be a cul-de-sac. Barbara has circulated among the dozen or so people who came to the cemetery and asked all of them. Mort leaves Doc to get there on his own and rides with Gerry and Vivian to give directions.

Barbara's daughter Helen is there when they all arrive. She tells Gerry and Vivian that she and her husband live just a few blocks away. She's dropped over to look after Aunt Carmen and Uncle Charles and put a couple of casseroles in the oven.

"I guess we're…what? Second cousins?"

"Close enough, I guess. I always get confused."

Vivian takes charge of Duane and Gretchen and herds them around. First they gravitate to Aunt Carmen and Uncle Charles. They feel Aunt Carmen is arguably the saddest person in the room, since Gerry seems far-too-much himself. However, she's not sad enough for them either.

"Peter," Aunt Carmen says to her son-in-law. "I found that chapel chilly. I don't know how you people stood being out in the cemetery. I'm still cold. Do you think you could find a nice little drink of rye for an old lady?"

Gretchen and Duane fidget. Helen takes the kids to the den and turns on the TV for them but Gretchen keeps popping in to see what's on. They hang around for half an hour and accept cups of tea, but then they plead horse-feeding as an excuse and leave. Vivian fusses over Joshua and Natalie on the way to the door.

"The poor children," she says when they've gone. "That Gretchen has about as much life in her as I don't know what and Duane's not much better, God help us. It must be Jack's side of the family. My crowd were easy-come-easy-go."

Gerry circulates, catching up on cousins.

They're cousins, but they look like uncles, he thinks. He sees his mother's dead brothers in a couple of chunky men in dark suits, the sons, who are now the age their fathers were when Gerry left home.

Some female cousins seem to have married clones of their brothers, fathers and uncles. In the kitchen, a cousin's husband reaches for the mineral water at the same time Gerry does.

"You're a friend of Bill Wilson's too, Gerry?" the man says, using the AA catch phrase. "I think Barbara told me. You mentioned you were on the wagon when you brought your mother to see her, a couple of years ago."

And I thought I was the only one in the family, Gerry thinks. He chats with the man and his wife. He catches up on kids, grandkids, a couple of divorces and a remarriage or two.

Nearby, Doc has found he does business with another of Gerry's cousins in the hardware trade. Rob knows another from the Masons, and his wife Mavis is talking fabrics to a knot of wives.

Barbara is explaining to Vivian how Gerry is considered the exotic member of the family. "He's got a real Newfoundland accent," Barbara says.

"I don't know about that," Vivian says. "He doesn't sound like where I come from. A bit townie, maybe."

In a family room off the kitchen, Barbara's husband Peter is showing Mort the player piano that came from the original family farm. "I did the restoration myself," Peter says. "It took me two years. I got a whole bunch of rolls on E-Bay."

It's early, still before six, when everyone is surprised to find they're hungry. "You'd think we'd had to dig the grave or something," Barbara says to Vivian.

The Ottawa cousins are used to each other's company. They fall easily into a buffet line and even know what cupboards to look in for glasses or serving spoons. They absorb Vivian and Gerry and his friends into their groups at the kitchen table, the dining table or at coffee tables in the living and family rooms.

After supper, Peter pumps the player piano. He gamely pedals through "Ride of the Valkyries."

"That's worse than riding the bike," he says. Others volunteer to pump and they run through Peter's collection of rolls, singing along with the ones they know. Bob's English wife Mavis brings the house down with "Bird in a Gilded Cage." Gerry gets a round of applause for "When You and I Were Young Maggie."

Vivian volunteers to pedal for "Till We Meet Again."

"Don Messer," somebody says. "Smile the while you kiss me, sad adieu…"

"Kit used to get such a laugh out of your Uncle Cyril about that song," Aunt Carmen tells Gerry. "He used to think the girl's name was Saddy Doo. 'What kind of name is Saddy Doo?' he'd say."

Gerry and Vivian stay and chat with Barbara and Peter for a while after the crowd thins out. It's quite late when they drive back to their motel.

"I'm glad we were with people after the funeral," Vivian says. "It's nice to get to know your family after all these years."

"For me too," Gerry says. "Some of those people I haven't seen since before Pat and I were married."

"It's a good thing you saw them. You won't be back here much anymore, I guess, not regularly anyway."

"Smile the while you kiss me, Saddy Doo," Gerry sings softly, as they pull into the motel parking lot.

fifteen

NOVEMBER 2004

It is not quite eight in the morning, two days after the funeral, and Gerry is juggling two big paper cups of coffee outside the door of the motel room. He sets them on the frosty bonnet of his rented car and digs in his pockets for the key. A clipped-looking older man with two small dogs on leashes comes out of the next room.

"How do you like the small Pontiac?"

Gerry hadn't really been aware he had a Pontiac. "Fine, I guess. I've only had it a week. It's a rental."

The clipped man looks at Gerry as if there's something immoral about rented cars. Perhaps Vivian isn't his real wife either. He loads the dogs into the back seat of a very clean car with a Canadian Legion decal on the back. The dogs have a folded blanket to sit on.

"White schnauzers," he says. "They're rare."

"Nice dogs," Gerry says non-commitally. The white schnauzers watch him out the back window. They seem pre-occupied with schnauzer thoughts and a sense of their own rareness and superiority. They remind him of two elderly, diminutive, twin bachelor brothers who were both elders at the church Gerry and his parents went to when he was about ten. They monopolized a vestry committee meeting over a suggestion to omit the confession of sin from some services. They were against the idea.

"Opinionated little runts," said Gerry's father.

"They're old and they're lonely," his mother had said.

Gerry finds his key and takes Vivian her coffee.

They spend their final morning doing last-minute errands. Gerry drops Viv at the retirement home to pack anything she doesn't want shipped by the movers. He drives downtown to drop off undertaker paperwork and spends an hour signing papers for Bob.

When they are done, Bob picks up Vivian's theme from the night of the funeral. "I hope you'll get back sometime, guy. It's always great to see you and Vivian."

"Yeah, I'm sure we'll keep in touch. I don't say we'll be up as often, but it wouldn't kill some of you guys to take a trip east sometime." Gerry wonders what he means when he says this. He's asked his friends many times over the years. Doc drove down in 1974, for his and Patricia's wedding. Mort had spent a night with them once, during the Joe Clark election in '79. Mostly though, the distance seems too much. He wonders how much he'll miss coming here. He and Bob shake hands.

"Take care, guy,"

"You too, buddy."

When Gerry gets to the retirement home, Vivian is waiting for him. She's got a suitcase of his mother's packed. It's a small suitcase that reminds Gerry of old newsreels of British kids being evacuated from London.

"You need a gas-mask bag and a name-tag," he says.

Vivian is looking at the photo album that he and his mother passed the time with on his last visit.

"I'm taking this," she says. "I'll put it in the desk and the movers can ship it. I called the kids and said goodbye and I called the phone company. They'll cut the phone this afternoon, tomorrow morning at the latest."

They take the room keys to the desk then and say their thank-you's to the staff. Vivian leaves contact names and numbers with the movers. Gerry punches the code on the elevator buttons that prevents residents on this floor from wandering off. It's the street number of the home reversed. The elevator is crowded with old people with walkers. It's after eleven-thirty and the slow-motion rush to early lunch has begun.

A few minutes later, they have driven down the street to their motel and tossed their bags aboard the rental car. Gerry takes the key to the office while Vivian waits in the car. He's been coming to this motel for ten years, since his mother moved into the home. He feels he knows the weedy-looking clerk, who, he gathers, is a ne'er-do-well member of the family that owns the place. Still, he supposes that in ten years he hasn't spent more than twenty minutes in this lobby.

It took that little to make it familiar, Gerry thinks. Now it's going to become unfamiliar even quicker.

A computer printer stutters out his bill, completing the process. Already he feels the motel fading around him.

Gerry and Vivian find themselves in early afternoon limbo. They have done everything they had to and their plane doesn't leave until nearly six. Between motel check-out and airport check-in, Gerry feels they're in a backwater of time, circling just out of the current.

They conceive a sudden nostalgic fondness for the Italian restaurant they went to a couple of nights before and go there for a leisurely lunch. In the shrunken universe they inhabit this afternoon, it's become one of their places. They eat for amusement, making an idiosyncratic meal of several kinds of antipasti and salads. Vivian has a couple of glasses of the house white while Gerry drinks San Pellegrino. He talks her into a crème brulée for dessert, and after a couple of cups of coffee they feel they need a walk.

Gerry chooses an Aunt Louise place for their walk, the arboretum of the experimental farm. They park the car at a look-out that gives them a view of ornamental streams wandering from the canal under bridges and through willow trees reduced to pale pencil sketches by their fall nakedness.

"We used to hike around here on Sunday mornings," Gerry says. "She'd take the other aunts to church and then pop up here for a little pagan fresh air."

"Let's walk," Viv says. "I ate too much."

They have the big park pretty much to themselves on a cool, sunny Friday afternoon. A few joggers and dog walkers pass them by, but for most of their ramble, they're by themselves. There's frost in the ground and the puddles are still skinned with ice although it's late afternoon. They walk along the canal for a way. It's been drained to a narrow stream at the bottom of its bed, just enough water for its winter tourist role as "the world's longest rink." They come to a set of locks. Across the canal is the university Gerry went to.

"God, it seems huge," Gerry says. "None of those office towers were built when I was here. It was just the quad there and a couple of buildings on the back and the residences along the driveway."

"Let's go across and look," Viv says. "I need to pee. I shouldn't have drunk all that coffee."

One set of lock gates is kept permanently shut to make a footbridge across the canal. The gate top is wider than the others and has double handrails. Gerry and Vivian hustle across like exploring children. They scamper across the driveway, hand-in-hand, and go in a side door to the basement of the student union building.

"Relief is on the way," Gerry says, pointing to a set of male and female signs with arrows. "The sign of the canny middle-aged traveller, the ability to find the loo anywhere."

"I'll see you in a minute," Vivian says.

"Me too," says Gerry.

They re-unite outside the washrooms and do a prowl around the older parts of the campus. Gerry discovers the geography of the university he knew thirty years ago, like a vestigial organ in the body of the present-day version. Mostly new has been piled on top of old, so by following the tunnel system, he can recreate his world of the late '60s.

"This was Juvenile Junction, sort of a speakers' corner and general hang-out. The Tunnel Rat's snack bar was down there."

"I was married when you were here," Vivian says, "married and expecting Duane. Jack was supposed to be working in Labrador City and quit because he said he had an ulcer."

"The year I got here, everybody was getting right into Tolkien," Gerry says. "Personally I always sort of cheered for the Orcs. I got tired of all the amazing escapes and wanted somebody to eat the damned hobbits. Anyway, there used to be some really good runes in Elvish painted on the tunnel walls over the stairs down here."

"When I think of all the stuff I missed," Vivian says, "I get so damned poisoned. Get a job or get married. That's what we were told. We didn't know any better. I should have been here too."

"And you'd be somebody else I've forgotten about or only run into now and then," Gerry says. He takes her hand. "I guess we had to go our own ways to run into each other."

They leave the university the way they came in, by a door close to the canal. A couple of girls waiting for rides by the door nudge each other at the middle-aged couple holding hands.

"They probably think we're profs, married to other people, having a little on-the-job affair," Gerry says.

They're still holding hands when they've walked back across the locks and the arboretum footbridges and climbed the hill to the look-out and their car. The afternoon shadows are getting longer and the sky turns shades of denim. A striped hot-air balloon floats over the Friday traffic as they drive to the airport to catch their flight to St. John's.

Gerry and Vivian check in at the Ottawa airport.

"Adamson, Vivian and Gerald," Gerry says, presenting the tickets and his wallet, open to his driver's licence. "Going to St. John's... Three bags to check and we'll carry the little ones."

Vivian leans around him to show her driver's licence too. They have travelled a lot together. They perform the check-in rituals unhurriedly, but deftly, dancing around each other, playing to each other, but contained, like old vaudevillians reprising the routine that made them famous. Gerry swings the heavy bags onto the scale. Vivian gathers the shoulder bags for quick redistribution. Gerry wonders how the counter girl likes their performance. He thinks they'll remind her of somebody in an English movie she saw on a late show. They still dress up a bit to travel.

"Gate twenty-eight. You can go right through."

Gerry is glad to be rid of the big bags. They were heavy. They both had suits for the funeral and Vivian had his mother's suitcase with stuff she was afraid to leave for the movers.

"Feels good to get rid of that load," Gerry says. Their talk is the smallest kind of small talk. It hits Gerry that it has been for days, a Popeye and Olive nattering that gets them around the big stuff. "Thank God you couldn't get anything else in the damn bag."

"It's just jewellery and little stuff," Vivian says. "Things that would get broken or lost."

"I never realized the Adamson family jewels were so heavy," Gerry says.

They find their gate and sit on slinky aluminium and leatherette benches waiting to board. The walls of the waiting area are floor-to-ceiling glass. They can see right across the airport in the late afternoon sun. Far off, towards a backwater corner of the airport, the hot-air balloon they'd seen as they drove to the terminal is slowly descending. It seems to have followed them in its aimlessly majestic way. The gas bag is striped and imprinted with the sign of a big real estate chain.

"Look, there's the balloon again," Vivian says. "It looks like a big Christmas tree ornament."

"Check the tickets," Gerry says. "With the bargain bookings and all the last-minute running around, that could be our flight."

They lose sight of the balloon as it drifts downward behind a row of hangars. Their flight is called a few minutes later.

They have changed planes in Halifax. They are somewhere off the south coast of Newfoundland. The plane has the snugness of nighttime as it tunnels through the dark sky. The interior seems cozy, almost fire-lit, with only a few reading lamps turned on. Gerry's is off. Vivian's is on. She's reading the in-flight magazine. Vivian tells people that she is not a nervous flier, but she doesn't sleep on planes. The magazine isn't holding her. It's full of articles about Japanese gadgets for the business traveller. She's a person who needs things to do. Gerry suspects he's a person who just needs things to happen.

"Are you tired?" she asks, looking at him in his nest of shadow next to her cone of lamplight.

Gerry doesn't answer right away.

"No," he says finally. He's a bit surprised, but he's not tired. He's been sitting thinking about the last seven days. Their events seem to be receding the farther east they go.

"Are you okay?" Vivian asks.

"Yeah, I am," Gerry says. "We did okay there. I think we did about as well as could be expected. For a fifty-something orphan, I think I'm holding up pretty well."

"You always do the right thing." Vivian pats his hand. "You're good that way. You just seem to know what to do."

Gerry looks for an implication that there are ways in which he's less good, that knowing what to do is not a trump card under Vivian's rules. He's looking for a fraying of the accord they've lived under for the past week.

"Eventually," Gerry says ruefully. "Give me long enough and I'll figure it out eventually."

He wonders how long is long enough. He fiddles with the lever on the armrest and leans his seat back.

How long did I have to rehearse this? When did I start doing the right things? What has it got me?

Suddenly he feels tremendously tired and tries to relax. It seems to have taken a very long time to get here, to this time, to this seat. A life recedes in the plane's invisible wake.

"You've been uptight, I know," Vivian diagnoses.

"Yeah, I guess I have. It's like for the last, I don't know, the last year or so, I've been frozen, waiting for something to happen. I feel lighter."

Gerry leans back and thinks about waiting and doing the right things.

The plane bumps heavily, seems to skitter sideways slightly and bumps again.

"I hate this," Vivian says to Gerry.

"I know, kid. It's just a little rough." Water streaks the window beside him and beyond that the green of the wingtip light is only a stain in the speeding murk. The plane's white strobe pulses off the walls of the cloud tunnel they seem to be caroming down. "It's not a very nice night out there."

The plane's hydraulics squeal and the cabin tilts, levels and tilts again. Gerry supposes the computer is flying the plane. Somebody told him computers do the final approaches now.

If we crash and burn, was it worth it trying to get here? a morbid bit of him asks. Is this the place you could die trying to get to? Could you have stayed where you were?

The plane rips its way out of the belly of the cloud like a movie alien. The lights of a subdivision scroll by under them, like the too-fast credits of a TV show. The airport fence rushes under them and they hit with a solid thump. They're forced forward in their seats as the brakes grab with a rumbling shudder. They effortlessly make the transition from plummeting sky beast to big, tame, three-legged bus with fins.

Once upon a time, in the old EPA days, that landing would have got a cheer, Gerry thinks. We must be getting jaded.

He looks at Vivian, unclenching beside him. She smiles a small guilty smile. She knows you're supposed to trust the technology. Studies have been done. It's safer than walking, breathing even.

"We're home," she says. "Home again."

"Back where we belong," Gerry says.

I t's almost Christmas again, a month since Gerry and Vivian got back
from Ottawa. Gerry finds himself doing some pre-holiday filling-in as
a morning producer at the radio station. The Atlantic Accord shit is
hitting the federal-provincial fan, and upstairs they've opened the phone
lines for the last hour of the show. They're giving out the numbers to
call, but somebody has decided to ring Gerry on the office number.

"They shouldn't be taking down the shaggin' flags, they should be
burning the shaggin' flags."

It's not my job to decide if this guy has managed to get drunk before
nine in the morning, Gerry thinks. I used to be able to do it myself.

"I was on hold for fifteen minutes on that number they're giving
out," the man says.

"Well, I can transfer you back upstairs," Gerry says. "But I'm afraid I
can't guarantee you won't go back on hold. It's a stacking system.
You get out, you go back to the bottom and we're really busy. A lot of
people are upset with the feds, just like you are."

"I bet you're not fucking upset, buddy. You're trying to keep me off
the air. I bet you're not from here. Where are you from?"

It's been a long morning. Gerry wonders why he isn't supposed to be upset with the feds too. It's not genetic. He's probably lived here as long as the drunk on the phone has. The man has an aggrieved, Generation-X voice. Gerry thinks of his own adoptive tribe of X-ers. Vivian's kids count Ottawa's Alberta elk. They make their electronic widgets and make pious, ex-pat nuisances of themselves in Ontario. Darren's Donair and Pizza has probably created half a dozen federal jobs in employment and taxation.

"Hey, personally I think the feds are off-base here too."

"You aren't from here, buddy. Where do you belong to?"

"Outer space," says Gerry, and hangs up. "And a very merry bloody Christmas to you too."

Gerry had half-expected his caller to ring back on yet another number and complain. He doesn't, but Gerry's end of the conversation has been overheard by enough people for it to become office gossip. He's asked about it.

"Just some obnoxious drunk," he says. "I'm sorry, I lost it. I don't need to be sworn at in the mornings by some asshole."

That explanation is allowed to stand, given that there's no aggrieved listener who wants to make an issue of it. However, Gerry finds himself being looked at askance. It's suggested that it might be too soon after his mother's death for Gerry to be back at work. Perhaps he'd like to have some more time off at Christmas. He can't explain that he's feeling less stressed, getting lighter all the time.

Vivian meets Gerry downtown in the space debs' coffee shop on a colourless December afternoon. They're supposed to be buying a carpet for Melanie and Darren. Darren has landed a baker's job with another pizza joint and they're trying to fix up their place. Viv and Gerry are going rug-hunting this afternoon.

Gerry had expected Vivian to be upset that he's not working, but she's not.

"You need a break," she says. "We both do. It's been a hard fall."

Gerry orders them veggie sandwiches with sun-dried tomato and African peanut soup.

"Bob called from Ottawa, this morning," Viv says. "He said to tell you he's getting on with the will and you should get a nice little bundle. It'll be sometime after February. He says he's got to sort out your mother's income tax."

"Just as well, if the station thinks I'm losing it. It's time to be a greeter at Wal–Mart and write."

They are paying their bill when Leona from the writing group comes into the coffee shop, stamping her boots. She's got a school satchel over her shoulder. She fumbles in it and puts up a Xeroxed notice on the coffee shop bulletin board.

"Gerry," she calls. "I'm starting up the group again after Christmas. Are you interested?"

"I could be, Leona. Maybe Nish getting published was contagious. I'll give you a call."

Leona joins them. She'd met Vivian at a party she gave when the group wound up last spring. "Make this guy write big stuff," she says in a heartily confiding, gym-teacher voice. "He should let go, loosen up. Merry Christmas, you guys."

"So should you loosen up?" Vivian asks Gerry, after Leona has gone and they're standing in the street.

Gerry looks east to Signal Hill, lowering over the east end of town. The hill, he supposes, is like *the big stuff* Leona is talking about, a dirty big fact, popped out of the earth, smacked around by waves and weather. Still, as he looks at it, framed by the Christmas decorations on the street lamps, what interests him is that the top of the hill is bathed in weak winter sun, while farther down, a snow squall is dragging a smaller, private winter across the lower slopes.

Maybe I'm a landscape writer, he remembers telling Philip last spring. Maybe changes in light on the scenery are all I do.

Then there's loose itself. Should he loosen up? God knows, his collection of George and Paula and bar sketches is loose. Patricia and he got loose from each other.

Mom got loose, he thinks. The home ties are loose. I've got a loose attachment to...hell, you name it. How loose do we all have to get?

He knows that the telepathic strand they seemed to have when they were in Ottawa seems to have parted again. It's been stowed away in a past that already seems remote. A deal seems to have been made. Vivian has done her part. He, apparently, has done his. The system worked.

Will a week in a motel, arranging a funeral, be one of our golden moments? Gerry wonders.

"So do you need to loosen up?" Vivian repeats.

He realizes he hasn't answered her, not out loud anyway.

"I don't know," Gerry says. "Let's go find some carpet for the kids. Maybe we can start getting some of the Christmas groceries on the way home."

They found a carpet, with, for them, relatively little bickering. With only days to go until Christmas, the act of buying it and taking it home seems the last normal thing they do in a season that goes suddenly claustrophobic.

The first really cold night they have, the pipes freeze in the house next door to Melanie and Darren in their row-house. Somebody who's had a few beers has a late-night go at the pipes with a blow-torch and sets a wall on fire. Melanie and Darren's house gets smoke and water damage and the power is out in the row. Melanie, Darren and Diana are now living next to their rolled-up Christmas carpet in Gerry and Vivian's basement.

Early one morning Gerry paces the house, up before everyone else, padding around in his socks with a coffee mug and taking emotional stock. The previous night he overheard Vivian on the phone telling Tanya in Calgary how good he'd been in Darren and Melanie's emergency. Tanya's staying out west this Christmas.

"We'd gone to bed. He just got up and was over there at three in the morning and picked them all up," Vivian said. "Just threw stuff in garbage bags and came on."

Gerry feels unfairly lionized. What else could you do with family driven out of their house? Of course you take them in.

It makes him grumpy that Viv is boasting about something so normal. He wonders if it's a warm-up for the lowered expectations of the nursing home: shoes on right feet, socks match, still housebroken. Isn't he a wonder?

"He wipes his ass every morning too," he says sourly to the empty kitchen. "And the prize for being such a little paragon is a basement full of Darren and Melanie."

As if to confirm his mood, he goes down the basement stairs and peers around. The new rug lies in a roll, stuck diagonally across the basement floor, a misplaced Yule log that seems to take up more space than it needs to. Next to it are the garbage bags of clothes and linens, salvaged from the smoke and water.

Diana is the most visible piece of human debris. She's sleeping on a couch. Her clothes are neatly piled on the desk next to Gerry's computer. His files and his cardboard box of old notebooks have been shoved under the desk. Only Diana's hair is visible above a nest of blankets. She seems profoundly asleep, like a hibernating animal. Gerry feels dispossessed, that she has a better claim to this space than he does.

Darren and Melanie are in what used to be Tanya's room. Their door is ajar but all that is visible of them is one of Darren's arms protruding from under the covers. There are two beer bottles on the bedside table. A tangle of clothes is visible on the narrow strip of floor he can see. He can distinguish a sweater, winter socks and a thong. It strikes him that Melanie in a thong is better than tepid, errant Darren deserves. The idea of a thong-less Melanie under the covers is disturbing. The room emits a smell of tobacco smoke from Darren's heaped clothes. Darren's still a smoker.

He could have stayed where he was after the fire. What's a little more smoke to Darren?

Gerry goes back upstairs, refills his coffee mug and resumes his prowl. The house seems smaller than it did. Part of the problem is the addition of his mother's furniture, a desk and a couple of antique chairs. The desk has taken over a piece of the hall and the chairs are backed into gaps between couches and the Christmas tree. The effect is cluttered, shop-like. Sitting in the living room for a bit, Gerry feels pushed knee-to-knee with family ghosts past and present.

The ghosts start coming alive. He hears first his and Vivian's bedroom, then the bathroom doors opening and closing, followed by plumbing noises. Viv is up. Vaguely, under his feet, he senses the gurgle of morning cartoons from the basement TV. Diana is awake and stirring.

He thinks he hears real voices join the TV squeals and sound effects. Darren and Melanie are moving as well.

In the bosom of his family, Gerry thinks, listening to the random morning noises, the ill-defined stomach rumbles of their family-ness. In the bowels of his family.

The atmosphere of the house seems to flow sluggishly this morning. Its turgid eddies bring them all together in the kitchen.

Vivian is bustling around.

"You want some toast?"

Gerry thinks that, this morning, he doesn't like the smell of toast. It's one of those love/hate smells. Sometimes it's a comfort and sometimes the essence of breakfast squalor, like itchy, airborne, atmospheric crumbs.

"No thanks, kid. I'll just get some more coffee."

Diana is at the kitchen table now. She's eating cereal while her grandmother fries an egg.

"Do you want an egg, Diana?"

"No thank you."

"I've got it fried. Gerry, you have it," Vivian says and shovels the egg onto some of the toast he didn't want.

Gerry takes his orphan egg sandwich and his coffee cup and heads for the basement again. The smell of toast follows him. He passes Melanie on the stairs.

"Good morning, Gerry." She kisses him on the cheek going by. "What's on the go, Mudder-maid?"

"Good morning, kid. Get some toast and eggs. We seem to have a special on toast and eggs this morning."

Darren is at Gerry's desk in the basement. He's drinking pop and playing a video game on Gerry's computer. Gerry, who used to drink coffee with whisky for breakfast, cringes inwardly at the pop.

"You need a new computer, Gerry," Darren says. "The graphics load really slow."

"I mostly use it for word processing," Gerry says. When I use it all.

He's tempted to ask Darren to move so he can look at his e-mail and maybe do some writing, but he can't bring himself to. He's crushed under tons of toast smell and feels a million years old. He doesn't need a computer. He should be out in the back yard, chipping mammoths onto stone with a piece of antler.

"I don't know how you can write all that stuff you do," Darren says. "Who's going to read it all?"

"Archaeologists," Gerry says. He puts his sandwich and coffee mug on the washer, leans around Darren to haul out a boxful of notes and files and goes to hide in the workshop part of the basement.

Gerry's workshop is a workshop in name only. The furnace lives in it and, although it has a tool bench along one wall, it's too small and too warm to do anything more than pile tools, boat equipment and junk in. Today he roots around behind a pile of boat cushions and digs out a laptop computer that Vivian got when she went with the real estate company she's with now. The laptop has been redundant and replaced by a newer model for a couple of years. Gerry took it over with the idea of putting navigation software on it and taking it sailing. It turned out that the software had evolved too far for that to happen, but you could still write on the computer and save things to disk. Gerry unplugs the charger for his electric screwdriver and plugs in the laptop charger in its place. Perhaps he'll get out of the house sometime and do a little coffee-shop writing. He sometimes envies the people who click away at keyboards at back tables. They seem quicker and more efficient than his Chinese notebooks. Feeling he's done something, but not quite knowing what, he reclaims his sandwich and coffee. He sits on a tool box and finishes them, like a child eating a treat in a secret hiding place. The furnace cuts in with an asthmatic-lion purr and wraps him in white noise and warmth that is comfortingly isolating until it becomes too much and drives him back upstairs with his plate and cup.

"I'm going out," he says, running his dishes under the tap at the kitchen sink. "I've got some last-minute shopping to do."

Gerry's shopping stalls in the space debs' coffee shop. He's sitting with his notebook, trying to do the physics that has made him too light to stay submerged in his house, even, he suspects, in his life. He hasn't really much shopping to do.

"The statutory gifts are bought, the big items that people need," he tells the space deb who gave him his coffee. Shopping is one of the topics the space debs are programmed for.

"Yeah, me too," she says.

"I got Vivian a down coat she wants," he says. He thinks he may have introduced Viv here at some point. "Boots for Melanie, that's the daughter, and a sweater for her husband. I got the granddaughter a paintbox. She ought to get something she doesn't have to follow the instructions for."

"That's nice."

What he doesn't say is that he's stumped on the fun gifts. He's walked the length of Water Street, looking at everything from designer jewellery to dollar-store kazoos and can't feel a spark for any of it.

I have no feel for what anyone might want, he writes in his book. *I only can get what they need. I'm like somebody handing out supplies to a lifeboat crew. It's all so deadly serious.*

He's stopped in a couple of import stores where he can normally get stocking-stuffers and has picked up some cheap Indian bangles and strange little wood carvings and decorated boxes, but in their plastic bag, they feel like doomed trade goods for a tribe of clever cannibals. They'll see through their chintzy good humour and put him in the pot.

A page or two back, his notebook prophesies his cannibal musings. Idly web-searching, he had tripped over a quote from a science fiction writer called Stanislaw Lem. Gerry has never read any of Lem's work, but he wrote down the quote.

Cannibals prefer those who have no spines.

The coffee shop is warm and steamy. He decides he'll stay there a while.

Christmas day arrives mild and drizzly, less a dawn than a gradual paling of the dark. Gerry gets up in the half light and is making coffee in the kitchen when Diana comes upstairs from the basement.

"Merry Christmas, sweetie."

"Merry Christmas." Diana is a quiet kid, a watcher. Gerry feels a kinship. She's carrying the gift she was allowed to open the night before, some kind of hand-size electronic game.

"Are your mom and dad awake?"

"No."

"Well, your nan isn't either. They'll be up soon, I guess. We'll get at the big stuff then, but why don't you check out your stocking now?"

"All right."

Gerry takes his mug of coffee and they go into the living room. He plugs in the tree and sits in what's normally his reading chair in the corner of the room. Diana digs through her stocking.

"I got a tattoo set." She holds up a packet of paper transfers. Gerry's pleased. It's one of his import shop specials.

"You'll be like Lydia the Tattooed Lady."

"Who's that?"

"A lady in an old song. Lydia, oh Lydia, oh have you met Lydia? Lydia the Tattooed Lady..." Gerry waggles his fingers by his mouth, tapping an imaginary Groucho Marx cigar. She giggles.

They sit and exclaim over each new discovery in the stocking. When it's empty, Gerry fetches a damp dishcloth and they give themselves artificial henna tattoos on the backs of their hands. Then Diana settles in the corner of the couch with her video game, and Gerry returns to the kitchen to make the dressing and get the turkey in the oven. He's just finished when Vivian comes down the hall for a coffee.

"Good morning, kid. Merry Christmas."

"Merry Christmas. What's on your hand?"

"A tattoo. Diana and I were up early."

"You're as big a kid as she is."

Diana bounces into the kitchen, waving her game. "Look at the score I got."

"Oh my, that's pretty good," says Vivian.

There's a mumble of voices underfoot in the basement.

"Go down and see if your mom and dad are awake," Vivian tells Diana. "We'll open our presents now."

There is numbness in possession. Sitting in his favourite chair by the Christmas tree, Gerry feels anaesthetized by things. He's passing out the presents and feels like a sociopathic traffic light, divorced from the flow he controls.

He's wearing a breathable rain suit that Viv has given him for the boat. "You can't go wrong with extra large," he says. "I've got room to move. You need that on the boat."

"I could have got yellow," Vivian says, "but I thought the blue you could wear more. The jacket will make another windbreaker."

Gerry thinks that if he ever falls overboard in the blue and grey suit, he'll be invisible: lots of room, waterproof, but impossible to find.

Getting loose big-time in a bruise-coloured ocean.

Vivian is wearing the down coat he got her over her flannelette snowman pyjamas. "This'll be great for showing houses in the winter. It's warm but it's light."

"We're insulated," Gerry says. "Thoroughly insulated."

He feels insulated, isolated actually. A bit of old Beatles floats into his head. He thinks of the nurse selling poppies in "Penny Lane."

Although I feel as though I'm in a play, I am anyway, he thinks.

"There's more there for the kids," Viv prompts.

Although their big gift to the kids is the rug that lurks in the basement, Vivian has been shopping since the fall. She actually started when he left for Ottawa when his mother fell. She's got clothes and cosmetics for Melanie and a white, fur-trimmed ski-jacket for Diana. She's topped Darren up with socks and a sweater and what she still calls dress pants. Gerry is old enough and urban enough to have worn suits to work in the old days before working clothes for reporters took on the look of an upscale day-care. He still says "slacks" or even "flannels." It seems to Gerry that every Christmas Darren is re-outfitted from scratch. He also seems to absorb the new clothes like some sort of sartorial black hole. Gerry never seems to see him in anything but black jeans and white, short-sleeve cook shirts from the defunct pizza and donair. Gerry knows Darren was outfitted last Christmas. He wonders if Melanie gave the clothes away or if Darren abandoned them somewhere when he went to Alberta. Maybe Viv should just collect them on Boxing Day for re-distribution next year.

Gerry fishes a small, soft parcel from under the tree and passes it to Darren. "Socks, Darren. It definitely feels like socks," he says. "You can never have too many socks."

"That's right," Darren agrees. "Socks are great."

They fall into a lull after the presents are open. With only the five of them and no guests, they can't sustain the avalanche momentum that has accompanied other Christmas days. Melanie is peeling and cutting up vegetables. Darren is playing with Diana or, at least, with her new video game with her in the same room. Vivian is dressed now and is making neat piles of everybody's gifts. She feeds wrapping paper that is badly torn into the fireplace and stuffs what's re-usable into a plastic shopping bag.

"We'll find that the day after Boxing Day three years from now," Gerry says.

"You never know," says Vivian and keeps piling and sorting.

They are like a theatre company that has enough voices for the main parts, but no chorus. The theatricality of Christmas seems overwhelmed by the scenery of the house. Gerry remembers being told that theatre extras mumble "hubbub" and "marmalade" to make the noise of a crowd or mob.

"Hubbub and marmalade," Gerry says and skulks off to hang his new rain suit with his boat stuff and hide in the basement for a while.

With Darren and Diana occupied upstairs, he has a chance to get at his computer for a bit. He has decided he wants to put together a disk of book-bits to feed to the laptop he's incubating in the workshop. This morning there seem to be more pop-ups on the computer than he's used to. He suspects Darren of cruising for porn but decides, with Christmas charity, not to check the search history and confirm his suspicions. Instead he cruises his own files, his personal underwear drawer of fragments. He makes up website names for fragments and chapters as he takes them off the main-frame and salts them away on the disk.

"X-rated ex-wives," he mutters to the screen. "Red-Hot Old Friends and Geriatric Love Slaves Go West of the Overpass."

Gerry's pleased to find his bits and pieces take up more than one disk. He hadn't thought there was that much stuff. He feels like the spy who has micro-filmed the plans. He's got it all in pocket-size, ready to slip away.

Why am I making an escape kit?

Then he remembers that it was last Christmas that he told Vivian he was going back at his book.

Not my disk-and-a-half, he thinks. It's a long time since the fuse was lit on this particular firework. Perhaps she's tired of waiting for the explosion. Bombshells that don't explode become paperweights.

Noises of Christmas dinner preparation continue overhead. Gerry puts his new disks in a side-pocket of the laptop bag and calls up his e-mail account. He hasn't looked at it in a week or more. He doesn't get a lot of e-mail because he doesn't send much. Today, though, there's a reply to one he sent to Philip wishing him a Merry Christmas.

I was at my Humanist Discussion Group Christmas party the other night, Philip wrote. *There was a lot of argument about whether we should have one. We finally called it a solstice party and went ahead.*

Gerry reads on.

I met this woman who is a sort of new-age Wiccan and after far too much humanist plonk, we wound up in her apartment. What rough beast whose hour has come...

"Slouches towards Bethlehem to be bored," Gerry says sourly.

Before you say, 'Why Wiccan? Why not RC or Seventh Day Adventist?' I say it just feels right. It's time for me to stop being alone.

Or start, thinks a cynical Gerry and then instantly feels guilty.

She works in an alternate used bookstore and she says I can get a job there too. They want somebody to sort out some of their classics and take a look at their computer accounting.

Gerry remembers The Vales of Har and The Books of Thel from his first life. His imagination smells the peculiarly alternate-bookshop mixture of mildew and cat.

Good luck to you both.

I've told Charmian about the dinners you used to invite me to. I said you were a pretty fair amateur shaman in the kitchen. If we can get some money together we might get down to see you next summer. Merry Christmas (or solstice) to you and Vivian.

Gerry wonders what it feels like to be at the start of something again, when reconciling Yeats and crystals and the Goddess seems possible. He tries to remember the miraculous foreign-ness of someone new, the magic unfamiliarity of everything from her body to the layout of her bathroom.

He is suddenly aware that he and Vivian have made love only twice since they got back from the funeral. Once was after they had a fight over where to put the furniture they'd shipped down. The second time was in the cold dawn after they'd ferried Melanie, Darren and Diana home after their fire.

It sometimes seems to Gerry that they need a row or a disaster as an aphrodisiac.

For-giveness or for-titude equal fore-play, Gerry thinks. Good luck, Philip and Charmian. Good luck to you both and the books and the cats and the mildew.

Christmas dinner is a reminder you're old and jaded.

Gerry remembers being a kid and drooling at the prospect of Christmas dinner. He wonders if it was just that kids are naturally hungrier or if it was a sociological thing. Snacking hadn't been much of an option for a kid in the 1950s. Fast food hadn't fully arrived and kitchens were strictly controlled by Depression-trained mothers. If you got a snack at all, somebody made it for you and you were guaranteed it wouldn't spoil your dinner or supper or whatever the next meal in line happened to be. Gerry remembers the prospect of bland mega-food at Christmas being something you could daydream about. Now it's a lot of stodge that you'll still eat too much of. His annual Waldorf salad is as close as the meal gets to what they usually eat. Tomorrow he'll co-opt the leftovers into something less bland.

"Turkey curry tomorrow," he says.

"That's a waste of good turkey," Vivian says. She believes, implicitly, that turkey is good.

"I'll just do my share of the bits and pieces with a few veggies."

"Yecch," says Diana.

"Yeah, yecch," says Darren.

"Don't come looking for any when I get it made then."

Gerry and Vivian have yet to evolve a traditional Christmas dessert. Vivian gave up baking when Gerry took over most of the day-to-day cooking. One year he bought a steamer and attempted a proper Christmas pudding full of suet, peel, crumbs and rum. It was voted down as too heavy. This year he's bought a little red-wrapped pudding from the grocery store. The pudding is about the size of a softball and comes in a plastic basin that can go in the microwave. There's a tin of hard sauce.

"It's like survival pudding," Gerry says. "If you were going to put Christmas pudding in a life-raft, this is what you'd use." As it is, he eats most of the survival pudding.

The short solstice afternoon draws in quickly and the drizzle turns to snow as darkness falls. Vivian and Melanie are putting dishes in the washer with a litre-and-a-half of white wine between them. Darren is stretched out on the couch and Diana is watching TV amid a tangle of gifts on the living room floor.

Gerry decides to go for a walk. He puts on his coat, an old tweed cap and a pair of waffle-soled hiking boots and sets out by the kitchen door. His footprints in the new snow of the driveway are the first to escape the house today. Like some hatching dinosaur, he leaves the turkey-scented, vinyl-sided egg and makes his transient mark in the outside world. He stops at the street and turns to look at the house. The lights of his giant wreath sparkle and the front door and picture window drip icicle lights. Looking at the kitchen window, he sees Viv and Melanie pass back and forth at the sink, only the tops of their heads visible from street level. The house is like some illuminated novelty, a peepshow, observable but inaccessible. Gerry pulls his cap down to keep the fluffy snowflakes out of his eyes and sets off up the street.

It's fully dark when Gerry returns to the house, stamping snow off his boots on the deck and letting himself back into the scented warmth of the kitchen. Vivian is sitting at the kitchen desk, a smudged wine glass beside her, talking on the phone. The glass is one of a set of big, balloon-shaped ones that somebody gave them. It's one of only a few survivors of the set. The stems are too narrow for the big globes and they have broken with dignified restraint, one or two per holiday, for a couple of years.

"It's Duane," Vivian says. "They're coming down. Here, talk to him." She hands Gerry the phone but stays seated at the desk. He has to stretch the phone cord around her. He's reminded of the cartoons where somebody detaches the steering wheel and hands it to a passenger as the car careers out of control.

"Merry Christmas, Duane."

"Merry Christmas, Gerry."

"Your mother says we're going to be seeing you."

"Yes, that's right. I've got laid-off. Things are slow in the field just now. We just found out a week ago," Duane says, not sounding regretful enough for Gerry. Gerry also notices Duane always says yes, not yeah or yep or any of the short-hand affirmatives. It's as if he's relaying something solemn, something just this side of "yea verily."

"That's too bad," Gerry says.

"No, Gerry, I think it was a blessing." Duane's voice warms. "I've been talking to some of the people at Pastor Bob's ministry. They think they can find something for me to do back home."

"The move will upset the horse," Gerry says surreally.

"We sold the horse. A friend of Gretchen's from the church bought it."

"Too bad, or no, I guess, great really." Gerry is unreasonably nostalgic for a horse he's met once. Irrationally, he wants loyalty to the family stable, the tribe's trusty steed. "Put on Gretchen and the kids, I'll say Merry Christmas."

For a few minutes there's a confusion of people put on the phone, not knowing who they're talking to. Gerry finally makes his way through Duane's little family and hands them back to Vivian and Melanie.

Through much of Christmas evening, Gerry is by himself. Vivian and the kids disappear to the basement to play Christmas CD's and call extended family. He sits in the living room, scented with the Christmas tree, and toys with the idea of joining them or even of calling some of his own family that he rediscovered when his mother died. He discards the idea. They're fading back into the haze of the past thirty or so years. Besides, he doesn't really want family just now, extended or otherwise. He's got a basement full of it.

"I'll be home with bells on…," the CD player rumbles underfoot in the basement. Vivian is singing along.

Gerry picks up a coffee table book on sailing from his pile of presents and looks at pictures of expensive boats that all appear to be crewed by male acrobats and the space debutantes from the coffee shop.

"Boat porn," says Gerry to the Christmas tree. "It'll never take off in Newfoundland until somebody invents the thermal thong."

On TV, the Alastair Simm version of *A Christmas Carol* unwinds. Gerry has tried to correct himself of being a Scrooge-snob. He tries not to pronounce on its superiority at parties. If asked which version he prefers, he'll plump for the Disney cartoon or the Muppets. Now, however, watching Scrooge pine for Fezziwig's party, he unaccountably finds his throat choked and his eyes full of tears.

Gerry is asleep when Vivian comes upstairs to go to bed. She wakes him when she staggers slightly and bumps into the bedroom door. He hears her grunt as she pulls her sweater over her head and he feels the mattress cant sharply as she flops into bed.

"Are you awake?" She's switched from wine to beer in the course of the evening. He can smell it. He thinks beer is one of those smells like tobacco, smells that were warm and welcoming twenty years ago and are mildly sickening now.

"Now I am." He hopes he's not being too obviously sarcastic. "I was just dozing," he lies, to soften the tone.

"I don't think I'm going to take the tree down this year."

Gerry has visions of a sort of Miss Haversham's Christmas tree, bald and shedding garlands in the height of summer. He lets her declaration lie there, hoping she'll fall asleep or change gears.

"Leave it up, boy…Love Christmas."

"Yeah," says Gerry, waiting. The gear change comes without warning.

"We should sell this place to Duane and get something smaller. He'd do all right on the difference between what he'll sell for up in Ottawa and what this place is worth."

Gerry feels the universe wobble. In the past week or two he's felt smothered in the house. Now the suggestion of getting rid of it makes him feel exposed.

"You've been talking about this with him?"

"I'm going to leave the tree up," Vivian says again. He waits for an answer to his question but none comes. He doesn't push. This isn't the time. A snore comes from Vivian's side of the bed, then another. He nudges her slightly. She stirs, settles again and the snore stops.

"We'll talk about it," Gerry says. "Goodnight. Merry Christmas."

It takes him a long time to go back to sleep. When he does, he dreams he's standing outside the house again, as he did when he went for his afternoon walk. There are no curtains on any of the windows. He can see Duane and Gretchen inside, and a crowd of strangers singing. When he goes to the door, it's locked. They don't hear him when he knocks.

In front of the dresser mirror, Gerry performs the half-remembered magic of tying a black bow tie. He is sweating slightly, holding his head up and trying to make his fingers perform the magic middle part of the process where the knot starts to bite in the centre and the ends take on definition. It's his third try and the two previous attempts have come out lop-sided or too loose. This time he judges the tensions right and gets a hard, tight knot between two reasonably equal wings of black, just enough crookedness to boast that this bow is tied by hand and not clipped or strapped-on. He sighs and shrugs the tension out of his shoulders, feeling the unfamiliar braces on them. He shrugs again, takes his dinner jacket off the back of the bedroom chair and puts it on. His image in the mirror is black and white. It seems to him that his face and hair are the monotone grey of old theatre marquee photos to match the puritan formality of his evening clothes, a middle-aged face, to be charitable about it.

"Behold the penguin in all his sober glory," he calls down the hall to where Vivian is putting on her face in the bathroom. They're getting ready for a New Year's ball at a hotel downtown. Her office has booked tables. It's been a good year in the real estate business.

He walks down the hall and looks in at the open bathroom door. Vivian stops putting on eye shadow for a moment and looks sideways at him.

"You're all ready. You look nice." Vivian likes Gerry to wear the dinner suit he's had since they started taking occasional cruises some years ago. She was surprised when he bought one.

"You could rent a tux on the boat. It says so in the brochure."

"A tux is a rented dinner jacket," he quoted from somewhere. "I don't want to look like the senior prom."

Surveying his shirt front above his cummerbund in the hall mirror, Gerry is reminded of the Shepard illustration of Toad in *Wind in the Willows*. He doesn't mind. He feels pleasantly anachronistic.

Vivian emerges from the bathroom. She's wearing black with a sparkle of encrusting-jet. A short jacket of the same material covers her shoulders. She looks encased, like something Egyptian or perhaps some rather splendid insect.

"I'm too old for off-the-shoulder," she says. "God, I haven't had this girdle on in a while. I hope I can sit down."

Melanie and Diana look around the corner from the kitchen.

"Wow," Melanie says.

"Wow," Diana echoes obediently. Darren comes up from the basement in his pizza baker's whites. He's getting ready to go to work.

"All dressed up in your tuxedo, eh?"

"Come take our picture by the tree," Vivian says to Melanie. It vaguely irks Gerry. He wishes perversely that their dressing up could pass un-remarked.

"Taxidermy is more enduring," he says grumpily as Melanie herds them in front of the tree and the camera flashes.

Traffic feels light as Gerry drives them to the hotel, the *de facto* designated driver by virtue of being on the wagon. The cars they meet and pass have a ships-in-the-night feel, bound for their own mysterious islands of revelry or to the garage at home to let the cabbies have their big night. It's years now since Gerry and Vivian have had to wait in hotel lobbies or the downtown slush to get a New Year's cab home. He's always perfectly, predictably able to drive. There are times he thinks Vivian resents this.

"You're always ready to go home," she'll say, half accusingly, at the end of a party.

"I spent a lot more time out than you did in your last life," he'll say, as long as they're not arguing about it. "Home's got novelty value."

They drive past a sign from Viv's company on the lawn of a house.

"You know we can get a hundred and sixty for our house right now?" she says, the street lights flicking over her.

This is a topic that's been bubbling to the surface for a week now since it first came up Christmas night. In the past, Gerry has railed against selling the house. Now, for some reason, the proposal that Duane will buy it seems to put him at a disadvantage. Unreasonably, he feels he's being put in a position of denying Duane and his little tribe a roof over their heads. He doesn't want to have this discussion at the start of a party, particularly a party with Viv's office.

"That much, you think?" he temporizes. "But of course then we'd have to find something else."

"There's lots out there," Viv says. They pull up at a stoplight. He says nothing, waiting for the light to change. When it does, they drive on in silence.

Vivian isn't wearing boots and the hotel parking lot is full so he drops her at the main door and drives slowly out a back exit and parks in the lot of a dark office building across the street. A few other lone men in dark overcoats are doing the same thing, establishing parking outposts on the frontiers of festivity. They straggle back across the road to the hotel, looking like some off-duty platoon in their uniform trousers with the shiny stripes and the flashes of shirt front where their coats open.

The doorman salutes Gerry. He's been a fixture at the hotel forever and Gerry has been to hundreds of events here over the years. In the old days he's poured him into cabs. Latterly he's greeted Gerry when he has fits of fitness and signs up for a month or two at the hotel's health club and pool. The doorman is beaming. For once, the people he's ushering into the building are dressed up to the standard of his Cossack fur cap, buttons and braid. The lobby has a *Dr. Zhivago* look to it, men in black and white, women in Christmas tree colours and glitter. Gerry feels substantial and worldly walking in. He thinks of Rod Steiger in the Komarovsky role and is tempted to twirl his moustache. He's always felt Steiger's illusion-less villain stole the movie from Omar Sharif's frostbitten, runny-nosed poet.

Patricia or Jane or Rachel or Fiona will walk in and shoot me during dinner, he thinks. Except they won't because why would they? What would matter enough?

"Hi Gerry," calls Sally, a reporter he knows. She's seeing a Scottish engineer with one of the oil projects these days. He's got her interested in salmon fishing and gets along with her kid. Tonight he's at her elbow in kilt and hose. Sally is an explosion of dark curls over bare shoulders and a soft-line, 1930s-style dress that seems to drip off her.

"Hi Sally, good evening…" He fishes for the name for a moment. "Duncan."

"You clean up nice," Sally says, nodding at his evening clothes. "You'll ruin your reputation as a boat bum."

"And you look like you're expecting a very discriminating ape to pick you off the Empire State Building. Keep an eye on this one, Duncan, she's trolling for Kong."

"I know," Duncan says. "I feel quite inadequate and all."

Gerry feels a warmth for them.

"Have a good time, guys. I've got to find Vivian. See you on the dance floor later."

When he finds Viv, she's already found some of their dinner party. They're in the ante-room of the ballroom and Viv's boss, Chuck, has been to the bar to order. He's shuttling back and forth, passing drinks around. Gerry notices that Vivian has taken a rye and ginger instead of her usual wine.

"And that'll be what for you, Gerry?" Chuck says. "You want a Coke or something? The rest of us are on the hard stuff."

Chuck is short and trimmed. He's a keen after-dinner speaker and reputed to be a dirty hockey player in his old-timers' league. When he smiles it's a brief Edsel-grill stretching of his lips, as though he's checking out some new dental work in the mirror.

Hands up, those who can remember the Edsel grill, Gerry thinks. A Mercury sucking a lemon.

He feels he's been discussed in advance and is reminded that he's always thought Chuck was a macho little shit.

"No, Chuck, I might as well go on the hard stuff too tonight. I'll take a Perrier with a twist and cut me off if I start to sing." He gives Chuck a grin that he hopes looks insincere and gets a warning glance from Vivian.

Chuck's wife Natalie is taller than he is. A vee of golf- and tennis-weathered skin points downward into the considerable cleavage of an aubergine-coloured dress. Gerry tries to imagine them in bed. Ancient jokes about horny mice and acquiescent elephants float through his mind.

"Vivian tells us you're thinking about moving into a new home," Natalie says. It seems to Gerry that everybody involved with Viv's work is incapable of saying "house." They speak only of "homes."

"Yes, yes, I guess we are." He decides since they have talked about it, what he says is true. "Although I'm hoping we can swap the house for a really nifty boat."

This gets only a polite laugh. This crowd doesn't make jokes about homes.

Gerry floats with the stream as they go in to dinner. The hotel New Year's party always gets a lot of strays, odd office parties and odd couples, people who have no genuine plans or real places to be. At a distance, he spies Roger and Vanessa who visited him on the boat. They are with a group of similar old-young couples. Gerry thinks they look like an ad for one of those mail-order Russian bride services.

He watches Sally and kilted Duncan being led to a table for two that appears to have been added to the seating plan as an afterthought. They're too new a couple to fit somewhere else.

But we're an odd couple too, Gerry thinks. We're here because we don't fit anywhere else.

They've been together the best part of twenty years but that's not quite long enough to grow new traditions. They got together as they turned forty and had come from different places. They had a second-time-around newness that shut them off from old friends. Now, whatever else people their age do at New Year's, they've been doing it together for a decade or two longer than Gerry and Vivian. Only-child Gerry doesn't much mind drifting around the edges, but Vivian likes a crowd she knows. At a pinch the gang from the office will do, and sometimes Gerry finds himself turned off as she comes on too strong to blend in.

"...tigers," Chuck is saying. It's also an evening for people like Chuck to rent an audience.

"That's right. We're tigers." Vivian agrees.

"We'll have the tethered goat to start and a couple of coolies still alive," Gerry says to the air in front of him. "We want to play with them a bit first."

"Play with them a bit first," Chuck picks up. "That's good."

Gerry swivels his grin around the group like a nasty child with a magnifying glass, looking for new insects to fry. The group concedes him some brownie points for bloodthirstiness.

A man called Glenn is talking to him. "Vivian says you race your boat." Glenn has a small round head on top of a stand-up dress collar. Gerry is reminded of the penguin waiters in *Mary Poppins*.

"Yeah, we actually managed to win a couple."

"I hear you write," says Glenn's wife, a health-clubby, short-haired woman in sea green. "I read." She says it in a challenging way, as though there might be a causal connection, as though she might have caught something unpleasant from him.

Gerry wonders if Glenn and Glenn's wife do this good-cop, bad-cop routine often, engaging the same person in two simultaneous unrelated conversations. Then again, the way they ignore each other's conversation, maybe it's just some grudge match they've got going. Who can suck the victim dry first?

"My book group's reading *This Bucket Here*." She says it as if she's telling him she eats bran for regularity. "I like Newfoundland writing."

"My nephew's got a J-24," Glenn says. "Man, can that thing go."

"I never get on the boat," Vivian confides from his side. "Gerry doesn't want me on it. I think I got out once last summer."

"What are you writing, Gerry?" Mrs. Glenn demands.

"A novel."

"Is it fiction?"

"Well it's a novel, isn't it?" Gerry says. *It is fiction, isn't it?*

The waitresses bring the starter.

"What is it?" Glenn asks.

"Trout in drag," Gerry says and concentrates on taking it apart in small forkfuls.

Gerry decides the meal is a cunning attempt to cater to the tastes and aspirations of the guests. Perhaps a survey was done or a focus group convened. The Pilates crowd feels virtuous over the trout fan-dancing in phyllo and a soup that seems to be mostly hot orange juice with some shreds of carrot. The main course is a new-age-garnished, but identifiable hunk of beef for the marketplace carnivores. The dessert is a spun sugar concoction. It delights everybody because it looks as though it's made of plastic but turns out to be edible.

Gerry decides that conversation is dead. The talk is factual and faintly competitive.

"This is very good."

"Yes. We had it this way in Cancun."

"You bought it where?"

"We got in there on the ground floor and it's gone nowhere but up."

Gerry wonders if there used to be more ideas at parties or if he's just being nostalgic. For one thing, thirty, or even twenty, years ago he was partying with younger people. They didn't have much to throw around except ideas or maybe slogans. This crowd has matured into social Sumo wrestling. Wrap your jewellery, politics and bank account up in a silly loincloth and let them lumber around the room bumping into things.

"I've always hated that house," he hears Vivian say.

Has she? Our house? When did this happen and why and what business is it of Edsel-mouth Chuck and Natalie?

"Those old houses are more bother than they're worth," Glenn's wife is saying. Gerry wonders how she knows what sort of house they have. He feels conspired against.

The evening lurches into the ten-thirty doldrums that strike parties of people with short attention spans. Dinner hasn't lasted long enough to take them to the silly hats and noise-makers. The talk is refrains and variations on earlier themes. Little knots of shop-talk develop, and spouses, miffed or relieved, fend for themselves in other little knots. The jazz combo that is half of the evening's music starts to play. The rock band will come on after midnight. The partiers are faced with the prospect of an hour and a half of self-directed fun until midnight. They scuttle for the lavatories and the bars.

Gerry finds himself alone, stretching his legs in the lobby. He feels mildly combative, marshalling his calm among the potted palms. If sides are being picked, it appears Vivian has picked the gang from the office and he's picked himself.

I could camp here, he thinks, looking around the indoor undergrowth of the lobby. Raid by night and harass them when they least expect it. A palm court commando: they seek him here, they seek him there.

Like the forlorn hope of some archaic army, the dancers struggle to hold the middle of the floor in the cut and thrust of public fun, battling to survive to midnight. Gerry and Vivian are in the thick of things. She seems to be dancing too hard, a shade ahead of the music. Her face is flushed and self-contained, cut off.

"You didn't have to look so surprised when Natalie asked about selling the house. We've talked about it."

"Yes, I know, but I didn't realize we had a cheering section. How many of us are going to live in the place?"

The music stops suddenly and they're left in half-clenched positions, bar fighters trying to look innocent when the lights go up.

"Fifteen seconds," yells the girl singer from the band. "Ten, nine, eight…"

"Never mind, kid, we'll find something. I was just kidding."

"…three, two, one, Happy New Year!"

The band breaks into "Auld Lang Syne" and a waiter tugs at a rope to free a reluctant net of balloons overhead. It sags at one end and releases a couple of balloons. The crowd guffaws. The waiter looks flustered and tugs harder. The net tears partially free of its moorings and dumps its balloons on the crowd. There is the sound of a small war as the dancers stamp them to rubber shreds.

Vivian stands stiffly, angry now. She suddenly seems close to tears. "You spoil everything."

"I guess I do," he says, somewhere between contrition and despair. "I'm sorry. We'll look."

The singing strands itself on the chorus. "For auld lang syne, my dear, for auld land syne…"

"We'll look, okay?"

She lets herself be kissed.

"Happy New Year."

They dance clumsily into the new year.

The party is breaking up in the lobby. Gerry has collected their coats from the cloakroom. He's got his on and Viv's over his arm. A few moments before, they'd agreed it was time to go. Other people had already started looking for coat-check tickets. It's a point of honour with Vivian not to be the first to leave. It's a point of honour with Gerry to humour her. Now, though, she's got a second wind as the group lingers over its goodbyes.

"You'll have to come to dinner," Viv is telling Natalie.

"In your new house," Chuck says, playing with his car keys.

"Yes, that's right, Chuck, and maybe we'll celebrate Gerry's book. With what his mother left him, he shouldn't have to work now. He can write all the time."

Gerry cringes and shakes her coat like someone trying to attract a young animal's attention to a feeding pail.

"Why did you have to say that, about the old lady's money?" Gerry asks as they drive home. He decides he isn't angry so much as tired. All at once he's exhausted. He recalls himself to what he's doing and swerves the Honda slightly to give a wider berth to a couple standing in the gutter. The girl has a lime-coloured formal under a short leather coat and she's throwing up. Her escort leans towards her as though he's giving coaching tips.

Happy 2005, Gerry thinks.

"Why not? It's true, isn't it?" Vivian asks. "You've got no excuse now."

"I guess not."

The car makes its slow pinball way through the streets that are corridors of black trees and Christmas lights.

I've got no excuse.

seventeen

JANUARY 2005

Gerry, Vivian, her sister Nellie and a real estate agent named Carole stand in their socks on a cold expanse of plastic-looking blonde hardwood. They've been looking at a new house.

"The floors are beautiful," Nellie says. She's come to visit and has become part of the new house project. She's volunteering to stay and help clean up the old house for sale. In exchange, she gets to look at new places with them. "Beautiful floors."

"Aren't they?" Carole says. She's trying to read the dynamics of the little group of sock-footed worshippers. She knows Vivian's in the business. Gerry looks non-committal, so she correctly assumes that Nellie is moral support and cheering section.

"What do you think?" Vivian asks Gerry. She says it like an ambulance attendant, talking to make sure the patient is still conscious.

"It's nice and bright," Gerry says, thinking that if Gretchen and Duane are going into their house, they should arrange a floor swap. This house has the shiny gym floors of their place in Ontario.

"Viv, I don't need to stay with you guys," Carole is saying. "It's one-ninety-five but I think they'll move on that. Look around and just stick the key back in the lockbox when you're done. Call me. You've got my cell."

"One-ninety-five, eh?" Nellie says, looking shrewd, as though she's being asked to come up with the price.

"Thanks Carole," Gerry says. If he can add nothing else to the process, he can be polite.

Carole gets back into her snow boots, hopping one-footed, a hand braced against a door frame. Then she leaves them to it.

"It would look better furnished," Vivian says tentatively, still watching Gerry for symptoms of dissent.

"We've got the stuff to fill it," he says. She looks at him sharply for signs of sarcasm but he's poker-faced. He's thinking of empty places he's moved into over the years. "In a way, I kind of like it empty. It's got nothing but potential."

"The things you do get on with," Nellie says. "Like it empty."

A few days later, Gerry is back hiding in the coffee bars again. For the first time, he has brought his geriatric laptop to a coffee shop. He still hasn't fully made the transition from Chinese notebooks. One is open beside him as he translates the last few weeks into a George reflection.

Fragment: New Technology

George unplugs the charger for the electric screwdriver so he can plug in the one for the laptop. It's not going to cost him a screwdriver. The electric screwdriver hasn't worked for more than a few minutes in a couple of years now. He killed it with attention, popping it back on the charger as soon as he'd used it. It built up a memory and now can't absorb more than a few minutes of charge.

Ellen and I have built up a memory, George thinks. Doing the right thing wrong makes me bloody useless, incapacitated by the knowledge of what used to work.

Gerry saves the half screen and flashes up another.

Fragment: Liking It Empty

Once, a very long time ago, George had a room with a table, a chair, a bedroll and a half-dozen books. His knapsack hung on the back of the door with a set of nesting mess tins and a single-burner butane stove in the side pocket. He lived in it when he met Paula. The chair and table belonged to the house. She admired his simplicity. When they split up they left trunks full of simplicity in other people's houses.

Half as long ago he'd had an apartment where he'd owned nothing but some bedding, the kitchenware, the bathroom curtains, and a short shelf of books. He brought Ellen to it in their early days. She pitied his neediness. They are buying a new house to store its antidotes in.

Gerry patters to a stop on the little keyboard. The bits he's written seem small and stunted. He feels nostalgic for the days when he could conjure up ten pages of an old love affair reworked. If he admitted it, the days of love affairs seem very remote. He gets up and takes his cup for a refill. The space deb behind the counter smiles at him. For years now, Gerry has flattered himself that he's wearing pretty well, that pretty young women respond when he tries to be charming. He knows better than to come on too strong.

"My wife tells me I shouldn't hit on women I have socks older than," he'd kid them, "or should that be 'than whom, I have older socks?'"

It was gently self-deprecating, spelling out the realities of wife and age but leaving the hint that Gerry knew a bit about hitting and being hit-on. Today, though, he sees the girl's smile and remembers that no one frowned at the inmates in his mother's old-age home.

I dribble this coffee down my front and I'll still get a smile as she mops up.

Gerry takes his coffee back to his table and closes the lid of the laptop. It seems awkward to have it in front of him in the coffee shop, vaguely prosthetic, a crutch or an artificial leg. He never misplaces his Chinese notebooks, but he feels he could accidentally close the laptop and walk away, forgetting it on the table.

Forget your crutch and fall on your face.

It's a winter evening and Gerry has gone to earth. After supper he slithered away to the cramped, cluttered, incubator heat of the basement workshop. More and more, he finds the complete useless-ness of the room suited to what he is, or isn't, doing. The furnace blower cuts out, leaving only the sustained sigh of the warm air in the duct-work guts that branch out over Gerry's head. He feels that the warmth radiating outward is desiccating him, draining and mummifying him. He thinks of the grey fur husks of dehydrated mice you find on high, dry shelves in old houses.

They've made an offer on the new house and it's been tentatively accepted. The deal has gone off to the lawyers. Gerry's part in the process has been saying he doesn't mind. They're waiting to see what Duane and Gretchen can get for their place in Ontario.

When Duane and his tribe move in, I'll be here like mouse jerky, he thinks. He's not sure if he minds or not. He feels cramped and yet safe here. A part of him wants to become part of the fabric, like bones in a crypt. Another part wants to shed it all.

Tonight, in theory, he's sorting out his novel-stuff, filling a carton with notes he wants and throwing out the rest. He's got a plastic disk case beside him. From time to time he pops disks into the laptop to see what's on them.

The house is fairly quiet. Darren is at work and Melanie is over at their house, getting things ready for a move back. The power has been restored and the insurance has given them a cheque. She put Diana to bed before she left. Tomorrow is a school day.

Semi-consciously he tracks the movements of Vivian and Nellie upstairs. They'd sat at the kitchen table long after supper had finished, talking about what the new house needed. Now the kitchen water pipes and sink drain have stopped talking to themselves overhead. The dishes are done. A strengthening telepathy of creaking floorboards takes the women down the hall and into the living room over Gerry's head.

"You know, he's like he's dead, girl." Nellie's voice is strangely intimate in the workshop. The builders never bothered to run ducts to all the registers in the living room. One, over the work bench, is just a grating to let the warm air up. Nellie is apparently on the couch right above it. Her voice has the clarity of a theatre aside. "It's like he had nothing to say about that lovely new house at all. It's not natural. I don't know how you put up with it."

"Gerry just can't handle change," Vivian says. "He'll be all right. He likes everything just the way it is, but I know we can do better."

I'm not the only one who isn't crazy about the idea, he thinks. Duane and Gretchen chose to see taking over the house as a cross they have to bear to come home and do God's work.

"Well I suppose he could stay where he is and look for another job," Gerry had said a week or so before. They'd just had a late-night discussion on the phone, with everyone on the downstairs and bedroom extensions. "I wouldn't want to force him to live here just so I could have the fun of moving."

"He wants to come home," Vivian had said.

"Home is good," Gerry observed bleakly, "I'm quite partial to mine."

On the phone, though, he'd had to sound as though Duane was volunteering for a particularly worthy leper colony by condescending to take his house.

"You'd think he wasn't glad that Duane's coming home," Nellie says overhead, recalling Gerry to the present. He realizes he's putting note-books and his box of disks into a large gym bag he uses for hauling boat stuff. "Sometimes it's like he doesn't want to be with you and the family at all."

"Gerry's all right," Vivian says, but it seems to Gerry that she doesn't put much fire into the argument.

He rummages through dairy cases of boat stuff and finds the little ceramic heater the kids gave him for the boat a couple of Christmases ago. He chucks it in the gym bag and pulls a rolled sleeping bag down from a high shelf.

Move over you mummified mice!

He feels an unreasoning rage at Nellie, meddling in this move as a little break from the monotony of outport living in Burleigh, a chance to nose around in new houses she can't afford and snoop in this one. He goes upstairs feeling as if he's been sanded until the nerves are on the surface.

"Good night," he says, passing the living room and going down the hall to his and Vivian's room where he flops on the bed and reads an old copy of *Wooden Boat*.

After an hour or so, he undresses, gets into bed and flicks off the light.

"What's the matter with you?" Vivian says, flicking it on again when she comes to bed. Gerry has been lying clenched in the dark. "You never said a word, going to bed."

"To be expected from somebody who might as well be dead," he says tonelessly. "Besides, I'd hate to upset Nellie's planning of where I'm going to live."

"We agreed moving would be a good idea. The kids can use the house. We should be someplace better."

"Yes, yes, I know, but shit, it gets on my bloody nerves."

"Don't start. This house gets on mine."

They argue in forced undertones. Nellie may be Vivian's ally but she doesn't feel like giving her too much of a show. They fall silent, apprehensive of where the argument is going. The silence stretches.

"Look, kid, maybe I just need to get away for a little while, maybe do some writing."

"Oh, that's great, just when we're getting ready to move. The house is going to close anytime, and besides you haven't written anything in months. I bet you haven't done a damn thing since we got back from Ottawa."

"I have, but you're right, not much. I need to go away for a bit and try. I feel like I'm swelling up, like I need to go lance it."

"You don't care about me. I've got the kids coming and Nellie here…"

"You asked Nellie in," he says. "But no, I'm not running away. I just need to get out of the house for a bit. I'll keep in touch. The minute I'm needed for the house I'll be right back."

"It looks great, us buying a house and you don't even want to be here."

"I'll be here. I've said I'm up for moving, but I just need some time. I feel like I'm smothering."

"I smother you, do I?"

"No, kid, I think I smother me."

"You're making a holy show of me in front of Nellie."

"Shag Nellie! What do you care what Nellie thinks? She's still looking down her nose at you because you don't bake bread any more."

"I made good bread."

"But you don't have to anymore," Gerry says, urgently pushing the words into the room's dark, trying to bridge the yawning foot between them in the bed. "I'll be there when I'm needed."

There's a sniff from the other side of the bed. Vivian rolls face down. "Do I get on your nerves that much? Go on then."

Gerry is compelled to reach out and touch her. Her shoulders are shaking. "No, kid, I told you. I get on my own." He tugs her to get her to face him. "I just need some time alone to get human."

She lets herself be half-turned towards him. There is enough light from the window to show her face, wet and crumpled.

"I do love you, you know. If you don't want to move we don't have to." Her voice comes from against his chest. "You're not a bad man, Gerry."

So my wives keep saying, he thinks. Who are we trying to convince?

"If you have to, you go on. I'll be okay with Nellie and the kids."

"I'll be back when it's time to get serious about it."

"You go on then. I'll tell Nellie some work came up for you."

They curl into each other and for the first time in a while, go to sleep in each other's arms.

Gerry gets up before daylight the next morning. He pitches some clothes and a washing kit into a gym bag. He moves quietly, trying not to wake Nellie in the spare room or Melanie, Darren and Diana in the basement. Sleep-junky Vivian gets up a little while later and joins in his morning game of stealth. They drink tea at the kitchen table under a wide-based cone of light from the hanging lamp and talk in voices that are just above whispers.

"Where are you going?"

"I don't know. I'm just going to drive around a bit until I feel my shoulders unclench. I'll be in touch though. I'll call, wherever I get to."

"I suppose I should be glad. I know you'll just drive around. I don't need to worry about you going off with somebody else."

"You make me sound like an altered tomcat. That's not altogether flattering. Patricia would have worried."

"You were different then."

"I suppose."

Gerry drags his gym bags of book-stuff and clothes to the door. He rejoins Viv at the table and is finishing his tea when they hear Nellie moving around. Eventually she comes down the hall to the kitchen. She's wearing a home-knit sweater over flannelette pyjamas. Her feet are in shapeless knitted slippers.

"What are you fellahs doing up then?"

"Convention of the living dead," Gerry says, but Viv gives him a dirty look.

"Gerry's got to go on the road," she says. "He got the call last night. Somebody got sick at the last minute. You'd better get going, hon."

She kisses him matter-of-factly, as if he's being sent off to school.

"Yeah, right, see you, love, see you, Nellie."

"Say hello to George and Paula," Vivian says. He's surprised. He didn't think she remembered the characters in the bits he's read to her from time to time.

"Who are George and Paula?" Nellie asks.

"Some people Gerry works with." Vivian smiles at him, a bit forlornly.

And there he was gone, he thinks.

Gerry drives into the morning, not knowing where he is going. He stops at a Tim Hortons and fills the big insulated aluminium mug the garage gave him for servicing the Honda there. Normally Gerry has no trouble wasting time in coffee shops, but today he wants to be moving. He climbs back into his SUV and sets the mug in the holder. He'll run on just the smell of coffee.

He pulls up at the parkway, bustling with commuter traffic. The in-town lanes rush back towards his neighbourhood. The out-bound veer away south to skirt the hills which have a dusting of new snow.

His coffee suspended within reach beside the instrument panel, Gerry is reminded of the days when the space race was news. There would be pictures and TV shots of the astronauts in their fitted couches in their capsules. They were plugged into their tiny environments, working where they slept.

"This is Major Tom to Ground Control," Gerry sings and turns into the out-of-town lane. The vehicle is warm and he feels a part of it. He remembers somebody telling him that the downside of being an astronaut was that they lived in diapers inside their space suits. The space toilet didn't arrive until later.

Cruising into infinity in Pampers, Gerry thinks. This too may come.

South of the last bypass, the traffic thins out and Gerry is following the winding two lanes of The Irish Loop. The shamrocks on the signs tell him so. He remembers covering the fuss when the signs first went up. The designer had put four-leaf clovers on them instead of shamrocks. It cost some ungodly amount to get them all redone.

The sea is close on his left-hand side and there is little snow here, this early in the winter. He rolls past spruce that all lean one way from the sea winds and dips into communities of candy-bright houses and hauled-up boats, turned into still life by the winter.

It's the kind of driving you can do unconsciously, a steady hundred K with enough steering to keep the eyes and body from getting bored. The head can be where it likes.

Gerry wonders where he's going and when he's returning.

If I'm returning floats just out of reach in the back of his mind. He thinks back to last night's "You're not a bad man." Vivian and Patricia have both said this. Is it an absolution, an acceptance of a mediocre reality or a wave in a rear-view mirror as the distances grow?

At mid-morning, the distances have grown. The road has stopped dipping into little harbours and has turned inland, striking out across the barrens. The road signs have big-antlered caribou silhouette warnings as if prehistoric cave painters had got into the sign shop. The road is lined with sticks to guide the snowploughs, but there is little snow. What fell in St. John's as snow was apparently mostly rain here. The barrens stretch away in all directions with only sparse, shrunken, frozen drifts, like white hairs in the brown pelt of blueberry bushes and moss.

Gerry pulls over on a wide spot of gravel shoulder and sits and looks at the huge, windswept flatness extending to the pale bowl of winter sky in all directions. The wind buffets the car. Gerry feels you could fall off the earth here. There is nothing to hold onto to resist the upward suck of space. He slurps the last of the barely warm coffee from his thermal mug and wills himself to get out of the car and stretch.

The wind is from the southwest and it's mild for January. It's like a sustained bass note on an organ, an ambient frequency, felt rather than heard.

"Hey," he yells tentatively. The wind sucks the syllable away as though it never existed. He calls up thirty years of radio presentation workshops and puts his diaphragm into a great shapeless roar that lasts until his lungs are empty. It sounds fragile and babyish, swallowed by the space. He feels shriven.

Maybe this is what prayer's supposed to be, he thinks, roaring at the sky until you feel good.

Gerry sticks his coffee mug back in the car and slowly walks out on the barren ground. It's like a carpet under a magnifying glass, a jumble of frozen mossy hummocks, tiny water courses hidden in the folds and rib-like mazes of sand and gravel that seem randomly bulldozed into place by the wind-scour. The white noise of the wind seems to be drawing him out of himself through his ears, an infinite sky poultice. He picks his way along the gravel ridges and hops across the rivulets that criss-cross the barren ground. An old rugby song comes from nowhere to his lips.

"Why was he born so beautiful? Why was he born at all?" It becomes his barren anthem. "He's no fucking use to man or beast. He's no fucking use at all."

His feet dance to his words and the unwritten score of the tumbled ground. His arms pump for balance as he scissor-hops along his invisible trail. When he stops and turns, the Honda is a green bead, strung on the skyline half a mile away.

"No fucking use to man or beast. He's no fucking use at all," he finishes, slightly breathless. "World without end. Amen."

He stands until the sweat he's worked up starts to chill. He can see the highway for miles in either direction. A windshield flash on a hill crest miles away tells him that someone else is traversing his universe. He zips up his jacket and walks slowly back towards his car.

Without the counterpoint of his man-or-beast hymn, the walk takes longer going back. He picks his way now, rather than dances, looking at micro-forests of moss, the Lilliputian lake systems of the potholes and the diamond sparkles in the gravel and ice. The car he spotted crossing the crest is coming up a low grade towards his vehicle as he walks the last fifty yards. It slows just perceptibly and he sees heads turn his way, wondering what he's returning from, out on the barren. He imagines they'll think he's been poaching or having an *alfresco* crap out under the big sky. Religious pilgrimage probably doesn't occur to them. The car passes in a private tornado of sound and dwindles on down the endless road. Gerry climbs into his own vehicle and watches until the car is out of sight. As he does, he sees movement on a low ridge. Three caribou briefly trace the skyline like passing sailing ships. Then they move down-grade and fade into the camouflage of the other light splashes and shadow-play of the barren. Gerry takes them as a benediction and pulls out onto the long empty road. For the first time in a long time, he doesn't feel cramped. It occurs to him that Viv would have liked to have seen the caribou, so perhaps he's planning to bring some of this trip home.

"He's no fucking use to man or beast," he sings as he drives across a watercolour vastness.

It's mid-day and Gerry drives down a long hill in second gear. He leaves the barrens behind him at the top of the curving hill and rejoins the sea at the bottom. He crosses a long beach-rock barachois and crosses an iron bridge over a swirling river mouth. A settlement hangs on the road like a string of wooden beads, the softball field a ceramic pendant on the other side of the road. There are few cars moving. An occasional ATV potters along the shoulder or brazens it out on the pavement. It is not the sort of community with work for many people. The cars that belong to the houses are away at jobs somewhere else. Gerry tries to imagine a commute across the barrens every morning at dawn. It seems surreally daunting, like a razor-edged steel butterfly.

Gerry decides he's hungry and pulls up at a corner store with a padlocked gas pump in front. Inside, the place is a shrine to failing small-retail. Half dozens of this and that stand in sparse, nervous groups at the front of deep shelves that were built to hold sacks of flour, cases of canned goods, toys and rubber boots and rope. A push-button cappuccino machine with a sign proclaiming the name of the supplier sits next to a couple of half-picked-over cards of last season's trout flies.

Extract from the Analects of Adamson, Gerry thinks. The sage does not buy a cappuccino in a place that sells bait.

The woman behind the counter looks like a too-clean polyester bathroom decoration and has a mouth pinched from saying no to credit. She just manages a watery smile as Gerry selects from her sorry stock of snacks. Vienna sausages in the can, Doritos closing on their sell-by date and bottled juice, ditto, are as good as it gets. Gerry pays and they exchange small talk about the weather and lack of snow. An overloud bell on a spring announces that he's escaping out the door, another cash customer headed out of town.

Some way up the road, Gerry parks at a provincial picnic ground by the ocean to eat his junk-food lunch. He hooks the centre sausage out of the tin with the small blade of his Swiss army knife and thinks about the woman in the store, resenting him for being there, for buying a piece of her shrinking empire, for disturbing her contemplation of an impeccably tidy ruin.

Declining ambition makes you just as mean as big ambition, he thinks. How mean am I?

Mid-afternoon shadows are getting longer when Gerry noses the Honda along the back road into the community where he keeps his boat. A few minutes before, he'd sat at a crossroad and tried to decide where he was going. A part of him plumped for a heedless run west, nights in motels, maybe even onto the ferry and on to God-knows-where. Sensitive waitresses would take pity on the nomad for the night and ride beside him vicariously as he drove off in the morning.

"Yeah, right," Gerry had said aloud. Did he really need more field notes to add to the gym bag or paper riding behind him? He pulled across the Trans Canada on the overpass and headed for the smallest piece of his world.

Gerry pulls into his hibernating yacht club and parks. He walks around the tall shapes of cradled boats and down along the docks. The marina and boatyard are relatively free of snow. The thaw and rain at Christmas and the presence of the sea have kept it to gritty drifts on the shady side of cradles. Out in the basin, away from the current of the river, there's a skin of new ice. One fat grey seal lies on it in the middle of the little harbour, a grey-mottled sausage with a self-indulgent cartoon-dog face. It reclines on one side, flippers clear of the ice, conserving heat. Gerry decides it's an old seal, withdrawn from seal society. He supposes the sea trout in the river have attracted it.

"Just you and me, buddy," Gerry says to the seal. "Two fat old patriarchs, tired of our herds." The seal doesn't pay him much attention. It seems it's only a coincidence of ice drift that the sharp end with eyes, nose and whiskers points towards him, like the bottle in spin-the-bottle. In the trees behind the clubhouse, crows shout. Gerry meanders back along the docks to his boat in the yard.

Long ago, Gerry started making a point of always leaving all the boat's various keys in the Honda's virginal ashtray. He'd been caught too often, remembering that keys are on the hook by the fridge at home just when he tops the hill that leads down to the marina. Now he takes one and unlocks the padlocked chain that holds a homemade ladder to his cradle. He props it against the hull and scrambles up to inspect the cockpit. There's a thick loaf of hardened snow between the seats. Leaves have slowed the cockpit drains, and ice has built up on the cockpit sole. It's preserved the snowdrift on top of it. Gerry climbs over the life-lines and stands on the seat to uncleat one end of the blue plastic tarp he secures over the leaky sliding hatch in winter. Then he climbs down. He rummages another key out of the Honda's ashtray and goes and unlocks the clubhouse. In a storage room he finds a snow shovel and carries it back to the boat. Then he collects a tool box from the back of his car. The fact that it's there is not good planning on his part. It's been riding there, rattling since October when the boat came out of the water.

"The sage keeps to the deed that consists in taking no action," Gerry says to the empty boatyard. He climbs back aboard with the tools and shovel. Five or six shovelfuls and some determined chopping clears the little cockpit of snow and ice. Then he unscrews the winter plywood he keeps over the hatch splash boards.

Who says being a slob doesn't pay off? Gerry thinks as he lets himself into the boat. He'd meant to take the cushions off some nice day in November, but then his mother had her fall and he'd gone to Ottawa. When he came back, nice days seemed to get scarce and then it was Christmas. He'd come out on a sleety Sunday when it was too wet to put cushions on the roof rack. He'd just screwed the plywood on for security and left the cushions aboard.

Maybe I knew I'd be coming back.

As dusk sneaks into the yard, Gerry establishes his position. He digs out the boat's extension cord and plugs in the small electric heater he keeps aboard. The inside of the boat smells musty. He turns the heater on high to dry things out. The battery is out of the boat, so he pinches a small table lamp from the club house and takes it aboard. Then he climbs back down the ladder and heads across the road on foot to buy supplies.

Gerry and the woman behind the counter of the nearest convenience store find each other only vaguely familiar in winter. It's as if he's a migratory species, blown off course or inadvertently wintering over. He doesn't fit the winter ecosystem of the town.

"I guess you're working on your boat?" she says. Her usual "Nice day for a sail," is not applicable in January.

Gerry does the kind of unexpectedly expensive shopping you do when you start from scratch. He buys salt and pepper in expensive, convenience store sizes, teas and more sugar than he'll use if he stays all winter. He picks up onions and potatoes in pricey small–store packages and oriental noodles, assorted canned goods, bottled water and a jar of instant coffee which he knows he won't like, even as he buys it.

When did tastes in coffee change? he wonders. He remembers freeze-dried instant being almost a gourmet taste in the '70s. Now none of it tastes good, and he knows he'll drive to the nearest service station for something brewed.

He tops off his order with a plastic jug of alcohol for the stove. He has to root for it behind cases of paint thinner. It's a summer item.

The woman behind the counter looks at him uneasily as she takes his money. This is not a convenience store order. This is the commissariat of a one-man retreating army, someone who doesn't have a fixed address. She feels a twinge of the distrust the settled and successful have for nomadic losers. It starts to snow as he leaves the store, lugging handfuls of plastic bags. Big soft flakes at first but smaller and harder by the time he gets back to the boat, making a faint slithering rustle as it blows across his elevated fibreglass burrow.

Gerry simmers a can of meatball stew with Chinese noodles for supper. He's ready for something hot, unhealthy and hearty. He spent a chilling gloves-off ten minutes filling the alcohol stove in the cockpit so as not to slop fuel around the cabin. The interior of the boat takes on the smell of onions and gravy and damp wool. The interior of his shell is taking on his defining scents.

Funny as a fart in a diving suit. A grade school joke floats through his mind as he does the small things necessary to prepare a hot meal, eat it and wipe up a pot and plate after. He feels pleasantly stuffed after he eats. He has eaten everything he's cooked. His spaceship regimen allows for no storage of leftovers.

Afterwards, with a large mug of tea beside him, Gerry hunches at the playhouse-size galley table with a sack of notebooks beside him on the berth. He pops a disk into his laptop and tentatively pokes a few keys. He calls up fragments he's committed to disk, long ones that have been taken to the writing workshop and some that are no more than a file title.

Capture the rapture with Duane and Gretchen, he's written, and attached the name of a website that claims to give an accurate "rapture speedometer" to judge how the end of the world is coming along. *Picnic in the Park with Ellen.*

Fragment: George Alone

George sits at the laptop and listens to the wind outside. For days he's felt like a shell-less oyster in a whirlwind of broken glass, too irritated to wrap any of it in nacre and stop the itch. Now, alone, the storm of shards seems to have abated. He feels almost lonely for the irritants he needs to make a pearl.

What's an oyster to do?

Gerry blows a soft Bronx cheer and stops typing. He highlights the George fragment and hovers over the delete button, then relents, flicks off the highlighting and saves. The laptop is like playing a doll's piano for fat-fingered Gerry.

The hell with it. Save it. You can always throw it away later.

He turns off the laptop and leans back on his berth, nursing his tea mug.

Gerry wakes up in the middle of the night to the purr of his space heater's fan cutting in. The element glows red inside, like a cigarette end, drawn on hard. The heater is only an arm's length away from Gerry tucked up in his sleeping bag along one side of the boat cabin. He's wearing a watch cap as a night cap, keeping his head warm where it protrudes from the end of the bag. The cabin is small and thickly insulated. It doesn't take much to heat it. Now it's cold but only the cold of a country kitchen before the fire is lit.

Gerry decides he needs to pee, and outside and down the ladder in the snow is too much bother. He unzips the bag, turns on the lamp and sits on the edge of the berth. He roots in the galley locker and finds a bottle of water. He empties it into the kettle and then kneels on the cabin sole, hunched and prayer-like as he holds the neck to his cock and feels the bottle become heavier and hot in his hand.

When he is finished he screws the cap on and puts the bottle by the hatch step. He rolls back into his sleeping bag with a satisfied feeling of having dealt with a survival issue.

"House-broken under all and any circumstances," he says aloud to the fibreglass over his head as he turns out the light.

A tractor-trailer growls by the boatyard, heading from the tank farm down the road to the highway. Gerry squints to make out the luminous face of his watch. It's only half past midnight. Elsewhere, people are just turning off the late edition of the news and getting ready for bed. He's been asleep since nine or so.

Despite the snow, the boatyard lights shed quite a lot of light through the plastic hatch in the forward part of the boat. He can make out the dim shape of the bag of papers he'd brought aboard and the flat, plastic sandwich of the laptop on the galley table.

"Tomorrow," he says aloud and moulds himself and his cocoon of bag to the curved bulkhead, feeling warmer now with an empty bladder. Tomorrow he'll make up his mind about that *George and the Oyster* bit. Tomorrow he'll start joining up the pieces he's got. Tomorrow he'll probably call Vivian and tell her where he is.